Growing Up
Nigger Rich

Growing Up Nigger Rich

A NOVEL

Gwendoline Y. Fortune

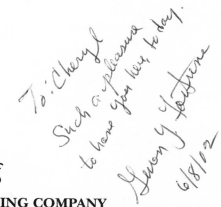

To: Cheryl
Such a pleasure
to have you here today.
Gwen Y. Fortune
6/8/02

PELICAN PUBLISHING COMPANY
Gretna 2002

*The word "Pelican" and the depiction of a pelican are trademarks of
Pelican Publishing Company, Inc., and are registered in the
U.S. Patent and Trademark Office.*

Library of Congress Cataloging-in-Publication Data

Fortune, Gwen Y. (Gwen Young)
    Growing up nigger rich / Gwendoline Y. Fortune.
       p. cm.
    ISBN 1-56554-963-5 (alk. paper)
    1. African American families—Fiction. 2. Parent and adult
child—Fiction. 3. African American women—Fiction. 4. Children
of physicians—Fiction. 5. Middle class families—Fiction.
6. South Carolina—Fiction. I. Title.

PS3556.O7534 G76 2002
813'.54—dc21

2001036911

Printed in Canada
Published by Pelican Publishing Company, Inc.
1000 Burmaster Street, Gretna, Louisiana 70053

ACKNOWLEDGMENTS

Those who contributed to the composition of this work are beyond counting: my agent Nancy Rosenfield and her editor Janet Tabin believed in it. From the beginning of my decision in 1985 to "write full time," many workshop and conference instructors, authors, and participants have read, listened to parts, and given invaluable suggestions. I am grateful to Pelican Publishing Company for being willing to bring my dream to reality.

Gwendoline Y. Fortune, Ed. D

CHAPTER 1

Gayla

A RED AND BLUE, LONG-BED pickup truck came up behind and skidded into my bumper. I cut my motor, opened the door, and jumped from my seat to check for damage. I wasn't hurt, but my car was two months old, and I loved its newness. Dammit, the light was red. Why didn't that idiot see it?

I glanced at the tiny scrape on my bumper. The pickup was right-angled to my car, its hood pointed left, just scant inches between the two vehicles. It was drizzling. Down from the cab came a pair of scuffed, tan, work boots topped by hairy, muscular, white legs and starched khaki pants hardly creased behind the knees.

"Sorry ma'am. My foot kindly slipped off the brake. You hurt?" A round head, short-cropped red hair and mustache, freckles, a thick neck slopping into narrow, fleshy shoulders followed the pants and checkered shirt, sleeves rolled up.

That accent, that Carolina drawl, reached out to me like a barbecue flame sizzles when meat spatters grease. Displeasure tightened my stomach, crawled upward, and tingled my spine.

"No, I'm okay. You barely touched me." I saw concern in the young fellow's eyes, which stopped my fear."You sure, lady? Lord, I hope so." The young man's face whitened, bringing his freckles to mole-like prominence. His hands shook when he pulled his driver's license from his rear pocket. I had swallowed my temper a zillion times before a face like his, a white face—especially a white male face—in a pickup truck.

"Well, let's see. How are you? Is your truck damaged?" I asked.

"No'um, it's pretty sturdy. It's my daddy's truck. I'm doing a delivery for him. He's got insurance. Don't you worry none."

Billy Joe Taylor, age 20, and I, Gayla Tyner, age 47, exchanged insurance and telephone numbers.

"If you have a problem, just give me a call, you hear?" Young Mr. Taylor seemed unaware of the caution stirred by his Carolina twang.

"I will. Thank you." I smiled over clenched teeth, my eyes not quite at ease. A Jane Austen quote squeezed into my head. 'One does not love a place the less for having suffered in it.' Maybe.

Back in the car I grabbed a handful of tissues, wiped the rain from my face, and completed my turn.

Yeah Gayla, I thought, here you are, back in the part of the world that you hate. Holding in my anger was a lesson I learned in Carolton, South Carolina. So, what in Hell's Bells was I doing back here, "down-home," "big-foot country," after all the jokes I'd heard about the South—where I was born. I had felt split in two even after I left. But down here, even if I was right, I was wrong—black and wrong.

I didn't grow up always happy in a town where I was, alternately, a precious child—because I was the daughter of Dr. J. C. Hughes—and teased or ignored—because I was "colored." Billy Joe Taylor didn't look or speak as if he were born into class privilege. I was. It was a dubious honor.

The last cloud moved beyond the sun. Two-storied old, red, gray, or buff buildings were faded Technicolor. Old white men in summer wash pants, pastel short-sleeved shirts, and suspenders walked hesitantly from under protective store entrances. I glimpsed young black men. I sensed something different. Young black men walked with their heads up, and some older ones who wore hats kept them on when they passed white women.

My decision to come "back home" to spend my sabbatical from teaching in Michigan brought on a growing malaise. I had not taken a sabbatical in more than seven years, so the university extended the usual term for an extra month, if I wanted it. My youngest child, Pamela, was at Howard University, in D.C., her first year at college. My adult home needed me less, my childhood home, more.

It wasn't only a dislike of my Southern roots that made me carry a perpetual bottle of antacids. I needed to resolve a tension that plagued me. My father and I were like a pair of scissors, matching sides and cutting edges. Our separation began very early. Once, I was pedaling my tricycle with my little sister, Janis, standing on the back. I bumped the doorframe. Janis fell and started to cry. I fell and bumped my head. Our daddy came running and picked up Janis. He said to me, "You mustn't hurt your little sister." Daddy always worried about Janis.

He needed me now. Mother needed me. I wanted to help her. I needed to want to help him.

I drove back home from Ann Arbor two weeks ago, rented a small apartment, and furnished it with items scrounged from my parents. Mother insisted I use the twin bed, dressing table, and mirror that had been in my bedroom when I was a teen. I settled in to work on neglected and tangled tasks for my elderly parents.

A new courthouse stood in the same place where the first one burned the year I left Carolton for college. Its Doric columns had been salvaged, scraped, painted, and placed exactly as they were before the fire. Are burned, reconditioned, wooden columns and scared people alike in any way, I wondered?

I looked at my watch and pushed the accelerator. Damn this lingering feeling about being late, my fear of displeasing my father. I had silently vowed not to be drawn into our old games. Still, when I was with my father I had a nagging emptiness and censored myself, squelching words that surged upward. Just once I'd like to tell him, "I'm grown up Daddy. I have been a long time. And I'm not always wrong." I couldn't be having a mid-life crisis. Could I? I wanted—needed—a little space, time to be alone, to think.

George, my husband, had begun to appear in my dreams. After more than twenty years together and three children, we ought to be ready to play together again. Returning to Carolton might help me get insight into my sense of ill ease, the men in my life—my father and my husband. I tugged my antacid tube from my purse and made a usual twenty-minute drive in fifteen.

A black, wrought-iron marker leaned a bit: "Dr. and Mrs. J. C. Hughes, Jr., 9119 Laney Drive." Rain had not reached the distance from downtown Carolton. My car pulled heavily against the steep grade from the graveled, country road to the crest of the circular drive. My mother and father were bending, straightening, and walking slowly in their vegetable garden behind and west of their home.

A sand-colored, brick house crowned a grassy hill. Inside, the rooms were generous, high ceilinged, and cool in hot weather. Daddy insisted that we say "home," not "house." I never knew if saying "home" was Dad's rule because it was Southern or middle-class.

Scruffy and Brownie sprawled in front of the open garage. Carolinians call dogs like Scruffy "a sooner," because he'd as soon be one breed as another; he's pretty much German Shepherd. Scruffy stared, wagged his tail twice, and ambled away. Brownie was Mother's lazy, arrogant, pedigreed cocker spaniel. She barely moved to avoid being run over. Maneuvering around her cinnamon, silky, well-fed slowness, I stopped the car and started toward my parents.

Daddy turned when he heard my footsteps on the graveled driveway. Mother shaded her eyes to see who was coming up the hill. My father hated to admit that he didn't hear as well as he once had. He was a short, well-proportioned man. His light-yellowish complexion and green eyes were striking, even at nearly eighty. Daddy carried himself with the poise of a man who was accustomed to being noticed.

He waved, "Morning, girl." Daddy called most women younger than himself 'girl.' On occasion he'd say, young lady. "Got a nice mess of garden peas here," he said.

Gardening warded off boredom for my parents who no longer needed to rush to their offices. Together, they'd picked less than a cupful of a late planting. Neither of them had a green thumb. I decided I wouldn't mention the accident with Billy Joe Taylor.

My lips brushed the cheek my father offered. He and I had the same long chin and our smiles were the same. I coveted his eyes. My sister, Janis, had Dad's emerald-green eyes. Mine were an ordinary brown.

"Where were you yesterday, Gayla Marie Hughes Tyner? You didn't come. You didn't call," Dad said.

"Good glory, Daddy, I decided to run over to Charlotte . . ."

Behind his shoulder, Mother winked and wiggled her fingers at me, a familiar 'cool it' signal. "J. C., Gayla's good to come visit with us. Now, we don't want to scare her back to Ann Arbor, do we?"

"Mavis, I want to be sure she's safe. Females have to be careful running 'round by themselves." He pointed a bony finger at my face. "You're too damned independent, always have been. Your mother and I take our vacations together. You shouldn't be down here without your husband. I want to see George too."

Dad didn't see me wink in agreement with Mother's caution. Different color eyes notwithstanding, Mother and I have the same slanted eyes—Indian eyes Grandpa called them—and similar visions from within those eyes.

I took the pan with the little green balls rolling across the bottom, "Thanks, Dad. After all, I'm going to be here four months, except for Christmas break. George is deep in a new project for the university and the space program. It's secret, as usual. I don't know the details."

Mother reached for a speckled, black-and-white-enameled tin and her weeding spade and tucked them into her gardening pocket. Unlike Dad, whose baldhead was sunburned red because he forgot to wear his hat, her wide-brimmed, yellow straw hat rested squarely on curly white hair. Her Polynesian brown skin was soft, and at seventy-four, hardly wrinkled except around the eyes when she smiled. My sister, Janis, and I were fortunate to have brown skin, Mother told us. "It doesn't dry and crease like white skin."

Heading toward the house, Mother scanned upward. "Sun's getting high. I don't care to be burnt to a crisp."

We took off our shoes in the mudroom. "A bit Chinese are the Hughes; we honor our ancestors and take off our shoes." Mother and I sing-songed familiar words. Daddy was silent. Laughing, Mother tapped my butt with her sun hat.

Alice, the latest in a long line of housekeepers—"the cook," Dad said—called from the kitchen, "Y'all want a tall, cool drink?"

"Not yet, thank you, Alice." Mother slipped her feet into pink, Daniel Green, house slippers. "We'll catch our breaths first."

In the pine-paneled den, Mother's size-five feet rested on a maroon leather ottoman, a mate to Daddy's dark green one. "Picking peas, watching you come up the hill made me think about when you told me, 'if I ever go to the electric chair . . .'" she said.

I had heard the story a hundred times over, but as always, I went along.

Mother leaned into the worn, cool cushion. "Oh, yes, electrocution country all around. Newspapers, radio, criminals, kidnappings. People joked about 'goin' to the chair.'" She sighed and closed her eyes. "You told me you wanted your last meal to be fried chicken, peas and carrots, corn soufflé (shoo-flay, she pronounced it), Jell-O, chocolate cake, and a glass of milk."

"I don't know if anyone jokes about 'goin' to the chair' anymore," I said. "My taste runs more to broiled fish and a salad, but I'll take the peas and carrots. No butter, please."

Dad strode across the den rug. He had stopped by the bathroom to wash the perspiration from his face and hands. The odor of Irish Spring soap spread behind him. He dropped into his green chair and opened his paper. Before lifting it to his face, he droned in his doctor's voice, "You're too thin now, girl. No butter?" His sunburned head was a distinct contrast to his bare, pink feet. He patted his waist. "Look at me. I eat what I want. I'm not fat. No butter . . ." He rattled his paper and dropped his head behind it.

"You look great, Dad." I smiled with what I hoped was agreeable exuberance. Not wanting to prolong his critique of my diet, or of myself, I turned to leave the room. "While you two catch your breath, I'll check that broken window in the guest bedroom." I hurried down the hall to measure a window I had seen when I was "borrowing" furniture. Hunters, in the nearby woods, had shattered it.

For the first time since George Tyner and I married, I was on my own, no children, no work, no routine. George reluctantly agreed for me to spend my sabbatical from the university with my parents. George didn't think I could do anything without his advice and approval. My sabbatical would give him a chance to miss me.

I measured the window and headed back to my parents. Most of their friends were now dead or in nursing homes. Mother didn't see as well as she had, and Dad was beginning to misplace and forget things.

"What did Pam have to say?" Mother said the moment I returned. "You heard from her, didn't you?" Mother's eyes were bright. News of her grandchildren cheered her.

"College is fun, not as hard as she feared." I filled her in even though she knew every detail of Pamela's first days away from home. "George Junior is getting used to working and I haven't heard from Antony since getting here. He forgot to pack enough toothpaste and he doesn't like the taste of the ones in Europe. They're all fine," I said.

"That Antony ought to have stayed in school." Dad lowered his paper, frowned, and shook his head. "Only reason to go overseas is if we're at war."

Mother's voice was quiet but firm. "Antony is a lot like Gayla. He likes adventure. That's why she went all the way up to Pennsylvania to college."

Daddy held his newspaper close to his eyes. He grunted. I grinned at Mother. "I have to run." With a quick kiss on the top of Dad's head and a hug for Mother, I retrieved my shoes.

Alice stood in the kitchen door. She was a tall, comfortable and comforting woman of about fifty. "Y'all ready for that long, cool, drink?"

"No thanks, Alice," I said. "Mother and Dad may want something by now. See you later."

Scruffy chased my car down the hill, barking and snapping at the tires, his head inches away. I stopped, got out, grabbed a handful of small rocks, and threw one near him. The dog stared, and after several more stops and stones, he left the chase. I'd be very happy if I could stop everything I didn't want as easily as I stopped Scruffy. I'd never throw rocks at George or my father. Maybe Daddy was right about Antony. My mind danced from one thing to another. George criticized me for "hopscotch thinking." He says I drive him crazy by bouncing from one topic to another.

Antony—our middle child, headstrong and independent as a firstborn or a baby in the family—was taking a year off. "Everyone does it," he insisted.

"Not us," George had said. "Especially not our people. We African American—used to be colored, used to be Negro— people have to stay on the case to make it in 'the man's world.'" He was only half joking with his litany of names our people had been called at different times in history. George and I were together on that point, to no effect.

"There's a whole other world out there, Pops. Don't be Neanderthal." Antony winked and hugged me. "That's not your style, Mom." He looked at his father. "I prefer to call us 'people of color,' Dad." Tony was trying, as usual, to turn a problem into a joke. Now, our Antony was bicycling around Europe, en route to Africa, sketching and taking pictures. "I'm going to be a planetary person," was the way he put it.

I came back to Carolton to sell our old family house on Lowell Avenue, where Janis and I grew up near the end of the Great Depression, which at the time we didn't know was going on. We weren't poor like most of the people we saw.

My first reason for taking a semester leave of absence was to help Mother and Dad. But unbidden, ignored, and buried questions were surfacing in my mind. What was happening between George and me? I was beginning to feel that we were living on different planets.

My family, the Hughes, was one of a few Negro families who did not owe our livelihood to the white-power world. Daddy's father had been a prominent minister in the county. To the white world, he was a well-known "colored" minister. White people would call Grandfather "Reverend" or "Doctor," but he would never be called "Mister." Daddy was, luckily, a "real" doctor, or he'd have been plain "J. C."

"Professor" Ellis, the school principal, drilled us in Friday assemblies, "Enunciate distinctly, say 'nee-grow.' That way white people can't slip and say nigra. That's too close to nigger," he'd lecture from the stage of the auditorium of Deerpath School. Ellis wasn't a professor either, but "Professor" wasn't "Mr."

We lived in a nine room, sprawling Victorian house. We had live-in housekeepers, two cars, and traveled somewhere away from the South every summer. These were prerogatives I took for granted in the world that Janis and I inhabited. When I moved out of our cocoon, I learned how small our world was. The total of our class was about four school principals, teachers, a couple of insurance agents, the undertaker, a handful of preachers, two dentists, our mother the pharmacist, and a few struggling entrepreneurs: barbers, a cobbler, tailor-pressers, grocers, and restaurant owners. That was our Negro middle and upper class—maybe a hundred, in a city of about twenty thousand, colored and white.

Grown-up and back in my womb of contention, I welcomed the opportunity to fathom who and what I was. When I looked at myself, my family, and my neighborhood, I knew I was privileged. My family, like nearly everyone we knew, was two, three, and four generations removed from the grinding degradation of slaves and sharecroppers. I should have been filled with a sense of belonging, even arrogance. I wasn't.

Education, property, and prestige did not bring a sense of self-esteem. The schizophrenia—of segregation and enmity surrounded my world like a foggy morning on the banks of Lake Dillard.

By two o'clock, the sun was high and hot. I passed the oldest cemetery in the county on my way to the bank to meet Dad's real-estate agent. Across the street from Restview Cemetery, a house, nearly obscured by giant trees and unkempt shrubbery, was barely visible behind years of neglect. I saw something or someone move. The cemetery aroused childish fantasies. I looked straight ahead.

Myrtle Lee

Myrtle Lee Urmann was hidden on her sagging front porch by an overgrowth of shrubbery that had not been pruned or trimmed in twenty-five years. She took a slow swallow of bourbon from the cut-glass tumbler. She paid no attention to the gray film on the outside of the beautifully-carved glass in her hand. Myrtle Lee Urmann no longer cared if the glass was washed, or if the lovely furnishings in her house were dusted.

Myrtle Lee talked to herself a lot. She'd been alone so long there was no line between thought and the spoken word. "There she goes. Since she came back from up North, she spends lots of time riding around town. I've seen her looking all around a dozen times. She's going to write a book about us, I bet. Old lies never die. She's gonna spread the story of Henry Lee and me, a black man and a poor white trash, folks like to say. Miss fine colored lady wouldn't recognize me. If I told her that we used to play together she wouldn't remember. I do. McGuire Street for me. Lowell for her. I didn't know back then that Lowell was a name for the rich people's street and McGuire a name for the poor folk's street. Henry Lee, I sure do miss you." The last words were silent, inside her head, but Myrtle Lee didn't know or care.

"Damn Mama, anyway," she mumbled in the haze of her morning round of trying not to remember. She wanted me to marry Mr. Stuart Urmann because he was a big shot-banker."

Gayla

I found the documents the real estate agent wanted in my parents' safety deposit box. Mr. Crutchen was a thin, nervous, blond man, beginning to bald. His upper lip sweated and he said, "Yes ma'am" at least two dozen times during the hour we sorted and studied papers. I can't stand "ma'am," but I hid my amusement at the irony of being called "ma'am" in South

Carolina. It used to be taboo like "Mrs., Miss, and Mr."

At a teller's window my attention was caught by a stout, mahogany man calling, loudly, to a slim, gray-haired, beige-brown woman.

"Hey lady, ain't you Maxine Lomax? What you doin' here?"

The woman searched for the source of the voice, cocked her head to one side, threw back her shoulders, and smiled in recognition. "Dan Scott, you old scalawag. I didn't know you right off." She pursed her eyebrows and, focused on the man's expanded stomach. "Looks like you been sopping a whole barrel of biscuits. Why, man, I came home to die, that's what."

Placing hands that could palm a basketball on his substantial waist, the man she called Dan Scott shrugged his upper body side-to-side and teased, "What you say?"

The woman lightly touched his colorful shirt. She smiled more broadly. "I hear the Sloans moved down from Philly, back out on their family farm near Plainland. Big Jon is back from California, and the Walkers retired from Chicago. Looks like everybody who left here in the old days is comin' home to die. Ain't that a caution?"

Together, laughing, the couple pushed open the heavy, bronze door to the street.

My head overflowed with images of people I had heard of or neighbors who went North and West or stayed in the military after World War II and Korea. They left Carolton to find jobs and better living than Negro people were allowed before Medgar Evers, Martin Luther King, Jr., and sit-ins. They were coming "back home." It didn't make sense to me why anyone would come back to old hurts that rested lightly beneath the surface, scars festering in every Southern drawl and Rebel license plate on the front of eighteen wheelers glimpsed through rearview mirrors. Were the painted signs that screamed "White" and "Colored" gone from the insides of people's minds as well as from the storefronts and waiting room doors?

I left the bank. Rain-washed streets by now had dried in the hot, autumn sun. An old, slow speech cadence was beginning to seep into my ears.

Louise would be home by now. Louise Hendricks and I exchanged Christmas cards and once in a while, we mailed each other letters. When I called, the night before, Louise said, "I'll be home right about three, come on over." Carolton was not the cold Mid-west; if you wanted to see someone, you didn't have to wait for an invitation.

I stopped at my apartment, freshened, and caught myself frowning in the mirror. I was a year younger than Lou, even if she was prettier. I, reflexively, reached into my purse for an antacid and shrugged. I didn't need one.

On my way across town, I noticed that Carolton had once been cleaner. Running through the neighborhood in shorts and sandals, I had once passed houses where colored people planted flowers in their front yards, even if the house was rented. Without sidewalks, flower borders were lined to the very edge of the streets. Cars and people passing would stir the blossoms with a rippling breeze—yellow, blue, pink, and red like waves in a multicolored sea.

I turned onto Spring Street, where the most popular girls had lived thirty years earlier. The houses were still neat, and strangely smaller. Then, newer houses began. Sidewalks separated lawns from streets. Houses and yards were twice and three times as large as the ones at the beginning of Spring Street. Lots were uniformly shaped. I felt lost.

I parked in front of an attractive ranch house and followed a stone path to the door. It opened before I could ring the bell.

"Come in, come in," a breathy voice said. "I heard you were in town." Louise swung the door wide.

"This is one nosy place," I said. "I haven't seen three people to speak to since I've been here."

Louise May Hendricks was beautiful; luminous black hair curled around her ears and forehead. She had a slim figure, skin the color of butterscotch, and deep-set, hazel eyes that were, at once, sad and glistening with fun. She didn't walk; she floated, elegantly on the earth. People in Carolton said Louise looked like Lena Horne, only prettier. Louise married Lloyd Brown during her sophomore year in college. "He was," she said, "too much in Marine blues." Lloyd died before he was thirty.

We embraced, shoulders only, southern style.

"You don't look a day over thirty, and I know your age, you know," Louise said. "And nobody can come back to this burg without the word getting out as quick as a lightning flash."

I inhaled and, smacked my lips. "Smells delicious in here." Louise beckoned me to follow to her kitchen. "Just a few peaches my mother brought from down in the country. What are you doing here, lady? You said you'd never stop in this town for more than a hot minute."

"First, let me look around," I said. "Your house is as lovely as it smells. Show me."

Louise's house was tastefully decorated. An alcove off the living room was lined with photographs: Louise's parents; her husband, Lloyd, in his Marine dress uniform; her sister; and one of a baby, lying, as if asleep, on a white lace tablecloth. Straightening already perfect alignments, she touched each picture as if in introduction.

"This baby is my aunt. I'm named for her." Louise said. "She died before a live photograph could be made. The old custom was to take a 'laid-out' picture.

"These old-fashioned, wooden frames aren't in with today's style," Lou said, "but they've been in my family a long time."

"They give your home a special air," I said. "Besides, have you ever been inside a black home where family pictures aren't all over the house, even the bathroom? We've lost so much of our past, we hold onto what we can."

"I hadn't thought of it that way." Louise rubbed a nonexistent spot of dust.

I stopped before a picture of a little girl. "This is you, I know, but it reminds me of someone else. Do I know a relative of yours?"

Louise stroked her hand down her throat, her face not quite a frown. "Not a legal one anyway. Answer me, Lady Gay, what brings you back?"

"Sorry, I'm admiring, and envying. I'm on leave of absence, a well-deserved R and R and a little time with my parents. They're not as hardy as they used to be."

"Sounds good to me. Everybody needs a break once in awhile. How is your gorgeous George?"

"George is fine," I said. I hoped my longtime buddy didn't notice that I was looking at a portrait of an elderly gentleman with a Santa Claus beard instead of into her eyes.

"If you say so, girl." Louise beckoned for me to follow her.

"Carolton seems so peaceful," I said. "Are things as calm and friendly as they appear?" She motioned me to a seat. "I can't get over Dad's real estate man, 'yes ma'aming' me the entire time we were together."

"You'll get used to it," she said. Louise and I sat in her sun-filled kitchen, the tantalizing odor floating up to the skylight. She served two bowls of warm peach cobbler.

"I'm sure everyone is relieved to get that segregation thing out of the way." I licked my spoon. Lou had taken a smaller portion for herself. "My dad used to say the South would be the best place for our people when that legal segregation stuff was done away with. He said, because colored and white grew up close together down here we understood one another better than immigrants and colored in the North."

"KKK feelings are lurking out there somewhere, I suppose." Louise tasted her warm fruit and sugary syrup. "Tar and feathers are gone, but it will be a cold day in Hades when Carolton has an African-American mayor." She reached for my bowl to give me another portion.

"No, no," I covered my dish. "The waistline can't take it. But let me know when the nightriders are on the way, will you? I hope there're no more dark-of-night chases because black and white people fall in love."

"Sure, like I have a direct line to headquarters. We haven't a thing to worry about," she said.

"Promise?" I asked.

"By the power of the creme de la creme." Louise clasped my hand in the secret grip of our high school club.

She washed our bowls. We swore we'd get together soon. Louise's phone rang just as she opened the door to let me leave. She blushed and quickly mumbled, "Bye." Until then, our visit had been Southern slow.

I felt strangely rushed. I felt that I sometimes made hasty judgments. The phone had rung, and of course, she would hurry to answer it. Except, Janis once said, "I've known you all my life, Gay, and you're usually pretty much on target. You're psychic." But maybe Louise was eager to answer the phone, that's all. Besides, everyone is entitled to secrets.

Driving through streets I once walked, skated, and biked brought me to our old, vacant house. It was drab and dilapidated. The gutters overflowed with dry leaves and the windows gaped, empty of glass. An ugly factory hovered three blocks away. Its garish, hideous, green, water tank marred the view of trees on a hill that once beautifully framed the evening sun.

Every room in our old, rambling house had been large. With "catty-cornered" furniture leaving lots of room, I chased my sister, our voices reverberating off twelve-foot-high ceilings. Mother was exasperated when her bookworm daughters took King Arthur, the newest Bobbsey Twins, Langston Hughes, or Louisa Mae Alcott into an empty room. She'd call and call, but deep in our imagined worlds, we couldn't hear her with the door closed.

I looked down the darkening street and checked my watch. I'd told George I would' call him before ten. Hurrying by the old cemetery, I noticed it wasn't as frightening as it once seemed. Hundreds of stories in there, for sure.

CHAPTER 2

George

GEORGE TYNER LIFTED TWO RECTANGULAR, yellow and blue boxes from the frozen food bin in the sprawling, daylight bright supermarket. He caught his full lower lip between his teeth, flattening the corners of his full, black mustache. He looked from one to the other of the packages.

George sensed someone moving closer to him. He turned to see Dr. Thalea Davison, her svelte, much above average figure in a coral jumpsuit.

"Your wife's on leave and you have the look of a man who isn't at home in a market. Need some assistance?" The woman pushed her ebony hair behind her shoulder. Her smile heightened nearly imperceptible sun crinkles at the edge of dark, almost purple, eyes.

"Hi, Thalea. I'm trying to figure out the difference between medium and large on these frozen veggies. Does confusion translate into self-pity?" George threw a frosted bag of broccoli into his cart. "How did your paper go over at the conference?"

"I don't recall a standing ovation, but it was well received," she said. "My colleagues can only take a limited number of reports on econometrics. But honestly, may I help?"

"Thanks, not really. Gayla left the freezer and pantry chock-full and I eat out often. I stopped to get milk and decided to try my hand at dirtying a pot or two."

He'd heard that Thalea Davison was recovering from divorce. Campus gossip was that it was her second. The rumor

23

was that she used her first husband to get her doctorate, her second to get to Ann Arbor, where he was a faculty member. Bets were out on when she'd turn up with number three. Davison had been on faculty three years and no one was making book on if she'd ever get tenure.

"I'm on my way out. Care for coffee?" George said, aware of an emptiness in him that was not for groceries.

"Why not? Kilgore's or Gareto's?"

George dropped the icy bag back into the frosty bin. "Who needs it," he shrugged. "Gareto's coffee is fresher this late in the day."

Sipping a second espresso Thalea said, "You've heard I'm divorced, I suppose?"

"You know the tangled vine. Should I offer condolences?" George wasn't sure of the tone he should take.

"No, indeed. It was a necessary ending." He thought her face showed no stress. "I've moved to an apartment on the west side of town, near the lake. No memories, no problems."

"You're farther from campus," he said.

"I like my privacy."

The mid-October evening was not cold. He and Thalea strolled around the small lake in the park across from her apartment. A flock of Canadian geese flying south landed, stirring the water to a series of half-moons. Several geese wandered, shaking, preening their feathers, unmindful of the two humans.

"I've heard that some birds mate for life. Do geese?" Thalea said.

"I'm not sure," he said.

Thalea picked up a tiny gray and white feather from the grass. "People don't seem to be much like birds."

"I guess some people are like some birds, flying from place to place," George said.

Thalea tilted her head in the direction of her apartment building. She smiled broadly beneath the streetlight. "Now that we've solved the major issues of life and love, would you join me in a nightcap before you go to your empty abode?"

George felt a familiar twitch at the corner of his lower left lip. He knew she was flirting with him. He knew he'd promised himself he wouldn't get involved in another affair. Damn, he thought, she's gorgeous. Gay will never know and she's miles away. He tucked her arm in the bend of his elbow. "Delighted, I assure you," he said and let her lead him into the chandelier-lit foyer.

Inside her apartment Thalea mixed martinis. They joked about similar experiences in the political inner sanctum of the university: competition, drinking, marital problems, and the occasional failure to gain tenure.

Thalea said, "Time passes fast when the company's good. Do you mind if I catch the late news?" She handed him another martini.

"Fine with me. My work takes all the thought I want to give. I don't tax myself with political goings-on." George settled into the beige sofa, its oversized blue flowers feminine behind his shoulders.

When the program ended, Thalea turned off the television. Red lights flashed on the stereo. Another martini and the blue flowers disappeared between them.

"I'm glad I stopped at the market," she said. "You don't think I'm brazen for saying so, do you?"

"I say, thanks for shopping." George brushed her neck with the back of his hand. Inhaling her unfamiliar perfume, he bent toward her. Thalea did not pull away. He held his lips to a pulse at the curve of her shoulder, feeling its increase when his hand traced the shape of her breasts. She relaxed into him. George marveled at the small differences between women; each mouth had its own definitiveness; each body fit just so.

"This room is confining." Thalea stood. George followed her. Her bedroom was, strangely, as masculine as her living room was feminine. The king-sized bed was low, made of an expensive, dark wood. A matching chest and armoire gave an almost oppressive feel to the room. The music was faint, but loud enough to discern Johnny Mathis's voice.

"Believe me, I didn't anticipate this." Thalea hesitated a moment, then moved close to George.

"You know what you want when you see it, and you don't hide it. I like that in a woman," he said.

"I'm glad you approve." She drew one arm over his shoulder.

"If you wear outfits like this one, you can expect the wish if not the fact." He unbuttoned her coral outfit and held it open to let her step out slowly, one leg at a time.

Thalea laid her clothes on a chair beside the bed. "I won't lie. I felt, if not now, then soon."

Entwining hands, they sat on her bed. She handed him his glass from the bedside table. She finished her drink, took his empty glass, and put both on the floor.

"Lights on or off?" she whispered.

"On, if it's all right with you."

"It is."

"Sweet Thalea," he breathed, gazing into almost familiar purple eyes.

CHAPTER 3

Gayla

I HURRIED TO MY APARTMENT and dialed my home number. It was later than I intended, nearly half past ten. Even if George was in the basement, he could get upstairs by eight rings. I planned to call again at midnight, but fell asleep.

My eyes opened abruptly. The clock glowed 2:46 A.M. A conversation between my teaching assistant and another student sprang into consciousness like a videotape in my head.

"How can you look her in the eye?" a young, unrecognized voice asked.

"You know the old saying, what you don't know won't hurt you," my TA, Melody, answered.

"Yeah well, my last roommate got in trouble for having an affair with her psych professor."

I drew a breath and exhaled slowly, the way the yoga teacher taught me. My TA and her companion didn't know I had come to the office earlier than usual to look up a letter I needed to answer.

Melody said, "I'm cool, sister. Professor T has been a juggler for a long time. I can tell."

Jangling metal jewelry and girlish laughter muffled the next words. I scraped my chair against the tile floor. The voices stopped. I took the letter from my desk and walked out of my windowless office into the central area that was an anteroom for the offices shared with three other faculty members.

"Good morning, ladies. Melody." I smiled and nodded to them. "We're early today, aren't we?"

"Morning, Dr. Tyner." Looking like kids who've misbehaved and been caught, the women spoke at the same time.

Melody stammered, "Can I get anything for you?"

"No thanks, I've found what I came for. I'll be back after my ten-thirty class."

Why was I thinking about this now? There were at least three male members of the faculty, that I knew of, whose names began with T: Tarkov, Tolliver, and Tyner. I heard Melody's silver and turquoise earrings skimming the shoulders of her purple knit tee shirt as she lowered her eyes to avoid mine. I finally drifted into sleep.

The next afternoon two children popped up beside a shrub at my door when I drove into the courtyard of the apartment complex. The taller girl said, "Hi, I'm Shaundra. I'm seven-and-a-half. You're new so we came to welcome you."

A smaller girl said shyly, "My name's Elizabeth. I'm almost seven."

The children offered to help carry packages from the car to my apartment.

"Are you a school teacher?" curious, outgoing Shaundra asked.

"Why, yes, I am." I hated that question. I had long ago become accustomed to whites who couldn't fathom an African American who spoke "good English" being anything except a teacher. But Shaundra was African American. I wondered what makes me look like my occupation.

The naturalness with which the girls held hands when they followed me to the door was refreshing. Shaundra had a glowing walnut complexion, tall and wiry for seven and a half. Her thick black hair, which glistened in sunlight, with burgundy-red highlights was intricately braided and sculpted in winding curves. Shaundra's mother was an artist. Shaundra's black eyes were self-assured and intent, above a high-bridged nose and full-lipped smile. Permanent teeth were beginning to change her small-child face.

Elizabeth's head barely reached her friend's shoulder. Shapely, sturdy legs supported her compact swimmer's body; devilish blue eyes were ringed by slightly curling, earlobe-length, blonde hair. Elizabeth had lost her first baby tooth, the left front one, but she grinned widely. I hoped that older kids wouldn't tease her until she hid her mouth with her hands.

I offered my new friends glasses of apple juice, if it was okay with their mothers. Shaundra ran to her apartment and came back panting, "It's okay, my Mom says, and she's sitting Elizabeth."

Shaundra and Elizabeth set their glasses on the floor to play with my doll collection. I hadn't taken time to arrange them in the apartment. Shaundra said, "This one is from Nigeria." Elizabeth lisped, "Nitheria" as she cradled Oya, the Yoruba queen. Oya, in black and red robes and gold beaded earrings, was the largest of the dolls I decided to bring to Carolton. The girls called her "The Mommy." Ten minutes later, tantalizing noises pulled them outside.

I had signed a month-to-month lease on a Sexton Place apartment. When I lived in Carolton, years earlier, I couldn't walk or ride through such a neighborhood without fear of being called names, watched from behind lace curtains, or chased by white boys who circled close enough on bicycles to make me fall off and scrape my knees. It felt odd, the ease with which I rented an apartment now.

Sexton Place boasted adult and family courts. I like the sounds of children playing and fighting, so I picked family. The kids in Court Four were popular. They attracted friends from all over the neighborhood.

I sat down to my broiled patty and salad and finished with strawberries and cottage cheese. The fruit, grown nearby, was sweeter here than in Ann Arbor. The sounds of the children were an intrusion and a reminder of the difference between the world of my recent visitors and that of Allison and of McGuire Street when I was six and seven years old. My child-hood friends and neighborhood wandered into conscious-ness, unbidden and as real and present as Shaundra,

Elizabeth, and their friends who played in the courtyard outside my window.

"Tit for tat, tit for tat.
You kill my dog, I kill your cat."
McGuire Street is two blocks long with a tail that connects it to
Lowell Avenue where Gayla, Janis, and their friends Drew and Tally
live. The first block begins at a dead end, the back of a grocery store.
Colored families live in one block; white families live in the next.
Houses are identical from one end to another: two-, three-, or four-room
frame, with chimneys dead center with openings for fireplaces or black,
pot-bellied, iron stoves that heat the front room and bedroom, back to
back. Fathers in both blocks leave before dawn, in overalls or work
pants, and walk across town to the cotton mills that circle Carolton.

Mothers care for four, five, or more children. They cook, wash out-
doors in backyards, and stop the children from fighting, then go inside
again to sweep balls of soft lint that grow like cotton candy under beds,
tables, and ironing boards.

Mothers in the black block go to work cleaning, cooking, and serv-
ing as nursemaid for well-to-do white families anywhere except on
McGuire Street.

White mothers wait tables at Sam's Homecooking and the Robert E.
Lee Hotel dining room. A few work in the mills, and they brush white
lint from their hair, stomping it from their shoes on the steps near dusk.
Adults on either side of Ashley Street, the cross street that separates the
two McGuires, do not trespass across the dividing line. But children
wander block to block, black to white, white to black, singly and in
troops of two or more, stopping when an infrequent car travels north
or south on Ashley, during gas-rationed World War II.

By rumor or surreptitious observation, names, ages, and life stories
cross the permeable boundary. Children are playmates from school, out
until dark on the long, hot summer days. Not really friends but tenu-
ous comrades, they are aware of an invisible, solid barrier wider than
Ashley Street. Six, seven, and eight years old, they feel the wall and
don't know what it is, or why it is there.

Allison lives in the white block on McGuire. The tiny girl is hydro-
cephalic. She spends her years in a stroller—a heavy, metal vehicle with
what was once white, solid rubber tires. Her brother and sister wheel the

stroller outdoors and casually tend to her. Allison drools if she falls sideways. Her sister or brother wipes her chin with the towel squeezed under the stroller arm. A crowd of multicolored onlookers come to watch and ask questions. Allison is quiet, her oversized head braced between soiled, rolled towels tied with grocery string. Her brother tells everyone, in front of Allison, that she will die when she is seven. The dwarfed child, sitting strapped in her closure, doesn't show any emotion when the children innocently and openly talk about her coming death. Her brother, Tim, says, "She knows." He seems to enjoy his role as expert narrator. Her sister, Myrtle Lee, a year older than Allison, is embarrassed.

Curiosity satisfied and wrapped up with a daily "Hey, Allison" flung at her, the kids continue their games. She watches them play hopscotch, baseball, an old broom bat, and marbles in the red dirt sidewalk. Mothers come out to call their own to supper. Once in awhile, a grandpa, his lungs crippled by cotton lint, does the calling in. The Hughes family is called "rich" by folks, like Allison's father, who works in cotton mills. Mill-Hill people, colored and white, live in "shotgun" houses. Daylight shines right through from the front to back door.

Word spreads into the colored block of McGuire, up the hill to Lowell, and throughout the neighborhood the day Allison dies, which is two weeks after her eighth birthday. The afternoon of her funeral, the Negro children watch from across the street. They would not have thought of going to her funeral in a white church. Allison's brother and sister, Tim and Myrtle Lee come down the front steps, all dressed up and crying. If they see their colored "friends" on the other side of the street when the pink casket is carried down the steep rickety steps, they don't show it. The onlookers have never seen Allison any way except sitting in her old stroller. Her casket is longer than the children imagine it should be. Nobody thought about how tall she might have been if she could stand up.

Allison's funeral is in a Pentecostal church where the members play tambourines and shout. People like Gay and Jan think this is weird. Class is their buffer against discrimination.

For a time, Allison is the focus that brings disparate children together long enough for them to plant feelings and memories. After her death, the visits over Ashley Street cease.

Every house on McGuire Street is a novel full of stories. JoAnn, a tough colored woman nearly six feet tall, with a laugh you can hear many houses away, falls down her long flight of front steps one night. There are no lights or grading in the streets where poor people live. JoAnn tears her left calf open from her knee almost to her ankle. The wound is jagged, uneven, without much bleeding. JoAnn walks several blocks to Dr. Hughes' to have him sew up the cut. The night is cloudy, cool, and late, the smell of whiskey thick in the spare room that the doctor uses as an emergency office. Hospitals are expensive, and the colored cannot be sure of their treatment in the hands of The County Hospital.

"Paper time. Where's my news girl?" Dr. J. C. calls.

Gay runs to the pile of old newspapers kept behind the back door for such regular happenings. A future doctor's practice cannot begin too early.

"Is this enough?" she asks, her chin holding down fluttering pages, arms aching.

"We'll see, but I think so." The doctor arranges a white, enameled, blue-bordered tray of sterile syringes, needles, curved shiny steel scissors, and catgut.

Blood does not bother Gay. Cleaning up crimson-soaked gauze and cotton swabs is normal on a Saturday night. Her father takes so many stitches in JoAnn's leg, his hand stiffens. He shakes his wrist, blowing on his fingers.

"JoAnn, you've got some tough skin here, girl. Like an alligator. How about letting Gay rest me for a spell?"

Winks, the tiger-striped cat, watches and rubs his back on the doorframe. He arches his back higher and jumps when JoAnn's laugh roars through the house.

"Course not. You strong enough, Little Doc?" She looks at Gay as if to say, after what she's been through, nothing can really hurt her.

Gay takes three sutures, sweat popping out on her brow. JoAnn does not flinch. Chewing gum snaps, loud and steady.

JoAnn's McGuire Street holds a fascination for Gay and her best buddy, Tally Johnston. Their parents warn them to stay away from low-class people: "poor white trash" and "shiftless colored." One afternoon Mrs. Johnston sends Tally to Handy's Store for a loaf of bread. His pa likes lightbread once in awhile, a change from biscuits and cornbread.

"Go right straight to that store. Don't you cut through that Devil street." Mrs. Johnston shakes a finger, white-floured from dredging the dinner pork chops, at the children.

Tally and Gay start off. The lure of a short cut is too much on that hot day. On the return trip they stop to sneak a look into The Beer Garden, a narrow brown-and-white-trimmed frame building with one small window in front, its door wide open. They slow to a pokey-walk to watch the patrons on stools in front of a counter that lines a long wall. Neon lights in the jukebox mark garish forms in the dark interior. A glass, chrome, red, blue, and green monster blasts music that Tally's African Methodist Episcopal Church member mother calls *"scandalous."* Alarmed by their boldness and rank disobedience, they edge closer to hear the forbidden music. They grab each other's arms, digging stubby and chewed fingernails into each other's flesh. How could that happy rhythm, the rich guitar vibrations that make them feel so good, be bad?

Inside the human cavern, a man dances with a woman, hands clasped around her back. Each palm rests lightly, fingers stroking over a cheek of her buttocks. She wears a clinging rayon dress, dipping loose in front, hiked up in back, her pink slip showing. Red tulips on the shiny fabric stand out against the yellow background of her dress. Four hazel-brown eyes wander upward, adjusting to the darkness. The couple hardly moves, swaying from hip to head. He is a short, light colored man, the kind called high-yellow, and is no taller than the thin, darker woman. A wave of sweet perfumed heat invades the children's noses.

"Yeah, baby. Groovy," he moans. From the darkness cracks a deep, gravelly voice, *"Hot damn, shake that thing."*

Seeing the bodies undulate like the snaking movement of whirly cars at the county fair, the boy and girl, nine years old on their last birthdays, feel warmer than the sun allowed. Strange waves stir their stomachs, down to their thighs. They turn to each other, gulp, and squeal. *"He's dancing with a lady with his hat on!"* They now know what *"low-class,"* and what *"low-down"* means.

The children bolt from their hiding spot near the porch of The Beer Garden. Confused, Gay crashes into the hedge at the corner of Mom Dutch's yard. Tally runs wildly, taking the longest way home. Mrs. Johnston is surprised to see them flushed and out of breath. She doesn't have time to ask why. Pa will be home shortly and supper is running late.

Behind her house the next day, Gay and Tally whisper about the music, the smells, and the dancers. They do not mention the funny feelings the dancers aroused in their bodies.

I was startled back to Sexton Place by the ringing telephone. I almost said, "Dr. Hughes' residence," the way Janis and I were taught.

"I let it ring six times." George said. "Did you just come in?"

"No, I've been day dreaming about the good old days," I said.

"You sound like they weren't all that good. How are you? Did you tell that lawyer what I said, how to minimize the tax bite for your folks?" George lectured with his boss voice.

"George, everything's fine. The market's slow, till spring. I'll let you know when anything breaks," I felt my jaw tense. "And George, there were good, bad, and funny good old days." I fished the antacid package out of my purse.

"I could have managed this little matter by phone and fax. You could have stayed here, at home."

"I know you could have and I could have. But they enjoy having me. Mother does anyway. You agreed that I could use some time off, and in . . ."

"Look, babe," George said, "I've stopped with the frozen dinners. They don't fill me up, and they cost too much."

"Are you trying to make me feel guilty, George? I left lots of casseroles and soup in the freezer and you like to eat on campus. I'll be home soon." I didn't like the apology in my voice.

Beneath his jocular effort, a childlike whine sneaked through. "With Pam away, you could give me a little more attention."

"I like your teasing, George. Thanks for calling. Bye, love."

CHAPTER 4

Gayla

EARLY THE NEXT MORNING, I drove to one of my favorite spots, a creek that used to wind through a pasture near a small grove of honeysuckle, oak, and pine trees. The creek had been incorporated into part of a nature preserve. I followed the meandering water for nearly an hour before I felt relaxed, refreshed, and hungry.

On the way back to town, blue lights circled ahead of me. A policeman in a yellow and black slicker waved traffic to the curb. Flares in each of his hands glowed surreal-like sparks into the overcast morning. The line of varying shapes and sizes of brake lights, among them a school bus and a truck or two, waited in the morning haze. I could not see why we were being delayed. Snaking onto the street from a wide driveway came a mix of black and white city police and tan and yellow county sheriff's vehicles. Impatient to get to work, drivers paced outside their cars and tapped their fingers on metal doors. A few stood around languidly, in no hurry. Her hair in curlers, a woman, embarrassed at being seen, slumped in her front seat.

A white and red rescue vehicle turned into the street from the driveway. It followed the last police car, red lights whirling, but without warning sirens. A traffic monitor held the waiting cars before official release. Two men in work garb dodged across the street emerging from the taped off area.

"What's the trouble, boy?" a male voice yelled from the stalled gathering.

"Boy got hisself shot to death by the police," a raspy voice answered, making its way to a pickup.

"Know who it was? White or black?"

A third man followed the raspy voice to the pickup. He joined the curious crowd. "Boy name of Billy, white boy from down Bakerstown. Seem like he run away from the police 'bout four A.M. this morning and they cornered him in the back of the church parking lot here. Boy wouldn't get out of his car till sunup. Jumped out with a gun in his hand and the police shot him dead."

People standing around or sitting in cars shook their heads. Some tugged at the remains of their morning meal with toothpicks. The officer at the front of the line motioned the halted traffic forward. Everybody got back in their cars and moved on. I edged ahead slowly, through the accumulated traffic, until I reached my turn.

The next morning I unrolled the newspaper. The headline read, "Man Shot Dead in Parking Lot." The story followed, "William Joseph Taylor, age twenty, of Bakerstown, was shot by local law enforcement officers in the parking lot of Calvary Baptist Church at 7:20 A.M. yesterday when he refused to leave his car at the officers' request. Mr. Taylor got out of his car with gun in hand and the officers opened fire . . ."

My doorbell rang. My young friend, Elizabeth, stood outside with her favorite doll in her arm. "Miss Gayla, my momma said can you come over for a spell? She wants to ask you a favor."

Holding hands, the small blonde girl and I crossed the courtyard. Elizabeth's mother, Beverly, paced in front of her living room window, a box of tissues in her hand. She dropped a wet one in the wastebasket.

"Thanks for coming. I hope I didn't interrupt you too much."

"No, no. Are you all right?"

"I didn't watch the TV news last night," she said, sobbing. "I was tired. I see a story in today's paper about a man shot by the police. Did you see it?" The tearful woman motioned me to a seat on a deep, cushioned, sectional sofa. She sat tensely, holding the tissue box.

I sat beside her. "I saw the paper, too," I said. "It's really odd, I was held up by traffic where it happened yesterday. Is he someone you know?"

"I'm so mad I can't stop crying." About five feet two, Beverly's nondescript brown hair had, no doubt, once been the same gold as Elizabeth's. My new neighbor patted her red-veined eyes, her eyelids swollen. "That boy was the sweetest kid you ever saw, wouldn't hurt a soul. I worked with him. He bagged and stocked shelves at the grocery store where I keep the books. Only job he could get, even though he had a year at the technical college. The big, new supermarket opened and our store had to cut back. We had to let him go."

I didn't know Beverly well. We chatted a few times after Elizabeth and Shaundra became my young friends.

"Could you, please drive me to Bakerstown to see his family? I know they're real broken up, and I'd like to pay my respects. My husband is out of town and my car is in the shop. Now, if you're real busy just tell me, there won't be any hard feelings. I don't know who else to ask. Elizabeth can stay at Shaundra's."

"Give me about twenty minutes and I'll take you, if that's okay. It's about ten or fifteen miles if I remember correctly."

I felt I had no reason not to go, not to be accommodating to a neighbor. My memory of Bakerstown was that it was a red-neck corner of the county. Negroes had always been careful not to exceed the speed limit when we drove through the Bakerstown speed trap—at the bottom of a hill.

An hour later, Beverly and I were in Bakerstown. A line of cars was parked in the driveway of a neat, yellow, frame house with green shutters. Cars were pulled onto the grass to leave room for others along the roadway. I felt uneasy among the yard and roomful of local whites. The men, with work-rough-ened faces and hands, wore dress-up pants and suits in which they appeared uncomfortable. The women's faces could have used sunblocker. I was introduced as "My college professor neighbor from up North."

"He couldn't find work nowhere." A man's voice cracked, on the verge of tears. Holding his wife's hand, the dead man's father, a thin, sun-scorched man sat in a straight-backed dining room chair.

Mrs. Taylor looked so like her husband they could have been sister and brother. Her pale gray eyes were dry, empty, seemingly running images of her son in a film loop. "He even went as far as Savannah looking for work. We told him it didn't matter to us. He had a place to stay long's he needed one. We wouldn't never let him go hungry. All the work is leaving this part of the country, like it done over and over before."

Neighbors, friends, and kin bowed their heads in agreement. A couple of men went to the front porch and blew their noses.

Mr. Taylor said, "Near dark, most days, he'd walk afar to the end of the field and look out at the sun go down and the moon come up, like maybe he was making a wish on 'em."

Mrs. Taylor's lips hardly moved. "He was a good boy. Even the critters come out of the woods close by him when he'd sit under a tree to rest. A good boy." She looked both too young to be mother to a twenty year old and very old, like her mountain and upcountry ancestors.

Her husband squeezed her hand. "I don't want to be dreaming up what's not so, but it's almost like he was asking for it. He sat in that car until daylight before he got out, nearly three hours. Like he wanted everybody to see him."

A late model sports car drove into the yard. The crowd opened up to let two young black men enter the overflowing room. The tallest ebony man, with prominent facial bones that gave his eyes an oriental shape, approached the parents. "Mr. Taylor, Mrs. Taylor, you remember us. We went to school with Billy Joe." He paused, lowered his head. "We heard what happened. I've been up in Virginia to college, and my brother here goes to Maryland State."

The brother, identical except thinner, squeezed his baseball cap into a ball. "We want you to know how sorry we are. We were good friends."

The young men shook Mr. Taylor's hand, nodded respectfully to the dead boy's mother, and murmured good-bye to the roomful of people. The shorter brother flinched; his head jerked in my direction when he caught me in his sweep of the room. His dark eyes narrowed.

Beverly and I repeated our condolences and left. Outside, a young woman, who had to be young Taylor's sister, was talking to mourners who were drinking iced tea around a green, plastic-covered card table.

"That gun wasn't even loaded, but don't nobody ever let on to Daddy and Momma. It would kill them." The young woman spoke softly, looking back and forth between the house and her plastic cup.

Beverly sniffled all the way back to Carolton. "Poor boy, poor boy," she murmured, blowing her nose as discretely as she could.

The next morning there was no follow-up story on the church-lot death. It was then that I saw and remembered the concerned eyes of the young man who skidded into me that rainy day, Billy Joe Taylor. I'd forgotten his name.

George

"Where does your wife keep her mixer?" Thalea stood on tiptoe to search into a cabinet above the counter in Gayla's kitchen.

"I'm not sure. Look in the lower cabinet opposite the sink, I think." George said. He thought women naturally knew their way around a kitchen.

Thalea bent down to search for the mixer. George smiled approvingly at the full, rounded butt she displayed to his gaze.

Standing before the polished, oak island, Thalea plugged the white cord into a receptacle. "Cooking isn't my strong suit, but I do have a few gems that I can whip up on short notice."

George removed his pipe from its usual place in the left corner of his mouth, laid it on the island, and slipped his arms around her waist. "Indeed you do." He blew behind her ear into her hair. The twitch below his lower left lip was annoying. He would ask his doctor about it next week. Maybe he could use a muscle relaxant.

"Talk to me, George. What's going on in that magnificent, highly-evolved cranium of yours?"

George slid his hands upward, cupping her breasts. "Women always want to get into a man's head. When I'm not working, I like to keep life uncomplicated. We're enjoying ourselves, aren't we? Isn't that enough?" He felt a slight lifting to Thalea's chest. He liked feeling as though his touch worked like magic. He smiled as he buried his head in her hair.

"You're avoiding my question, Dr. Tyner. I'm asking about *us*. We've been together almost every night for five weeks now. I wonder how you really feel about me. Just a hint will do."

George dropped his hands and picked up his pipe, slowly moving it from palm to palm. "You're the most exciting woman I've met in a long time. What more can I say?" He tapped his pipe on his forehead. "I've an idea. Let's go to Detroit this weekend for a hockey game. No, I've a better one; let's pop over to Chicago. The Cotton Club is a great hot spot. We can stay at the River Plaza and be close to everything in The Loop."

"George, you are the most generous man I know. Chicago sounds wonderful."

"I don't have anything after four-thirty Thursday," George said. He lit his pipe. He wished Gayla could hear him being called generous, just not under these circumstances.

"I have an appointment at nine on Friday. We can make the early noon flight," Thalea said.

When Thalea left, George wrote a reminder to call Gayla. "Did I call yesterday or the day before?" He went to the bedroom, selected two pairs of pants, and laid them on the bed. He chose the blue pair, and whistling, he hung the brown ones back in the closet.

CHAPTER 5

Gayla

CAROLINA RAINS COME SUDDENLY. The sun continues to shine and heat dissipates for a few minutes during the cloudburst. "The Devil's beating his wife," a child called across the courtyard as playmates scattered to porches and under trees to escape wetness. From my living room window, I mouthed the rest. "And if you stand in the corner holding a broom you can hear her crying."

The phone buzzed. Louise said, "How about running over to Atlanta with me? I want to shop for a new dinette set. Everything in Carolton is old-fashioned, colonial, and Queen Anne. I like modern, clean lines."

"What about Avondale? It's bigger than Carolton and closer than Atlanta," I said. "Or do you just want to get away for a day?"

"Smart girl. Besides, we'll have more choices in Atlanta. We can go over Saturday morning, shop, and do something different. It'll be fun to visit downtown. The Plaza has a revolving restaurant on top. How about it?"

"Sounds good. I am getting restless," I said. "I'll have to be sure to tell my father."

"Are you being polite or being a good little girl?" Lou said.

"You won't believe this," I said, groaning. "I went to Charlotte for a quick visit; he hit the ceiling. Dad thinks I'm a child. I want to tell him to buzz off, but I don't."

"Your Mom, too?"

"Thank God, no. Mother's cool, all the way. Wish I had her grit, or guts, or whatever, but I'm game," I said.

Friday Louise called, hurried and apologetic. "Something's come up. I have to run to Charleston for a couple of days. We'll have to postpone. Is next weekend okay with you?"

"I've nothing planned," I said. I wanted to know what was so pressing, but I didn't ask. If she wanted to tell me what happened to change her plans she would, in her own time.

Louise's house was in one of the new areas of Carolton. Her husband Lloyd hadn't lived long enough to become a great success; he couldn't have left her much. Louise was a private secretary who, I doubted, made enough for high style. I felt like the kind of nosy person I dislike.

Louise and I became friends at Deerpath High. We were part of a group of girls that we called "The Twentieth Century Club." Our motto was, "la creme de la creme." Twenty teenagers spawned internal segregation. After us more clubs sprang up, each with its own brand of bias.

We "Twenties" believed we were the most stylish, hippest, and prettiest girls in the school. Other girls were resentful and we were arrogant. I had no illusion about why I'd been asked to join. I was a shy fourteen year old, awkward with classmates three and four years older than I. I had begun school early and later was "skipped," a handy solution when schools and parents didn't know what to do with precocious kids. In a washroom stall I overheard, "She doesn't know how to dress, and she's too immature for boys to be interested, our boys anyway." I wasn't sure who was talking.

"Forget that," a voice I recognized said, "she lives in that big ol' house and we can have meetings and parties, I'll bet."

I stayed in the stall until they left, sneaked out the door, and waited until I was home to go to the bathroom. I wasn't comfortable with the sophisticates. Some of them, rumors went, had abortions already. Mother insisted I join the "Twenty Cs." "It'll help you grow up," she said. I never told her what I overheard.

Louise was a year older than I. My closest, and my only, confidante.

Henry Lee and Myrtle Lee

Myrtle Lee Urmann seldom sat in her front yard anymore. Nobody came to visit and she didn't go anywhere. The front yard meant Henry and the first time she'd talked to him.

Henry Lee is tired. He's walked a long and hot way. His car is in the shop and walking to collect insurance payments from his clients is not easy. His legs ache. The low stonewall is inviting—a place to take a load off before the last four blocks home. Henry Lee wipes his forehead with his handkerchief, which his mother leaves beside his bed every morning along with a freshly ironed shirt. A voice behind him stiffens his back. "Oh, shit," he whispers.

Mrs. Myrtle Lee Urmann's Carolina-white-lady voice is not hostile, but Henry can't hear its calm concern. "You look awful peaked. I can give you a drink of water if you want it."

Henry Lee turns, half wanting to run and half too tired to run. Mrs. Myrtle Lee Urmann holds a glass of water in her hand, rivulets of condensation wandering down its side. "Uh no—uh—I mean thank you Ma'am. My head is swimming from the heat." Henry Lee's head is also swimming because the white woman is smiling at him.

"Here, I was just getting a drink for myself when I saw you so beat down. Go on, take it, it'll stop the fainting feeling. I get that when I'm in the sun too long, like you." She continues to smile, not scared or mocking. She is the prettiest woman, colored or white, Henry Lee has ever seen.

Henry Lee notices that unlike other whites, who if they offered him a drink it would be in a Mason Jar, this lady gives him water in a cut-glass tumbler. Henry Lee knows cut glass. His mother inherited a set of twelve tumblers, with a two-quart pitcher, from her mother. The white family his grandmother had worked for gave his granny the beautiful set when the old white woman died. The woman said his grandmother had washed her glasses for thirty-two years and never broken one. If anybody deserved the set it was Henry's grandmother.

"Thank you very much, Ma'am," Henry says taking the glass and being careful not to touch her hand. She looks about ten years younger than Henry—young and happy.

Myrtle Lee laughs. "Don't worry, I'm not poison and I won't poison you." Her smoky blue eyes are innocent and amused.

Henry Lee drains the glass. "I must be getting on home. You're real kind, Ma'am." He puts the glass on top of the wall. "I can't thank you enough, Ma'am."

She picks up the glass. "You know I don't bite, either. You live around on Thomas Street don't you? I've seen you driving by. Something wrong with your car?"

"How'd you guess?" Henry Lee permits himself a smile. "Yes'um, the mechanic over at Dodson's says it'll be at least two weeks more before the parts get in from Detroit. I'll be walking for awhile." Henry doesn't notice he's moved a foot closer to the lady.

"Well, if you need to rest you can stop right here. I don't mind. My husband isn't home until later. I don't think he'd mind, either." Myrtle Lee waves her hands in the air, at nothing in particular. Jergens lotion floats to Henry Lee's nose.

Henry Lee has no intention of talking to the white woman ever again. To be polite he bobs his head, "Yes'um."

He doesn't have a pressing reason to pass Mrs. Myrtle Lee Urmann's house four times in the next two weeks. But it would have taken him a longer walk to go around her street to his house. By evening Henry is usually tired. "The lady," he calls her to himself, always sits in a swing inside the wall, mostly hidden by hydrangea bushes. She doesn't seem to know she isn't supposed to talk to a colored man. She is a Carolton native. That is clear from the way she talks. Henry Lee has lived in Pittsburgh with his aunt for a time. He'd sat beside whites on the bus—even women—but he was born in Carolton and knew better when he got back home.

Myrtle glances over her shoulder at the wall. She takes her glass inside to refill it. Gayla and her mother passed just then, driving into town.

Gayla

"I haven't been anywhere except to church in a month," Mother said, climbing in the car with me. Once, cocoa brown hair had framed her flawless complexion. That complexion was now complemented by white hair that needed no rinse to keep its shine. She wore blue: blue hat, blue dress, and blue shoes. White gloves and bone earrings completed her coordinated attire. "Okay Toots, let's see what this little number can do."

"You and Dad love your land yachts. Do we go to the mall or downtown?" I relied on her to know which place would be less crowded on a Saturday.

"Take Central downtown to the hardware. I need a new steelhead hoe and a bag of peat humus. The mall is all clothes and restaurants. You'd think people did nothing but dress up and eat."

The hardware store was run by the same family who opened it one hundred years ago. Carolton had removed the downtown parking meters and at every corner, wooden planters held multicolored flowers all summer and into the slow-moving autumn. Miles from the downtown "Square," the mall's canned music and man-made waterfall attracted more shoppers.

The McNeill's Hardware I loved in old Carolton was gone. Its high ceiling and solid wood shelves were not air-conditioned cold but sheltered naturally cool air, held within massive, thick walls behind green shaded glass. The dark pine floor smelled of flax soap and oil. I heard the pneumatic tube swish a capsule, filled with dollars, to a gray-haired woman in an iron cage on the balcony. Change and a receipt rumbled and whirred back in a miniature submarine missile on two vibrating wires. I was sure that if I stuck my finger in the tube I would be sucked in, like Alice down the rabbit hole.

The remodeled store didn't smell of soap and mystery. The new floor was an expanse of giant, shining, black-and-white, diamond-angled tiles. An electronic cash register took Mother's money. The cashier in the iron cage was gone. Minutes later a salesman, so feeble and bent I wanted to relieve him of his burden, loaded the hoe and two bags of peat humus into the trunk of the car. I offered him a tip.

"No'um, it's against store policy," he said

He looked older than my father. Nothing in his weathered, Scots-Irish face revealed how he felt about the way things had changed in Carolton. He smiled and tipped his hat. Maybe he'd forgotten or didn't like the old ways any more than I did.

Leaning forward to insert my key, I spied a recessed entry a few doors to our right. "Mother, isn't that the store where you had trouble?"

"You remember that?" Mother's voice lifted in surprise.

"I've a long memory. Sometimes I wish I didn't. When I'm reminded of what happened to you in this town I want to scream, hit something or someone. It takes nothing more than a Southern accent out of place, like in a drugstore in Ann Arbor."

Mother whistled forcefully and laced her white-gloved fingers. "You know how J. C. and I opened our offices in the colored block on High Street, two blocks south, where our Negro businesses were congregated: Jack's barbershop, Mr. Fleming's funeral parlor, the poolroom, and Mr. Powers' grocery. Upstairs, over the funeral parlor, our waiting room and my lab took up one room. J. C.'s office was next door. I was receptionist, pharmacist, secretary, and bookkeeper all in one. A pharmacist in those days wasn't a pill dispenser. I packed my own capsules, formulated my own mixtures."

"You had little waxed papers to pour powders into the empty capsules," I said. "Your scales had teeny little weights, and a marble mortar and pestle where you mashed stuff. Big, brown bottles on the very top shelves were labeled with red skulls and crossbones. I loved the spicy smell."

"I wouldn't like it much today, being a druggist in one of those chains," Mother said. "Reading from a TV screen all day ruins your eyes."

I noticed a dress shop with light and dark mannequins, two wearing Afro wigs. "Wasn't it the pharmacist in that store who called you nigger?"

"It was his clerk," Mother said. She peered into the back of the narrow storefront, past blonde, brown, red, and salt and pepper wigs. "The druggist was in the back. I asked for the doctor. It was a courtesy to call pharmacists 'Doctor' back then. The clerk looked up at me, looked over his shoulder and called out, 'Doc, there's a nigger up here to see you.'"

Mother twisted her gloves like a corkscrew. She continued in her soft, precise voice, "I stormed out of that store back to my office. I snatched my diploma and state license down from the wall and went back to the store. That young punk was slumped over the counter reading a comic book. I spread my credentials on top of his book."

Mother stopped and glared at the storefront. "I asked him, 'Can *you* read this? This is Latin,' I said."

Mother smoothed the bodice of her jacket. "I read the Latin to him and told that kid, 'When *you* can read *this* and have *these* then you can call me nigger.' He just stared with his mouth open."

She sat taller and touched her hair. "The druggist telephoned and asked me to bring my trade back, but I found a nicer place. Yes, that's the building." A serene expression spread over my mother's face and the twinkle came back to her eyes. She gracefully straightened the slight wrinkles in her twisted gloves and laid them on top of her purse.

"They forgot the whole thing I'll bet." I said. Maneuvering my car into light traffic, I decided to show her what my "little number" could do, if I could do it without getting a speeding ticket. On a quiet country road, we hit eighty for a few seconds.

"I love it," Mother said, reaching with both hands to hold onto the dash, her eyes bright.

A half-hour later, as we rounded the hill to her house, the lazy dog, Brownie, didn't move until she absolutely had to. Mavis Jean, the other Dr. Hughes, stepped out of the car and patted the door. "If I were a few years younger I'd get myself one of these little foreign jobs, a red one."

I put the hoe and humus in the garage and told my parents I was going to Atlanta with Louise.

"Now that's the way to do it, girl. Tell me what you're going to do." Daddy was content. During dinner he played Mills Brothers records, old 78 rpms. Once, he had sung first tenor along with the records. These days he chimed in once in a while with baritone harmony.

Back at my apartment my head throbbed with images of the insults Mother, Daddy, and so many had to accept when they were young. No, "accept" wasn't the right word. They never gave in nor gave up.

"You come for a job? Ain't nobody here yet." The ebony, baldheaded man stands inside the door, not sure whether he should open the door to the colored girl, all dressed up like it was Sunday.

"I'm here to take the State Board Examination. I didn't know how long it would take to get here, so I must be early."

"I don't know nothing about the examination, but the professors will be here soon. You sit back there." He points to a bench near the end of the hall and walks away mumbling to himself. *"Poor child, where'd she get that idea?"*

Fighting to stay awake, Mavis Jean MacKay sits in the dimly lit corridor. She's been up since four thirty in the morning. Fifteen minutes feel like an hour before she hears footsteps. A gray-haired white man in gray baggy pants brings a wave of humid, magnolia, and Prince Albert-tobacco-scented air into the tight space.

"Are you Mavis Jean? I'm Dr. Parker, the examiner. Come with me. I'll get you a seat."

Mavis is directed to a desk in a corner, away from the open window, in the very back of the room. Candidates for the State Pharmaceutical Examination file in, joking to keep their spirits up. Noting Mavis Jean, they glance away and find seats a far distance from her.

Three hours later the examiner announces time for lunch. *"There's a restaurant in the next block and a drugstore with a lunch counter right across the street, down two doors. Be back in one hour."* He does not look up when Mavis Jean, waiting until the others finish, puts her examination book on his desk. Dr. Parker puts all the exams in a book bag and leaves the room.

"Say, lady, you can sit here 'til they get back." The early morning voice reappears. *"I didn't know you really was taking that test, thought you was playing a funny. Look, there's no place for us to eat around here,"* the janitor smiles. *"I'm proud to see you doing this. Wish you good luck. We don't need no more bad."*

Mavis Jean moves to the chair he shows her, a cooler spot near an open window. She eats her sandwich and orange and drinks water from the fountain labeled *"colored."*

Waiting until everyone re-enters the room, Mavis Jean walks quietly toward her chair. One of the white candidates speaks to her. *"I heard you made one hundred on the chemistry exam."*

"It was nothing but high school chemistry," Mavis Jean MacKay, not yet Hughes, tells him. Later the candidate tries to pass a question to her. She ignores it.

I turned off my reading light, "Tough stock," I said aloud. Reaching to pull the covers over my head, I found my right fist clenched. Mother could be relaxed about denials and insults. A few years more and maybe I could, but not yet.

CHAPTER 6

Gayla

LOUISE AND I FINALLY MADE it to Atlanta; Louise selected a Danish import, teak with inlaid marble table and four contempo chairs.

"Wow," I wiped mock perspiration from my forehead. "Beautiful. Lloyd must have left you *loaded* or you have a rich relative in the bushes."

Louise blushed; a hand covered her lips. "It's one or the other." Recovering, she said, "I'll fill you in with the gory details one day."

My stomach indicated I had intruded into a place I shouldn't. "Please, don't take what I say seriously," I begged. "I don't mean to pry, forget it."

Louise forced a grin. She waved dismissal of my concern. "I know. You can imagine how difficult it is to live a life when you don't fit the expected pattern," she said giving a credit card to the clerk. Louise continued, "I'm being silly. You know the feeling, if not the details. I'm isolated from anyone I can confide in, except my mother and sister. Right now, you might say I'm your paranoid friend."

"You're not alone," I said. "The grandmas told us to not take on airs."

Delivery date set, we had brunch at the restaurant atop The Plaza, savoring the panorama from above the historic city. Tables piled with a sinful load of dishes stretched along greenery-decked walls. "I see why it's hard to find cheekbones around here, they're hidden by down-home cuisine," I whispered. Louise ate heartily, her one-hundred-pound, size-four figure was not at risk.

I was confused by her blush when I teased her about the price of her new furniture. Louise didn't mention our postponed excursion. It was none of my business, neither her affluence nor her personal life.

I inhaled the exotic smells of quiches, eggs Benedict, lox, and trays of pastries. "Atlanta was called the 'New York of the South' when we were kids," I said. "New York smelled of bakeries, kosher delis, taxis, and the excitement of freedom to sit where I wanted on the bus when I made my first visit to the Big Apple."

"I think of Atlanta smelling like college boys and fried chicken out on Auburn Avenue," Louise said. "Yes, sweet Auburn."

A polite, young white fellow cleared our table. "I can't digest how friendly the white people are," I said after he was out of hearing range.

"Our Atlanta was not downtown," Lou said. "I sneaked looks at all the neat-looking students strolling around the Morehouse and Morris Brown campuses."

"You mean neat guys, don't you?"

"Naturally, but I got ideas for clothes watching the girls. Sometimes," she winked.

"Our money spends anywhere, now. It's awful how African-American businesses took a dive just when our people could come downtown like we're doing." I felt a twinge of guilt.

"Let's get out of here," Louise said, standing quickly. Louise paid, waving away my card. "My treat," she said. "you drove."

"Okay, my tip, though," I said. I left a modest tip. "George says African Americans over tip, trying to prove we can afford it—and know how to do it."

The young black man who went for our car in the garage had a scowl when he delivered it to us. I said, "I suppose I should have driven my dad's big Caddy to impress him."

"Image is a big thing to a lot of people," Louise said.

She and I began the two-hour ride back to Carolton in my modest compact.

"How's Georgie Porgie taking care of himself with you away?" she asked.

"I don't think he's having problems," I said. "At first we talked every night, but I haven't heard from him in a week. George watches the old checkbook."

"A good-looking brown-skinned man like George, with education and with a professional career, isn't easy to find." Louise was serious. "Do you think it's smart to stay down here five long months?"

"It's fine, I'm sure," I said, dismissing the quiver in my throat. "We've been busy raising the kids and getting ahead in our careers. We're a great team. George spends a lot of time on research projects, traveling to conferences and consulting on top-secret stuff. He can't talk about what he does. I know he's doing important work. I'm proud of him and I don't pry."

"Girlfriend, listen to yourself. You can talk about more than the man's work. When's the last time you and George went away for some special time together?"

"Pam is at Howard and Antony was home until a year ago. I hadn't taken time to think about relaxing. That's why I'm in Carolton, for a change of pace."

"And George is there." Louise emphasized "there" with pursed lips and raised eyebrows. "Not smart, lady, not smart at all."

"I don't think about us the way you're talking. We're a team, I tell you. And as for fooling around, George knows I could never get involved with another man, and I believe the same about him," I said with a confidence I did not completely feel.

Louise squeezed my hand on the steering wheel. "I don't mean to stir the pot when it's simmering right along. Forget it. So much hanky-panky goes on in small towns like Carolton, it's second nature to think everybody else engages in the same goings-on. I'm happy for you, okay?"

"Okay," I said, returning the squeeze. "George can manage." My words were automatic. "Did I ever tell you about the time Mother brought Jan and me to Atlanta and we only stayed about an hour?"

"That was not a quick trip before the interstate," Lou said. "At least four hours downtown to downtown."

"Right, an all day trip."

"So, what was the big push?"

"A chocolate ice cream soda," I said, turning to watch Louise's mouth drop. "No, we weren't crazy."

"This one ought to cover about forty miles, am I right?" she said, settling back into her seat.

"No, it's short." I looked at the odometer. "One Saturday night after Daddy and Mother came home from the office, Janis started whining, 'I want a chocolate ice cream soda at a fountain, with seltzer water and a straw to suck through.'"

"Mother said, 'I'm sorry, baby, but we don't have a drugstore in Carolton where you can get a soda like that. I'll make you one. We have seltzer water.'"

"'No, I want a real one,' Jan said. 'I want to sit at the counter and turn around on the stool.'"

"Mother told Daddy, 'If my child wants an ice cream soda, she's going to have an ice cream soda.'"

"Then she said to Jan and me, 'We won't go to church tomorrow. We'll go to Atlanta and you can have your chocolate ice cream soda.' And we did. Daddy said Mother was trying too hard."

The ride passed quickly. I didn't know what Louise was thinking. My feelings were in that other Carolton. Reminiscing came often, now that I was "back down home." In Ann Arbor I never reminisced.

Old school, old family, old friends oozed up like dreams that feel as if they have a significance that is outside comprehension. The outside world loosened, but I wasn't ready to trust the strange oozings. Tomorrow might crystallize into a changed and still-changing world for black and white and brown people in Carolton who waited, watched, and weren't sure.

Carolton was laid out in four parts when Louise and I were kids. New suburban growth made the old neighborhoods less important. The neighborhood names had been East Carolton, Northside, Westside, and South End. No one ever told us why South was an end. A Southern town has an expectantly routine history—rich and well-to-do whites, poor blacks, and a heritage of caste and class. Carolton is in the Piedmont, the wedge stuck between North Carolina and Georgia.

Mrs. Flanders drilled our third grade class in segregated Deerpath Grammar School: "We live in the fourth largest city in the state. We are in upcountry, the foothills of the Blue Ridge Mountains, the tail of the great Appalachian range that defines the eastern coast of the Northern Hemisphere from Nova Scotia to Georgia." She'd tell us in a penetrating voice. "These mountains are the oldest on earth." Mrs. Flanders had a passion I couldn't grasp. She sounded like a preacher, the ones we saw when we sneaked to forbidden tent revivals. She paced from the window to the hall door in front of the class. "Most people think the low-country places, Charleston and Beaufort, are all we have. They are mistaken." Mrs. Flanders' pointer slapped against the faded blue and pink map to emphasize every word. The shape of South Carolina on a map looked like a piece of pie, the way I would cut it—crooked.

I felt Mrs. Flanders' pride, even if I didn't understand it. Her family had been in the Piedmont since before the Revolution, some of them slaves, some of them free, and as Mrs. Flanders' freckles broadcast, some of them European. I learned that being native to the Upstate was special. This special part of the world smelled of sweet pine and soft water, not of dead fish and sand like Charleston and the low country. Knowing I was special because I breathed mountain air wasn't enough when the ugliness of segregation intruded outside the classroom.

Oak Street was a wide, flat street where I loved to skate. Skating rinks were nowhere nearby. Friendly people sat on their front porches on Oak Street and watched us fall down, laugh, and play until dark, metal wheels flashing sparks against concrete. Four families, including the widow, Mrs. Hall, lived in the prettiest block on the north side of Oak Street. Full-grown oak trees and an occasional black walnut lined both sides of the street, branches touching in summer, shading the street, the sidewalks, and houses.

A white contractor offered to buy out the Negro families so he could build on the vacant side of the street. The Negro families wouldn't sell, so the contractor built and sold several houses on the other side of the street to white folk. Young Mrs. Hasgrove, limp carrot-red hair falling in her face, came almost every day to sit on the front porch with the Widow Hall. Because she was lonesome for her mother and because Mrs. Hasgrove's husband traveled, she brought her baby across the street.

In the same block in Carolton, the last house for whites would be followed by the first house for coloreds. White and colored didn't live checkerboard, except for Edna Parker and her grandson who lived in a yellow house not much bigger than a child's playhouse. Her house was in the Hutchinson's backyard—her "family," Mrs. Parker called them. Edna Parker's little house stood between whites' houses because the Hutchinson's backyard was exempt from the taboo. She was allowed to keep her orphan grandson "on the place." We Negro kids wondered about Mrs. Parker's grandson. He looked near white, and his grandmother was bittersweet chocolate.

One windy, cold March day when I was seven, we moved into a sprawling Prairie Victorian house down the block from Edna Parker's house and her "family," the Hutchinson's. We moved to Lowell Avenue, in the middle of a block where white people lived. Beds were being put up, clothes unpacked, and the last of the painters was finishing the railing on the front porch when a white boy, taller and older than I, with a pouty lower lip, blond hair, and beagle eyes came across the street.

"My name is Andrew Burroughs," he said. "Call me Drew." He, Janis, and I became instant friends.

"You jabber just like a jaybird," he told Janis. "I'm going to call you Jaybird." Most days after school we played together, in our yard. At four, Jan wasn't allowed to cross the street.

"I don't see why I have to walk all the way 'cross town to school. Your school is just two blocks away," Drew said.

"I don't know," I said. "Silly grownups make us." Drew agreed and so did Jan, although I don't think she understood either.

Sunday mornings Drew ran across Lowell Avenue, picked up the newspaper from our front porch, and walked through the unlocked door into our parents' bedroom. He nodded politely, "Good morning Dr. Hughes, morning Mrs. Hughes." Leaving them the news and sports sections of the paper, he came into our tandem bedroom.

"I'll read Dick Tracy," he said, squatting on the bed between Jan and me. "My turn for Dagwood," I said.

We argued over who would read each comic strip. Two years older than I, he didn't have to help me with the big words.

Drew wasn't as friendly with the other Negro children in the neighborhood. When he was visiting us, they didn't come to play. Nobody ever said anything mean. I didn't realize the isolation we shared.

One rainy afternoon as we pushed the porch swing so high our shoes stuck out in the falling drops, Drew said, "If y'all hadn't moved here, I was going to run away and join the circus. I've been practicing parachute jumping for my act." When the rain stopped he showed us how, by jumping off his porch roof with a blue and white beach umbrella.

Drew's sister was ten years older than he. She wasn't much fun for a boy who loved circuses. Their father owned a business and everyone seemed too busy to spend time with Drew.

Drew declared that brown-skinned people could stand more cold weather than white-skinned people, "because their skin is tougher, and it keeps out the cold." A feeling inside told me he was wrong. I didn't like cold weather, even thirty-degree Carolton winters, but I didn't have proof. Ignorance between us was total, and we spoke with presumed wisdom, every pronouncement total gospel.

Our friendship continued until one murky day after school. Drew was in junior high school, a longer walk. The white lawyer, our next-door neighbor, had a son Drew's age. Anson didn't play with the neighborhood kids. His right arm and side were crippled. Most games and play involved running and he couldn't run. When he came home from school, he went straight to his house. It was unusual for Anson to have visitors. That day he did.

Two boys, who Jan and I didn't know, sat with Anson and Drew under a giant tree, midway between our houses. Jan and I were playing Chinese checkers on our porch.

One of Anson's visitors saw us. He yelled, "Hey, niggers," laughed and repeated, "Hey, nigger coons." The second stranger joined him. Anson had a strange grin on his face.

The strangers kept yelling, "Hey, y'all niggers," laughing in their boldness. We didn't know what to say or do, confused at seeing our friend with the nasty boys. We waited for Drew to do something. He looked at the ground, played with a stick, and traced in the dirt. Jan and I went inside, closed the door, and peeked out at the boys.

The day turned darker than any day before. We watched from a window *in a guest bedroom until the group broke up, Anson and his awful visitors going into his house. Drew crossed Lowell Avenue to his.*

The next day was Saturday, our parents' busiest day. Country people and those from smaller villages in the county came to town to shop, go to the doctor and dentist, pay insurance, and see a movie. Our cook was busy somewhere away from us. Drew came across the street, onto our front porch. Jan and I saw him from our living room window. We had locked the screen door that was never locked.

He pulled on the handle, "Gay, Jaybird. Open up, lemme in."

We went to the door, glaring at our friend's tentative, sickly smile. Jan said, "You can't come in anymore."

"How come?" he asked.

"You know. You were with those guys calling us nigger," Jan said.

"I didn't say it. You didn't hear me say it."

"We know," I said, "but you stayed with them. You didn't tell them to stop. You didn't leave. You didn't say you were our friend." I didn't yell, but I felt tight inside.

I saw he was embarrassed. He didn't know what to do and neither did we.

Jan spoke behind clenched jaws, "We've been friends a long time. You ought to choose us over some ol' strangers. You didn't."

Seconds passed, filled equally with confusion and surety. Drew turned and walked away, throwing over his shoulder, "But I didn't say it."

For a long time Jan cried when she thought about Drew, especially when she saw him coming home from school. Jan had disagreements with our neighbor, Tally Johnston, and with me. Sisters are supposed to fight. She never had an argument with Drew. Jan liked the name he gave her. She was Jaybird.

Early on we learned to handle our own problems. Mother noticed that Drew didn't come over anymore. I mumbled something about, "He's doing after school sports." Tally spent more time with us after we no longer played with Drew. Tally agreed that Drew was "chicken." Three years we'd been friends, but I was growing up, too. I was more mobile and made friends further away from home. At ten, the real world often won. Sunday funnies were the only place where all the colors were on the same page.

Jan and I avoided Drew and he avoided us until the night the Burroughs' house caught fire. No one was home except the elderly grandfather and a sleeping Drew, when a fireplace popped a cinder. Drew climbed from his second floor bedroom window, in pajama bottoms, crawled out on the porch roof, and jumped to the ground, this time without his beach umbrella. His grandfather was sleeping on the first floor and managed to get outside. He had forgotten that Drew was upstairs. Our former friend ran at top speed, straight into our front hall. Mother found clothes for the shivering boy and kept him until his family came.

Watching him put on our father's oversized pants and shirt, Jan and I stood on the far side of the living room. A pair of Mother's shoes was closest in size for him.

The next day, Mr. Burroughs brought back the clothes and said thank you. The Burroughs family did not move back into that house. We didn't see Drew again.

CHAPTER 7

Gayla

I NEVER IMAGINED I COULD miss George's snoring. Carolton was quieter than Ann Arbor, where jets roared high up as they approached Detroit. I tried to read, gave up, and stared out into my small courtyard; a corner of my neighbor's roof flapped crazily in the wind. I gritted my teeth as I thought of how my dad had been a sucker for a roof repair ripoff. A quick fix artist bragged of being "born-again," tacked on a few shingles, and walked away with a couple of thousands. I'd be sure that the repairs were done right this time. Then, I remembered that Alice had asked me to bring a few things on my next trip out, so I dashed to the nearest market.

I had only a few items in my cart when I heard my name. "Gay? Ain't you Gay Hughes? Lord, I haven't seen you since you were *this* high." The aged, henna-brown woman with wide-spaced yellow teeth and clouded eyes suddenly brightened and searched my face. A cool, dry hand fastened itself around my wrist. I would still feel the pain minutes later when I opened my car door. The old woman's other hand raised a worn, peeling, walking stick. She held it waist-high, pointed, and parallel to the ground. "Yes, indeed, *this* high."

"Yes ma'am, I'm Gayla—uh—Gay." I vaguely recalled looking up into this or into a similar face without the cane and coarse, gray hairs that protruded from the smooth brown chin. Had she been a neighbor, member of the church, mother of a friend?

"Child, you remember me." Her words were not a question; they were a chastisement. I sure had better remember my elders. "I'm name of Hettie Sims. Your daddy was my doctor when he first came to Carolton. I had a boil on my neck, big as a goose egg. Your daddy was new and young, looked like a boy. He fixed it real good. It never came back. Dr. J. C.'s been my onliest doctor: mine, my husband, our young'uns, and the grands—them what didn't traipse off up North."

"I'm very happy to see you, ma'am. You're looking wonderful."

"Yes, Lord, I'm pushing eighty-five come January if I live and nothing happens. You tell your daddy you ran into Miz Hettie Sims. Now, you be good, you hear?" She lifted her walking stick, pointed its worn-smooth round knob at my midsection.

Mrs. Hettie Sims was one of the neighborhood women we playfully and fearfully called "the grandmothers." She smiled and chuckled softly. She knew I didn't recognize her.

A dozen times during my first weeks in Carolton this encounter was repeated—in the grocery, the post office, the bank, the new shopping mall. An old woman or man would stop, and in a way peculiar to this part of the south, recite with a voice of rising inflection that seemed to both ask and assert, "Is this here, Gay?" Men held their hands, hardened by manual labor, halfway down their thighs to show how tall I'd been when they last saw me. Features weathered by the burning Carolina sun creased into broad grins, and for a moment, a weight lifted. These old friends seemed to feel years younger in their recall.

It was odd to be recognized, the childhood me—a plain, skinny, tomboy with a mouth too wide for her face. They still saw the girl in the woman, whose face eventually caught up with her mouth.

Shoppers in the Bi-Lo Supermarket moved deliberately slow. My passing provoked smiles, a "Mornin'" even from white men and women. I pushed down old layers of hostility that wanted to break through and scream at weathered faces like these, whose eyes once would have ignored me or pierced me with disdain. Wobbly-wheeled, rain-rusted shopping carts were my reminders that things had changed. Clerks once lifted cans and boxes down from the shelves for customers.

Aged black shoppers lifted squinting eyes from price labels on cans of beans and corn. Their struggles to place me were like those of Pepe, the dog George and I gave to a friend when we moved from Seattle to Michigan. Two years passed, then when I visited the friend to whom we had given Pepe, the dog ran to jump on me. He stopped in mid air, turned away, the wag gone from his tail. Pepe had lost my scent. Long-separated from these townsfolk, I had lost their scent.

"Oh, I'm sorry," I said, apologizing to the woman who's cart I had bumped.

The woman didn't smile. She murmured, "I'm sorry, too."

She looked like a woman who had given up on taking care of herself. Even a quick glimpse was enough to see a once beautiful person.

Henry Lee and Myrtle Lee

Myrtle Lee's cart had bumped Gayla's. Myrtle Lee went shopping only when there was nothing left to eat in the house. She always sent a taxi to the state store for her bourbon. She didn't trust anyone to buy her groceries or to come inside her door, front or back.

She takes good care of herself, Myrtle Lee thought. Henry Lee would look just as good as she does if he was here. Colored skin holds up. She didn't recognize me. I know I'm a mess. Another time, I'm going to pretty up a little. She'll know me then. Henry Lee would know me 20 years, 30 years, no matter.

Myrtle Lee spent most of every day seeing, remembering, and re-creating her days with Henry Lee. It took nothing to turn her thoughts and visions to him. Gayla was only a more vivid prod for her.

Myrtle Lee Urmann doesn't offer Henry Lee a drink of water each time he passes her house, but she manages to be on the porch when he comes by, and she waves to him. Two weeks go by and on a Tuesday, she comes off the porch. "Is your car fixed?"

"No'um, not yet. Mr. Dodson's mechanic says there's a strike at the plant in Detroit, so he doesn't know when they'll get a delivery, probably two or three more weeks. I can't afford to do anything else right now. I've been with Carolina Mutual Life not quite a year. I have to go easy; I'm saving to get married at Christmas time."

"Now that's sweet," Myrtle Lee said. "I've been married nearly seven years. Don't want to sour you on marriage but sometimes it's not what it's planned out to be—well, not mine anyway."

"I'm sorry Miss Myrtle Lee. You're right, sometimes the best plans come out different," Henry Lee said. "I've waited longer than my friends to get married . . . wanting to be sure of myself."

"Oh, I'm not crying in my beer," she tossed her hair behind her shoulder. Her mouth smiled, but her eyes didn't. "I guess I should not have gotten married as young as I did. Know what? I've been thinking how my name is Myrtle Lee and yours is Henry Lee, but Lee is your family name. My mama just thought Lee sounded pretty along with Myrtle."

Henry said, "Yes'm, your mama was right. She gave you a real pretty name."

Gayla

I noticed the sad looking woman in the aisle next to me. Her hands shook as she paid for her groceries and left before I did.

I took the bags into the kitchen for Alice, who was somewhere else. I found my parents on the screened porch. "What have you been up to this morning?" I asked.

Dad glanced up from his seed catalog. "Why doesn't George come down? Don't you miss him? You two doing okay?"

"Sure, he's busy with some secret work, as usual. We talk, Dad. He'll give you a call when he has time, I'm sure. Guess what? I ran into some people from the old days and I went by Westminster Church. It was fun going on calls with you after Sunday service."

Legs splayed atop the ottoman, at ease in his green wing chair, Daddy forgot George. Old-timey reminiscing was more fun.

"I didn't charge for those calls either." He wiggled a long, bony finger at the womenfolk. "No one ever paid a penny, even if I stayed for an hour. That's service, girl, not one red penny."

"Jan and I were scared when you went inside patient's houses," I said. "You'd come back to the car and say, 'Don't touch me till I get home and wash up; I'm full of germs. I'm contagious.' Once in a while you didn't wait to get home. We'd stop at the office and you'd come out smelling of rubbing alcohol. I'd feel cold all over. Then you'd lean over and whisper to Mother, 'He won't last much longer.'"

"Most of the time Jan and I sat in the back of the Buick pretending we were princesses and you were our handsome Daddy King in your white linen suit," I cajoled. "Mother, you were our pretty Mother Queen in your flowered silk dress and straw hat, tilted over one eye. You guys were more beautiful than any pictures of kings and queens in books or the movies." I smiled from one parent to the other. Dad didn't smile back. Even compliments made no impression on him. I wondered if my father ever listened to me, or to anything I said.

Mother patted my shoulder. "I always took a book to read. The little children's eyes were surprised. They didn't know colored could be so, well, 'rich' they'd say. We weren't, of course. It's all relative. Some of the poor things looked forlorn—big round eyes, noses running, scratching sores—like pictures of starving children in Africa or Asia. We couldn't do much of anything, not much at all." Mother went back to her book.

I watched my parents, lost in their reading. They'd retreated into a pattern, in a room together, on individual paths. Our Sunday rides in the Buick lingered with me. I went outside, followed by the dogs, to walk the familiar, comfortable hills. Dogs, it seems, wag their tails in simple pleasure for a clear, warm day.

When we stopped for "calls" with Daddy, Jan and I sat ladylike quiet. Playing with dogs or children was not the thing to do. Sunday clothes meant Sunday manners.

Jan loved dressing up. Lying in bed one night, we heard fire trucks rushing past the front of our house. Jan whispered, "If our house ever burns down, I'm going to save my Sunday dresses." Fire came the year she was nine and I was thirteen. Jan and I grabbed our bicycles and dragged them out the front door, across the street, and straight into what had been Drew's front yard. We dropped the bikes and began to wail. The house wasn't severely damaged and was rebuilt with a larger living-dining room for the parties that Dad and Mother loved to give.

After Daddy's calls, we went home for dinner. Sunday was the cook's day off. Jan and I liked mother's cooking better than any housekeeper we ever had. Mother didn't cook the vegetables to mush.

Sunday after church is the time for long walks to different parts of Carolton. The monotony of "blue-laws"—no movies and an occasional ice cream cone from the side window reserved for "Colored" at Ye Ice Creamy Heaven—is broken by visiting. In warm weather, families rest from the heavy heat on front porches. Chain-hung swings squeak as people swing back and forth. Discordant rhythms of the swings play up and down each block. Rocking chairs and upholstered lounges beckon friends who nod and stop to chat. Cold lemonade and delicate, sugar-butter teacakes fill glass or silver trays on dining tables. "Come set a spell, rest your feet, sister."

Dinners are started and left in the oven and on the back of the stove before church. Two or three hours later, the womenfolk rush to their kitchens to tie on white aprons, starched and ironed stiff. Dress-up high-heeled slippers are kicked off until a guest appears, then, "Hurry, child, bring me my good shoes. Here comes company."

Merging and tantalizing people, dogs, cats, and lazy fat flies, dinner smells float between the metal squares of screen doors and windows. Sunday dinner is most often roast chicken, "Arsh" (Irish) potatoes whipped airy with butter and Carnation evaporated milk, stewed corn with okra, cornbread, and slaw.

Cardboard fans from the undertaking parlors move the heavy air. The most popular mortician is the one with his name on the most fans waving. Reproductions of The Last Supper or Mother Mary with Christ Child scare the flies away. Blue, red, and gold blurs Jesus' blond hair and pink face.

After dinner settles, mothers rest for a spell. Then they return to their kitchens. They call everyone in for hot cobbler, with vanilla ice cream melting into brown syrup. Carolton is filled with good cooks and appreciative eaters.

Scruffy and Brownie were panting from a romp after creatures too small for me to see. The dogs weren't underfoot, that day. I filled their water bowls and went to see if Alice had returned. She had put away the things I'd brought and was reading a magazine in the sun-filled breakfast room. In the den Daddy's newspaper rested on his face. Mother tiptoed to the green chair, removed his glasses from his head and put them on the TV. She left the newspaper. He'd feel her lift it and wake up. Our eyes met. We tiptoed into the kitchen to have a cup of tea with Alice.

After tea I said, "See you next time." We touched one another on the back. I knew Mother had noticed the shift in conversation I had maneuvered when Daddy asked about George. George hadn't called all week. Maybe he'd call tonight.

CHAPTER 8

George

ARMS AROUND ONE ANOTHER, THALEA and George strolled through Detroit's "New City." "There aren't many people around," he said, his arm rubbing her shoulder. "Sorry we missed Chicago. Next time, okay?"

Thalea surveyed a massive, blue, glazed, marble building and the expanse of nearly deserted, wide, concrete walkways and streets. "Those curved windows remind me of church windows, except these are clear glass," she said.

"I'm going to find a jazz club. Let's take a cab back to our hotel and ask about a good one. This is Motown, right? The action must be somewhere," George said. He didn't know if Thalea was a good dancer; Gayla was. At least she had been when they were younger. He wondered when that fun part had stopped. What the heck, he thought, new times, new things.

"Wait, I see something I want to check out," she said. "It's a pewter shop. Let's go in for a minute."

The shop was long and narrow. The dark red interior gave a feeling of formality and style. Dividing the space into two aisles, floor to eye-level glass shelves angled down the center.

Thalea wandered among miniature, dark figures of knights, birds, castles, and wolves. She paid no attention to the shelves along the wall. They held large castings of battle scenes.

"Oh, look at the owls." She motioned George to join her. "I love owls. They symbolize wisdom, you know?"

"Really," he whispered into her ear and kissed her neck. "I thought they caught rats and hooted."

Thalea pretended to be scared and pulled him to the rear of the shop. She lifted several of the heavy figures and turned them with admiration or a frown. George wandered back to the front. Moments later she appeared beside him. "My curiosity's satisfied. They have some decent pieces but I've seen better."

George hailed a cab and gave the driver the name of their hotel. Reaching for Thalea's hand, he placed a small white bag in her lap. "Here," he said, in a voice like a little boy who wasn't sure if he'd done something wrong. Inside the bag lay a tissue-paper-wrapped pewter figure.

A pair of owls perched on a tree branch lay in the creased paper. A smaller owl nestled close to the wings of a larger one. "How sweet. Mother and baby, aren't they?" She balanced its heft in her hands.

"I thought they were you and me." He was disappointed.

"Of course," Thalea smiled. "My mistake."

At the hotel George could not decide on a club to visit. "What do you say we take the ferry to Windsor? We can spend the night there. We'll make love in a foreign country. It's not Quebec, but we'll pretend we're French."

"You've already paid for tonight here."

"No problem. It's only money." He tossed two credit cards on the dresser. "Before we go, come here." He pulled her into his arms, kissed her, and drew her to the large bed.

Thalea laced her hands at the back of his head. She rubbed her fingers in his curly dark hair. "You're fun, George."

"We can take all the time we want. There's a ferry every hour. Ouch, we'd better put your owls on the dresser."

Yeah, he thought, I am fun.

J. C. Hughes

J. C. roused from a brief nap to hear the women talking in the kitchen. He peered through the sliding door, opened it, tested the air, and decided that the evening would be good for a walk. Most evenings when the weather accommodated, slight in stature and sprightly, J. C. walked outside to one of several pine-covered, red hills, which ringed the country-side. Now and then, he stopped to pick up an interesting pine cone or rock. Bracing himself with an ebony cane that had once been his father's, he poked through the decaying autumn ground cover and into a few animal holes hiding at the foot of tree trunks. During his private walks, J. C. talked to the ebony cane. Calling it "Poppa," he told it his dreams and problems and asked advice. A silver bird formed the handle of the cane. J. C. Junior pretended that his father was alive in his walking stick, although his Poppa had been dead for more than fifty years. J. C.'s favorite, and often-used, saying was, "My father was a great man. I want to be just like him." Family—the name Hughes and what it stood for in J. C.'s mind—was above everything else. That's why he kept the junior in his name years after his father died. J. C. Senior's favorite sports, his attitudes, and his actions were appropriated as closely as J. C. could keep them. He wouldn't say so, but he worshipped the man.

A chill in the air brought thought of the coming winter. "Poppa," he murmured to the cane, "you always had oyster stew for Christmas breakfast. Even if the Upstate is two hundred miles from Charleston I have our oyster stew, like you did." He smiled at the cane as he caressed the silver bird.

Carolina's long autumn allowed J. C. to stay outside until dark. He paused beside his secret seat—between two rough-trunked pine trees on the western edge of his land. He had discovered his personal spot shortly after he and Mavis Jean bought the wooded site.

"My baby, Janis, is gone," he said softly to his cane. "It helps me to get away from rooms still filled with her singing." He sank gingerly onto a smooth rock that jutted from the side of the hill, braced his back against one of the trees, and leaned Poppa's walking cane alongside the farthest tree. J. C. Junior closed his eyes.

"Poppa, Gayla is visiting us. She wants to help Mavis Jean and me. God knows, some things do jump ahead of me these days, but I don't know, Poppa. What do you think?" Crickets weren't yet rubbing their hind legs. Frogs wouldn't sing tonight; it had not rained in that corner of the country. J. C. believed he could hear Poppa extra clear on such a night.

"Calvin, you and the girl always had your problems. You're too much alike." Poppa called J. C. "Calvin" when they were alone. No one else did. Bubby was for his mother, siblings, and close friends to say.

"People always say she looks like me. I don't see it."

"I'm not talking about what's physical, Calvin. Don't fight me, son. The trouble between you and Gayla has been festering a long time, all her life. It's past time you worked it out, in your mind if nowhere else."

J. C. was distracted by a shooting star. The stars were clean white in the violet blue southern ceiling. He felt a moment's anger at the overly-bright, man-made satellite, unblinking toward the west. His eyes swept north, past Venus, to his friends Great Bear, the pole star below, Castor, and Pollux, north and west of his special place. Poppa had shown him every constellation above their heads before he was seven, names J. C. Senior learned from his mama, who was born in slavery. J. C. knew his father wasn't soaring around on great Mozar because he was there with him. Maybe Poppa was in both places.

J. C. turned back to the cane leaning against the tree. It sparkled. Almost seeming to be laughing. "Poppa, I don't mean to be sharp with Gayla. I hear myself criticizing what she eats, her hair, and her leaving George alone. She thinks I don't know things aren't right between the two of them. My words seem out of my control, as if they're coming from some other place, some strange voice. I remember my friend, Clothilde, when she'd get mad, she'd tell Gay, 'Pull yourself together. You're too smart for your own good.'"

From the cane or J. C.'s head, Poppa said, "Your friend didn't like Gayla's being smarter than she was. "I'd say your daughter is a lot like you, Calvin."

J. C. always paid attention to Poppa. Poppa was always right. "I'll work on it, Poppa," he murmured, gazing up to Mozar.

"Gayla's got her part almost worked out," Poppa said. "You

can do your part whenever you make up your mind, Calvin. How much time do you think you have?"

J. C. picked up his cane. He ignored the question. The cane pulsed under his hand. He brushed dried grass from his pants and sweater and balanced himself out of the trees and down the hill, toward the lights at the rear of his home. "Only a few days more before it will be too cold for my walk, I guess," he said to noone in particular.

At home, winded from his downhill trudge, J. C. chuckled and stamped a few stuck, dried leaves from his shoes. He and his father once walked hours without tiring. "Poppa was ten years younger than I am right now when we took our last walk," J. C. said aloud. "I'm not doing too badly."

Mavis Jean met him as he took off his shoes inside the door. "Thought it was time you came in. It's going to be a lovely night. What do you want, a dish of ice cream or something to drink?"

"I'll have some of that butter pecan if we've any left." He carefully shoved the cane in the umbrella stand. "You know, Mother, I'm glad Gay's home. I feel better knowing she's looking after things for us."

"Why don't you tell her how you feel? She'd like that." Mavis Jean opened the ice cream container that had been sitting on the drainboard.

Mavis Jean Hughes

Alice always moved their favorite chairs to the screened porch when the weather turned warm and to the den during colder weather, even though South Carolina was never as cold as Michigan. When J. C. and Mavis Jean built their country home, out from town, the quiet location made them feel as though they were on the farmland they loved when they were children. The interstate, ten miles away, had not ruined that feeling, although they could hear faint sounds from giant trailers.

J. C. turned on the television and settled back to eat his ice cream. Mavis Jean turned on her reading light and opened a new book, sent to her by her Quaker friend, Maude. Maude wrote that it was the King Arthur legend from a feminine perspective. J. C. would scoff if she told him that. She didn't, and he didn't ask. Within minutes of putting his empty dish on the floor, he was snoring.

Mavis Jean contemplated the man across the porch. They'd shared fifty-two years of marriage and two children—not counting their first one, the boy who lived only two days. She didn't like to think of Janis and the stormy night when an old man, who couldn't see well enough to drive and had been drinking, ran into the station wagon in which she rode. Jan and her friends, the Alton College trio, were on their way to sing at a small church in a town near Atlanta. Alton sent students to sing and speak in the Negro community and to seek funds from wealthy white groups who thought nobody could sing like "the Colored."

Mavis turned from her husband to look into the clear, starry night. The girls liked to sing in bed before they went to sleep. Janis had a gift. She could sing soprano, or alto, or tenor, even bass. She'd say to Gayla, "I'll take the downstairs notes. You take the upstairs ones." Mavis Jean thought J. C. was partial to Janis because she could sing, as he did.

I've never figured out why Gay and J. C. grated on each other, she thought. Jan had been an easy baby, smiling, cooing, and enjoying being held. Gay was different. She never seemed to trust that anyone could take care of her.

"Well, I kept my peace," Mavis Jean said aloud, J. C.'s snoring rumbled on. She watched J. C. emit bubbly rumbles, his upper lip and cheeks vibrating in rhythm. "He has no idea how much he's slowed in the past year, but that's to be expected. I'm not as swift as I once was, myself." Touching his shoulder, she called lightly, "J. C., don't fool yourself; night air is treacherous this time of year. I think we ought to go inside."

J. C. mumbled, "Poppa, I'm not cold." He realized where he was and said sheepishly, "All right, Mother, right away."

While J. C. prepared for bed, Mavis went through the kitchen to the extra room to say good night to Alice. Alice was the age Janis would have been and she and Mavis Jean almost talked like friends sometimes.

Alice looked up from the notepad on which she was writing. "Need anything before I settle in for the night?" she said.

"Not a thing, thank you." Mavis said. "Writing a letter to your Mother?"

"This one's to my sister. I'm the lucky one. God's watching over me."

"A problem? Anyway I can help?" Mavis asked.

"No'um. I know I'm no beauty, but I'm not about to let no rough-handed farmer use me for a workhorse and breeding mare, like her. My sister's all saggy after a houseful of babies and he won't let her go nowhere 'cause he thinks she might be cheating on him." Alice tied her chenille robe tightly across her waist. "It's him doing the cheating, if it's anyone. She's always busy cleaning and cooking for him and the children."

Mavis squeezed Alice's shoulder. "We have much to be grateful for." Her touch was almost a hug. She pulled back. "J. C. should be ready for bed by now. Sleep well."

Back in their bedroom, J. C. was climbing into bed. "Now this is different from our little old double bed we had for so long," J. C. said as he did four or five times every year. As soon as his head touched the pillow, he was blowing bubbles.

Mavis Jean tucked the thermal blanket under his chin. She thought, wonder what he and Poppa had to say tonight? He's worried about something, always talks to that walking stick when he's working out a problem.

J. C. Hughes

"Move along, boy. You're as slow as molasses on a cold winter morning."

"Poppa, your legs are longer than mine."

"And I'm old enough to be your Poppa, so it evens out, doesn't it?" The elder J. C. reaches a long-fingered, soft hand down to nine-year-old Bubby. The boy and man smile into identical green eyes. A few more minutes climbing and they stand on top of Mount Hermon, the highest point in Odum County. Like a stone rolled away from all the rest, the hill isn't actually a mountain, just an isolated outcropping left over from the primordial upheavals that formed the Blue Ridge mountain

range. It sets, a giant among small piedmonts. Poppa says, "This little mountain is like a big fish in a little pond. It's a little prideful, I imagine. I don't know what it would do if a real mountain came along and plopped down beside it." He laughed.

Father and son stare down the high space to the town of Odum. Main Street twists inward from the north. Large plantations sprawl, then smaller farms closer to town. In town, Colonial and Victorian houses sit importantly, a stately procession of achievement that ceases at the edge of the tiny downtown. A white-painted brick Episcopal church, its gold steeple towering, stands near the center of Odum. A gracefully curved walk extends to a poplar-bordered street to become one axis of a natural cross. From Mount Hermon, the Presbyterian and Methodist churches are set at opposite ends of the arms of the cross. Cradled in the valley, a mile south of the Episcopal church, are the tiny colored churches—Baptist, African Methodist Episcopal Zion, and Reverend Hughes' "John Knox Presbyterian."

"Son, see the Negro churches nestled at the foot of the cross, like the common people at our Lord's crucifixion?" The minister points his ebony and silver-handled cane to outline the cross.

Bubby doesn't understand the symbolism his father calls to his attention, but he answers, "Yes, Poppa."

"That's what you have to remember. The common people are the ground of God. You must serve your people. Ordinary people are the closest to God. Don't you forget it."

"Yes, Poppa." Bubby knows that everything his father says to him is important.

"See that big church on Ewing over to the left?" Reverend Hughes gestures to another axis of the streets. "That's where our white kin belong. My daddy was the son of the master of Hughes Plantation. His name was Robert. Robert was but sixteen when I was born. I might be ashamed; my mother wasn't married to him. She was only fourteen. That's not the Christian way. But she was a slave, and colored didn't marry white. Robert went off to fight. My mother said he was killed in the Civil War, at the Battle of Atlanta. His family always treated her and me kindly. The Hughes' will treat you well, almost like family, if you ever need them. I want you to come back here when you finish your education; stay in this part of the country; help your people."

"The Hughes family goes 'way back in this part of the country, on all sides—white and colored, Christian people, everyone. Too bad we don't know exactly where we're from in Africa. My mother's mama had a real big bottom—you know, her behind—so maybe we're part Hottentot."

Poppa places the walking cane and the wicker basket he has carried to the top of the hill on the ground.

Bubby doesn't understand why Poppa laughed when he said "Hottentot" or what a big behind had to do with anything. "Poppa, if we're family with the white Hughes' why don't we spend Christmas with them the way we do with Mama's folks, Grandma and Grandpa Glen and your mother, Grandmama Hughes? I see you talking to Mr. Dan Hughes, reading the Bible with him when y'all go fishing. Why don't they come over and we go there like we do with other family?" Bubby had noticed how his father and Mr. Dan had the same face, except Poppa was brown and Mr. Dan was red.

"Calvin, boy, some things just aren't done. And that's one of them. Maybe one day that'll change, in two or three hundred years. We're blessed to have them treat us kindly. Most colored like us don't know who their kin are, colored or white. Your mother's grandfather was sold into South Carolina by his own daddy. Come on, now, let's open this basket your mama packed. The walk up here has made me hungry as a bear." Sunlight glints the silver-topped stick. The boy blinks and covers his eyes.

J. C., senior and junior, sit under a maple tree. The smell of ham, unwrapped from brown waxed paper, closes all thoughts of crosses, churches, or relatives who don't come to Christmas dinner.

"J. C., time to get up. Alice is making country ham and grits for breakfast." Mavis Jean opened the curtains to let in the morning light. J. C. blinked and sat up. Mount Hermon faded.

"That's fine, Mother. We haven't had country ham in a long time."

"Young Dr. Porter says it's too salty for us at our ages. This is a special treat." Mavis Jean hung her negligee in her closet; an odor of rose sachet blew into the bedroom as she closed the door. "Alice says there's no point in living if you can't enjoy what you like once in a while. And I agree with her. Don't take too long."

"Humph, sounds as if I'm not a doctor, like I don't know about edema and pressure." J. C. pulled on his maroon robe, yanked the velvet sash so tight it hurt, strode into the bathroom, and slammed the door. The water was unusually forceful against the shower wall.

CHAPTER 9

Gayla

WHEN SHE HEARD MY FOOTSTEPS inside the hall, Mother called to me, "Mom Dutch heard you were home. She wants to see you."

"I had no idea she was still alive. How old is she?" I asked.

"Ninety-four or five, I believe. She's bedridden, has been for about a year. But her mind is as clear as spring water."

"Whenever I think of Mom Dutch, I see those floppy bonnets she wore. She looked like the woman on the Old Dutch Cleanser can," I said, remembering that the spring in Mom Dutch's backyard disappeared when the city made her fill it in and bring in piped city water. "I'll call her and set a time to visit. Thanks, Mother," I said, making a note in case I forgot.

Later in the day, I stepped up on the worn, dusty porch. "Lift the latch and walk in," called a strong but old-sounding voice. I knocked lightly anyway and proceeded briskly down the hall to a bedroom I knew how to find.

"I wondered when you'd get around to coming to see me." Cushioned by big, feather-filled pink and white faded pillowcases, Mom Dutch sat upright. The heavy, dark headboard curved like the bow of an ancient ship. A familiar grin, nearly toothless, welcomed me.

"You're as rambunctious as ever, Mom Dutch." I bent forward to kiss the molasses-dark face. The old woman smelled of menthol and snuff. Her cheeks felt powder soft, a delicacy brought on by age and a lack of sunlight. "Last time I was here you were in your chair in the living room."

"My legs don't do me any good anymore. But thanks to the good Lord, my head is still working." She sat bolt upright, not leaning into her pillows. "I'm the only one left." With a defiant lift to her jaw, she added, "and I'll outlast a lot more. All the neighborhood grandmas are gone, but me. The young'uns don't get their comeuppance the way we used to give it to 'em. They rip and run and tear around like little demons. Why, some of the young devils broke in on me eighteen months ago. My old dog scared 'em away. She died since then. I would get another, but I don't know how I can break in a new dog, with my legs not working."

I admired this woman. Once, I had feared her. Mom Dutch King never spanked, when all the old ones in the neighborhood were given that right, but her words cut clean through you, worse than the swat of a hand on your backside. And her eyes flashed like lasers. Mom Dutch and Tempy Bolden and Ma Johnston had been the trinity of grandmother surrogates on Lowell Avenue. "So you're the last of the Mohicans? I often think of you and the other grandmas. You helped us over many a rough spot."

"I didn't do anything special. When I was young everybody looked out for everybody. I learned that. What was I supposed to do, ignore you crazy, wild young'uns stealing my pears and leaving Ma Johnston's gate open so the dog could get out and the cat get in?"

We laughed so hard Mom Dutch choked. I handed her a glass of water. Holding one hand to her ample bosom, Mom Dutch gasped. "You were the worst of the bunch, catching pigeons so's you could have pigeon pie. You didn't know those tough old birds would never cook tender. Had to slow y'all down or you wouldn't be alive today."

"Too bad you can't amble up on the kids out there now. Somebody has broken all the windows in our old house."

"Your bunch never would have gotten away with breaking windows on an open street." She slapped the covers with a fist so strong the bed shook.

"Mom Dutch, how are you making it since you can't get around on your own?" I studied the stained and chipped

marble-top table, crowded with bottles and boxes of medicine, plastic tumblers, and dosage spoons. Dust spilled from
the table's rococo crevices, carved grapes and roses reinforc-
ing the eighteenth-century feeling in the house.

"Child, my neighbors and the church folks take good care
of me. I don't want for a thing. I get my meals, my mail, and
company regular. My nieces, Mary Sue and Nan, call often
enough. Nan gets over from Savannah once in a while.

"Wouldn't you be safer in a nursing home?"

"Somebody's always suggesting that. Why should I? I own my
home free and clear. I sleep peaceably. Don't have any problems. Just my legs don't work. Don't want busybodies fussing
over me. They'd tire me out."

She was beginning to tire, her voice turning raspy, with only
me there. "I'm going along now. If you want for anything give
me a call. I'll be around a while longer. It's good seeing you in
such excellent spirits."

"That's what the good Lord intended. I enjoy seeing my
children when y'all come home. But you little devil, you
turned out fine despite yourself." Eyes reddening, she smiled
her toothless smile. "Come back when you can. I don't want
for a thing, remember that. Gramma Ann didn't go to any
nursing home." She held up her arms, once powerful muscles
now hanging loose, and gave me a tight hug. "You look like
your mother." She settled into her pillows and closed her eyes.
"Just pull the door on your way out."

I passed rooms I'd glimpsed on my way in. They were crowded
with accumulated treasures. The furniture showed curves on
top of curves. A graceful walnut sideboard, its satinwood swirls
encircling shell-shaped brass handles, filled one wall of the
dining room. Differently shaped and sized chairs were sen-
tinels along the dark hallway, ball and claw feet and cabriole
legs bulging out from the bottoms of needlework-covered
chairs. More than a dozen, empty, paper-laced, frilly, Valentine
boxes filled the high mahogany mantle. The fireplace ashes
were cold, a residue from the winter. Everything smelled of
closeness and age.

It was not unpleasant.

Mothers give birth to babies. Grandmothers, whether real or assumed, make them human, especially in black neighborhoods. Women like Ma Johnston, Tempy Bolden, and Mom Dutch King were deep anchors, on and off Lowell Avenue. Mom Dutch's stoic, cheerful assent to her life was typical.

"Patience. That's what it is." My words were thrown up to the crisp air.

Mom Dutch's house nested close to the earth. The roof soared to narrow points. The hand-carved Victorian ornamentation was broken and gaping where sections had fallen. I gazed at the white house, faded to peeling gray—overgrown grass, and untrimmed greenery. Her pear trees needed pruning.

The grandmas lived with patience and faith that every problem would be settled in the "sweet by and by". My kids would say, "Don't sweat the shit." I could see George, Junior wrinkling his nose with distaste at the "naughty" word.

Neighborhood grandmas knew the limits to their free expression. They found creative outlets in flowers and in everybody's children. They assumed we would pass on what they gave to us.

Tempy Bolden lives in the next block across the railroad track from Mom Dutch and two blocks from the Hughes. Tempy buried two husbands before she was forty. She takes care of her youngest daughter and a grandson, her oldest son's boy, on the wage she earns as cook for one of the wealthy white families in Carolton. Tempy is not at all pretty— a handsome woman is the euphemism. Tempy is the oldest of three children born to "a beautiful quadroon and her black-as-night husband."

Nearing sixty when the Hughes moved to the neighborhood, Tempy is the children's friend. She is playful. Kids gravitate to Tempy like bees to nectar. She has the subtle balance of a grown woman who has kept her childhood zest, a motherly advisor, and a confidante who is trusted with secrets shared only with those of one's own age. Testing their mischief with their tall, sinewy, white-haired friend, children learn the thin line between devilment and the devil.

Meanness and cruelty are not tolerated by Tempy. On the other hand, she never loses her exuberance and curiosity. After work and a long walk home, five or six kids, including her grandson, are waiting for her in her backyard. "Come out and tell us a story." "Tempy, tell him he can't do that." Best of all, "Come play with us." Tempy is the best mumblety-peg player in the world. Tally opens his jackknife. "Play you a game?"

"You been practicing, huh?" She flips the knife from the back of her hand into the soft, green-carpeted ground.

Tally does the same. "One point."

Tempy flips again. This time the knife twirls from a bent knee. "Two points."

The solemn-faced boy concentrates, repeats his success.

"Equal." He beams.

"Elbow. Three points," Tempy says.

"That's the one I've been practicing." The small caramel face spreads with a Halloween pumpkin grin. "Gotcha."

Tempy places the point of the blade on the tip of her middle finger— a perfect strike into the well-kept mound.

"Four points," she says with a teasing laugh.

The boy can't get the heavy knife to balance on his small finger for a clean throw. He tries, bites his lip, squints, and holds his breath. Painful seconds pass. "I'll work on that one. You'll see."

Tempy rubs his hair back from his forehead. "I'll wait for you."

Sitting in the cool grass, stringing beans, she tells her visitors that she and her brother learned the game from their father. "One day Brother and I sneaked a snapshot of the two of us. We played mumblety-peg with the snapshot as a target. Before we knew it, we'd ruined it. We were scared we'd be whipped so we buried the picture under the back steps. We moved and lost the photo album. My brother died in the flu epidemic of 1918." She tries to draw him so the kids will know what he looked like. "He was a pretty boy," she says.

Tempy's house is filled with colorful quilts and handmade pillows. Tempy doesn't hand out cookies. She doesn't have money for extras. Tempy Bachman Bolden is never cross. If she is tired she tells her visitors, "I'm pooped. See you later, alligator."

Tempy's mother is the daughter of Mr. Bachman. Two children, Tempy's mother and a boy, are his by his mulatto house slave. Tempy tells her backyard visitors, "My mama and her brother had the run of the house. Bachman's wife didn't like it, but she was afraid to complain. When slave traders came looking for new stock, Bachman would have Mama and her brother dressed in their finest clothes, hand-me-downs from his white children. He'd cuddle his honey-skinned slaves on his knees and say, 'What do you think of these little niggers? Aren't these the finest little niggers you've ever seen? Make me an offer for 'em.'

"'Two thousand for the gal, a thousand for the boy.' The trader would rub the rosy smooth skin on Mama's thigh."

"Bachman would laugh and hug the children to him. He'd kiss their silky hair. 'Oh, no. You can't have these little niggers. These are my little niggers.'"

Tempy tells her story over and over. She always shakes her head when she says, "My mama was scared near to death every time her daddy played that game."

CHAPTER 10

Gayla

"WHORISH BLOOD, THAT'S WHAT IT is. Ain't nothing changed, I tell you, nothing." A raspy male voice tried to whisper, without success.

"Hush yourself. You're just an old-timey fool," a woman's voice said. "A body can be and do what they want. It's no business of yours or mine."

It's not that I choose to listen in on conversations, but it was impossible to ignore people sitting right behind me talking loud enough to be heard. I peeked in the mirror behind the restaurant wall and saw the couple who met in the bank a few weeks ago—he with the booming voice.

My bowl of split pea soup was the only item on my mind. My ears insisted on staying open.

"Well, I tell you this, Miss Maxine, she probably thinks nobody knows, but it's not likely that a body can look as sweet as that lady and not have flies around her honeypot."

Whoever he was talking about, I was glad the restaurant was nearly empty.

"Dan, you're awful," Maxine said. "Gossip is sport in this town. How do you know, for sure, she's got a white man?"

Dan's voice lowered but was still audible. "Got to be white. If it was a brother he'd be rapping all over town. Ain't heard nothing. That lady looks too pacified to be staring at the ceiling alone every night."

"You listen to me, Dan Scott. Everybody knows there's white blood in her family. You know it was never our women who started any of that messing around. White men been after colored women for ages, no matter what they looked like. It wasn't faces they were after."

"You're right about a long time ago. Only one time I heard it was the other way 'round. That Henry Lee that got himself run off, I'm speaking about now," Dan said.

Maxine shushed him. "That story's hearsay. I don't believe a word of it. If you don't know more than what you've told me, you can keep your speculation to yourself."

"I didn't mean to rile you. Curiosity isn't just for the cat. Men have wonderment, too." Dan's laugh rang across the room. Waitresses and the hostess stopped to look at him. The few customers stopped their forks or spoons in mid air. "How about me treating you to a strawberry shortcake? Real shortcake here, no sponges like I bet they have up in Philadelphia."

"White blood" played in my mind like a singsong. My pal, Louise, and the picture on her wall stayed in my awareness.

Two months I'd been in Carolton, still with an unease I couldn't put my finger on. I was also apprehensive about going back to my familiar routine. An old feeling of being pulled in two ways wouldn't leave. George Junior called from Seattle to say he wouldn't be able to get home for Christmas. At his first job for less than a year, he couldn't "swing it." Pamela would come home after she spent a few days with her new boyfriend Jeff's family in Baltimore. Antony was bicycling in Europe and visiting cathedrals and ruins in places like Dresden and Athens.

Days passed when I hardly thought of George. Other times I ached to see him. I didn't want to think of the tension I felt between us. All the pop psychology books in the stores did not speak to me; I had more important demands than self-indulgence. Black men had been damaged too much. We black women had to back them up.

George

George stared into the blackness outside his living room window. The house settled and creaked in the wind. Bare tree limbs swung in erratic waves. George liked sounds and people around him. Thalea was busy. Work had no harness on him tonight. Occasionally, a car's lights rounded the corner, but this week-night on and near campus was filled with the silence of studying. He was jolted into another place, before a dark glass that shielded a Mies van der Rohe complex. In a blue suit, white shirt, and discreetly-patterned red tie, George saw a figure pause in front of the door to "Suite 606, Science and Engineering Consultants."

The dark-haired, dark-eyed secretary wore a white polyester blouse and dime store blue earrings. She stopped typing when the man spoke.

"Good morning. I'm answering your advertisement in The Sun for Aeronautical Engineers. I sent my resume. You called. My name is George Tyner."

The secretary did not smile. "There must be some mistake. We have all the people we can handle right now." She scribbled on a slip of paper. "Here's an address that may be able to help you. It's around the corner on Plymouth."

George felt a flush of question and discomfort now, the same as then. He recalled the two men in the waiting area, their faces hidden in their newspapers.

George watched a younger version of himself go fourteen stories down in the elevator, and like a slide show, find and compare the scrawled address with the number on a dilapidated four-storied building. The sign beside the door read, "Altman's Custodial Placement. Walk Up Four Flights."

"I'll be damned." The young George tore the paper into bits and let the bits float in the air. He pulled his shoulders back, stuck his hands in his pockets, and began to whistle, his long legs heading for the next appointment.

A car horn sounded. Inside the comfortable room with shelves of books, awards, and art objects, George closed his eyes. His body shuddered. On his way to bed, he ran his hand across the oak frame of his doctoral diploma on the wall near the door. "I'll be damned."

Gayla

I didn't know why a pain for the man I married rose from the crevasse woven between him and me. During a backyard cookout, George had told the children, our guests, and me a story about one of his classes in college. George's professor had asked the class, "How would you calculate the stress factor of this 'I' beam?"

George said, "I raised my hand. He ignored me. I had figured the solution in my head. Others were working out solutions on paper."

I watched George's eyes cloud. George, Junior fidgeted.

George continued, "The Prof called on another student. Same answer I had, if he had asked me." George's jaw moved back and forth.

George Junior asked, "How come you didn't deck him, Dad?"

George laughed, "I would have liked to, but that's not protocol . . . look it up. The worst time was when he did call on me and I gave him my answer. He frowned and called on another guy."

"'That's right,' he said to the other guy." George paused and looked each one of us in the eye as if he wanted to be sure we got the point. "A voice at the front of the room piped up, 'But, Tyner just said that, sir.' The professor replied, straight-faced as a statue, 'It didn't sound that way to me.'"

George knew how it felt to be invisible. My Dad did, too. We all did. George deserved my understanding.

It was time for my flight home. I bought Christmas gifts for my folks, Alice, Elizabeth, and Shaundra. The children promised to see that no one broke into my apartment while I was away.

Ann Arbor felt good, normal—cold. Pamela peeled potatoes at the kitchen counter. "Mom, what do you bet that Jeff and I will be married when I graduate?"

"Five dollars. One dollar a year, and one for good luck." I leaned over the counter to kiss near the corner of my long-legged daughter's mouth and embraced her. If I acted unconcerned about her first, almost mature, love it would fall away.

"Be serious, Mom." Pam pulled from my hug.

"I am. I haven't seen you in three moons. I'm trying not to be a clingy mother."

Pam set the bowl of cut potatoes on the countertop. She draped her arms over my shoulders, "Ma, you've never been a clinger. You just don't seem relaxed, like always. Is everything cool with you and the Grams?"

"Certainly. I suppose it's living in two places, even if it is only temporary. I'm pulled in two directions." I hugged my five-foot-eight baby. Our children inherited George's height. That was good; the Hughes and MacKays were short.

"Okay, but if you need someone to talk to, I'm available." Pamela hugged me hard with a woman's look inside her girl's eyes.

Pam, my girl child, could do almost anything. I felt happy with her. She painted, danced, and sang. She would dream grand schemes and lose interest, but I was sure she would mature. I knew where she inherited the trait.

I am proud of our children: they're smart; they get along with one another. Antony gave us a few rough times during his early teens, but he grew back into his earlier sensitivity to people when he went to college. Tony is passionately interested in the Third World. In high school he made posters and did volunteer work for a maverick political candidate. He swiped my coffee pot, and when I missed it, protested, "But, Mom, they don't have any money. They're real poor." I let it go.

"Wake up, 'Grandma,' let's run." I turned on the lamp on Pam's jumbled desk. She was buried in covers with her head hanging over the side of the bed. "The snow has stopped and the air smells good. How about it?"

Making a face against the sudden light, she mumbled, "Sure, Mom. Ten minutes." Pam dug out thermal underwear, an old jogging suit, and Christmas-new running shoes.

Downstairs, we poured juice and made hot chocolate. We drank the juice and left the chocolate on the back burner for later.

Running, synchronized and easy, we waved and exchanged foggy hellos with neighbors who had braved the ten-degree weather. Pam was soon animated. "The loneliest looking place in the world is a college campus at break time. It's like a ghost town."

Green, silver, and gold decorated trees filled bay and picture windows. In one house two children peered out, their breath condensing and obscuring their faces behind the cold glass. They waved to us. We blew kisses.

"If those children had lived in my neighborhood on Christmas day, they'd have run to everyone's house calling, 'Christmas gift.' On Christmas Eve, Jan and I wrapped a piece of fruit, some candy, and a handful of nuts in gift paper. We filled a card table with the 'gifts,' and put it by the front door. Next morning, every kid who came by got one."

Panting a little, Pam said, "If that happened now, folks would think the candy was poisoned. Times have changed."

"Obviously, but is it good to fear everyone and everything?" We slowed to a walk. "When school opened after the holidays, teachers made everybody stand and tell what Santa brought for Christmas. Some kids would say, 'I got some nuts and fruit and candy.' Some told about bikes and skates and dolls that you knew weren't true. It was cruel of the teachers to ask. They had to know that Santa Claus didn't come to everyone."

We reached our yard. A "real" Christmas tree graced our window. I laughed at my dancer daughter. "How come you're winded? Your old mom isn't."

George was sipping hot chocolate. He placed the phone back in its cradle. "Sorry I didn't hear you ladies leave, or I would have joined you."

Pam and I rolled our eyes heavenward. Pam stuck out her tongue. "Says you. One day that naturally lean body of yours is gonna fool you, Pops."

George gave her a peck on her cheek. "You'll have to wait a long time before I'm over the hill, my girl."

"How goes all the highbrow stuff, oh great Professor Paternal Parent?" Pam returned her Dad's kiss.

"Nothing new. I'm glad I left Boeing years ago. I could never work on killing machines."

Pam slid into a chair beside him. "You could have made muy mucho dollars, Dad."

My brow furrowed, then I saw she was teasing. "I appreciate your father's integrity. George is frugal, and we've cooperated."

"Sure, I approve. Heck, you juggled three babies, your doctorate, and teaching. It's simply that I admire integrity and bucks in the bank." Pam reached for and juggled an apple and an orange from a basket on the counter. "See? No conflict."

"I'm not worried," I sipped chocolate. "My buddy in the department, Jan Sobieski, jokes about teaching being a service industry. If you think being a dancer will bring in lots of money, I suggest you look closely." George didn't respond to what I considered a subtle warning to our daughter.

"I can be the next Judith Jameson. I might join the Alvin Ailey dancers when I finish Howard." Pam lifted her head on her slender, graceful neck.

Christmas night Tony called, collect, to say Happy Holidays. He was having a fantastic time and would soon be in Africa. George Junior's gift was, "Please note, I did not reverse the charges."

Pam flew back to D.C. and George confronted me folding laundry. "That daughter of ours went out of here with more baggage than a porter." George flicked his pipe from side to side. "I didn't see all that stuff under the tree."

"She wanted a few things for the new semester. Pamela has matched and mated outfits from the time she could open a drawer. You know that, George."

He shoved his pipe into the left corner of his mouth. "She doesn't need all that stuff. How much this time?"

"Don't worry, it's from my personal budget. I saved for Christmas." I took a basket of warm towels to the linen closet. George came behind. He poked the logs to flame then tapped the spent tobacco into the fireplace. Red sparks were drawn up the chimney in random spurts.

"Sweetheart, the world's not going to end, and we're not going bankrupt if our daughter has a couple of new sweaters to look good for her new guy."

George put his pipe in a ceramic holder on the mantle, a new one I hadn't seen before. The pipe was new, too. He went downstairs calling up to me, "And I haven't been out of the house in the two weeks you've been home."

I didn't know what was bothering him. I hadn't asked him to spend every minute with me. The next day he brought flowers and tickets to a matinee in Detroit.

"I miss you, babe. The house is too quiet with no one in it but me," he said across from me at lunch.

"You look great." I caressed his face. "You've gained a pound or two despite your cooking. And you're so neat. I've always admired that in you. The house looks fine. We agreed to four months, and that's half gone. It won't be long." I leaned to kiss him.

George sipped his Perfect Manhattan. A handsome bronze man, his dark hair showed few gray strands. Like his father, African and Cherokee ancestry were apparent in his wavy hair and tilted eyes. Those eyes were opaque as they looked back at me.

"I've called you three or four times to one call from you," he said.

"Oh, Porgie," I teased, "Georgie Porgie Puddin' an' pie, you're imagining. I try not to bother you. You're at meetings or in class, and the expense of my apartment in Carolton keeps me careful. Please, let's not fuss."

On our drive home, I placed my hand on his knee, the closest I could get over the complex of buttons, lights, and bucket seats. I wanted our last evening to be a good one, summoning all our beautiful times to call back a closeness I sensed slipping away.

In bed George reached to turn off the light. He wrapped his other arm around my waist. The telephone buzzed and I picked it up. It was Louise.

"I know it's late, and I should have waited, but I wanted to let you know that Big Jon died yesterday. The funeral is tomorrow. They're waiting for the rest of the family to get here."

"He was in church Sunday, before I came home. I didn't know he was ill." I saw George's disgruntled gaze.

"He went in for a checkup and tests and had a heart attack." Louise seemed more upset than I would think about our old schoolmate. "He didn't talk about it, but that's why he retired early and moved home to Carolton."

"Gosh, I'm sorry. He was so outgoing and helpful. He told me he was remodeling his mother's kitchen the day before I left."

George tapped a finger against his glass and tightened his arm. Louise went on. "Jon and I were talking about all the people who are coming back home. Maybe he knew he had only a short time. He was home only about six months. Sorry to bother you, but I didn't want you to walk into the news the minute you landed, seeing the funeral is the same day."

"I appreciate your calling, Lou. I'll see you shortly." I snuggled close to George and wondered if people came home to die, the way elephants did. I replayed images from Saturday movies of giant elephants balancing and holding up an old or wounded comrade, bound by instinct to see that death occurred in the place of rest for the ancestors.

I tried but could not bring myself to be as involved with George as I wanted for our final night together. I hoped he didn't notice.

Before dawn, a chill cut through my chest. My teeth chattered. It was not a physical coldness, because George's arm was around me. Turning sleepily, he murmured what seemed to be "Sweet Sal." I'm always hon or babe.

At the airport George kissed me and held me close. "I'll call later to see if you get in okay. I miss you, babe, honest."

I caught and held my breath. If I asked why he added "honest," he'd be upset. I was edgy, I told myself, nervous to be leaving again. He didn't mean anything. My antacid foil was empty.

CHAPTER 11

Gayla

"LORDY, I'M PROUD TO SEE you. You look so fine." Mrs. Lowe's gleaming smile was identical to Big Jon's.

Friends crowded Mrs. Lowe's home. Her grandchildren, in unfamiliar surroundings, forgot to bend their heads going into the rooms of a house that was not intended for a generation of six-and-one-half-feet-tall boys. Startled looks and rubbed heads brought laughs of release to the mourners. Every room was a "living room," except Mrs. Lowe's bedroom. That was closed off, private, so she could retreat whenever she wanted. Four-poster beds dominated the bedrooms on each side of a narrow hall that ended in a large dining kitchen. Spanking-white and pastel chenille spreads trailed from the beds to the dark, stained, pine plank floors. Tufts of pink, green, yellow, red, and blue flowered designs portrayed girls in bonnets and branching trees that brightened the dark, wooden floors and mahogany furniture. Family and friends sat in clusters on the beds or chairs and leaned against tables and chifferobes. At the foot of each bed was a chest, called cedar even though it was pine. Folks talked of Big Jon's power on the basketball court.

"Man, he sure could shoot," reverent voices murmured and boomed. "He could dunk before the NBA ever heard the word." Mourners slowly wound their way through the clusters like searching bees.

"Yes, indeed. If he'd come along a few years later, he would have been the first Bill Russell or Kareem Abdul-Jabbar. Yes indeed."

A gray-haired friend sucked his teeth, his own brief glory days recalled. "That's a fact."

African Americans talk. We tell, we listen, we share, we pass on our feelings, fears, loves, angers, and most of all, our memories in words. Old folks tell whoever is within hearing range, "Child, I 'member . . ." and "Say now, do you remember . . .?" Memories are our life force: what we have been, what we are, and what we hope to become. Images are planted, grown, flowered, nurtured, and nourished by our telling.

In the kitchen, which Big Jon had not finished remodeling, volunteers from Mount of Olives Baptist Church heated, and sent out to the round, oak dining table, baskets of golden, hot, homemade rolls wrapped in large, white, starched, cotton napkins, a buttery aroma announcing their entrance.

Silver platters high with home fried chicken, cut-glass bowls of creamy potato salad edged with slivers of oily pimiento, and sliced boiled eggs sprinkled with paprika, lined the dining table and sideboard. Coconut, pecan, and sweet potato pies filled two card tables because there was no room for them anywhere else. The display gave a festive overlook to a somber occasion.

Gradually, hours after the long ride to and from the cemetery, the mood lightened. It wasn't exactly New Orleans, where the band plays "When the Saints Go Marchin' In" to send out the call to pick up on life because the one who's gone just crossed over and won't be back. Big Jon's spirit hovered in the tidy house. We could almost hear him saying, "Come on, live it up. I ain't never down." The mood swung from sadness to the joy of being together, from Big Jon to ourselves to how the Knicks, Hawks, and Celtics were faring.

Tally Johnston, my best buddy from Lowell Avenue, had married Big Jon's sister Juanita. They flew down from Hartford. Tally and I wrote and called, year after year, promising to get together. When we met this time, our tears were not only for Big Jon.

Tally and Nita chatted with Louise and me, the couple sprawled across a pink comforter on a bed that was once

Nita's. Lou and I balanced on pink, satin boudoir chairs without backs.

"My feet are troubling me." Tally loosened his shoelaces. "Too many days standing, running around good old Belmart Industries." Bouncing upside down on the red, shag rug, both shoes hit the floor.

Nita teased, "I say it's old age taking over."

"Shush, lady, I'm not ready for a wheelchair," he said.

"Odd that your feet are giving you trouble. Must be payback for being my trouble buddy," I said.

"How'd you come to be called 'trouble buddy'?" Louise asked.

Nita leaned against Tally's chest and laid a finger against his lips. "Let me tell it. You'll get into twists and turns and we'll be here 'til midnight and I'll never get a chance to talk." She stroked his cheek, then gave it a mock punch. "You see Louise, there was this ex-slave, Gramma Ann. She lived her last days on her granddaughter's porch next door to the Ma and Pa Johnston. Gramma Ann sat all day, rocking, smoking her pipe, and nosing on everybody and everything up and down Lowell Avenue and around the corner, as far as she could see. According to the old lady, Gay and Tally were always up to some trouble. So she named them trouble buddies." Nita stuck out her tongue at Tally, "Got it right, didn't I, old fellow?"

"Guess you did." Tally said, as if he wasn't too happy that Nita told the story right. "You do listen once in a while, anyway," he grumbled.

Dodging the pillow his wife tossed, Tally slid down from the high bed, sore feet and all. "Gramma Ann watched and told on us when we did stuff she thought we shouldn't, like climbing trees, stealing Mom Dutch's pears, and fighting. She'd yell at us and tell on us, if we were just having fun. We were always being called down by the older people back in what we called our dark ages."

"She had a cackly voice," I said, imitating the old woman. "She used to croak out, 'God don't love ugly. Y'all stop that right now. You young'uns hear me? I tell you, God don't love ugly.' I now know there are layers of meaning in 'God don't love ugly,' but back then, all we knew was she was stopping our fun. I even find myself coming up with some old sayings like, 'Um huh, yes indeed, I know just what you say.'"

"Watch it, girl," Louise said, "you might find out everything in Carolton isn't a drag."

"Never said everything was," I said.

Tally winced and rubbed one sore foot. "Gay, I bet you forgot the time you made me cry 'cause I didn't know my own sister's name."

Nita signaled Louise, "Get comfy, girl. A dark ages tale is coming. Told you the storytelling won't stop, long as these two are together."

"I remember," I said. "Jan and I couldn't keep the names of your sisters and brothers straight, you had so many. You said you had more in Philadelphia."

"Right." Tally's eyes widened. "I told you I had two brothers and a sister 'up-the-road,' Booker Junior, Walt, and John. You laughed at me."

"Right, I said, 'Whoever heard of a girl named John?'" Tally began to mimic childish voices. Talmadge Johnston was a natural born actor.

"Yeah, you ran cross the street home," I said. "Gramma Ann was on her porch, like every day, rocking and sucking her pipe. Janis and I ran after you. Gramma Ann stretched her neck to see what we were up to. Your mother was sewing in the dining room."

Tally said, "Uh huh. I asked, 'Ma, don't I so have a sister in Philadelphia named John?' Ma didn't slow the treadle on her Singer, just said, smooth and even-like, 'Her name is Evelyn. She looked so like Pa when she was born, folks came by, said, this one is sure enough a Johnston. It got shortened to John by the time she could walk.'" Tally beamed and repeated his satisfied comment as he had years ago, "Told you so."

"You haven't changed a bit, sweetheart. You have to have the last word." Nita stroked the chenille spread she'd folded to the foot of the bed back to its fluffy state and swatted Tally on his backside. She slid from the high bed. "Come on, Louise, that's enough dark ages talk."

"Sure." Louise said, "We'll be back when you two finish your memory trek."

Laughter floated down the hall. "Sounds like someone is going to pieces out there," Nita said on her way to the living room filled with talk.

Imaginative children, we had not lost the knack. Tally's mother seemed to still sit in her dining room in their white-and-green-trimmed frame house, the Singer sewing machine with brass drawer pulls shining in front of the double windows. Mrs. Johnston could look into her vegetable garden through lime green, dotted swiss, tieback curtains. Once in a while a breeze moved the ruffles. More often they were motionless in the humid Piedmont air. Mrs. Johnston's voice followed us as we ran to the front door. She didn't look up from her work. "Don't slam the screen door," followed us outside.

Tally lived across Lowell Avenue and three houses down from us. He and I were often mistaken for brother and sister, even twins. We had the same sand-colored hair Negroes called "red." Small boned and golden tan in complexion, we reflected a mixture of African, Scots-Irish, and Indian, a genetic fusing that was pervasive among colored people in our part of the Piedmont.

In large families, older children frequently left home before the younger ones knew who they were. Sometimes they were gone before the baby of the family was born. Tally was the baby that Booker Junior, the oldest brother, came "back home" from "up North" to meet.

The Johnston family was large. Ma was the pivot on which it turned. She gave directions—come here, stop that, do it this way. Ma expected and received obedience. Her children complied quickly or a bit slowly, according to how much they were like Ma or Pa.

Mr. Booker T. Johnston, Sr. was a gentle, solidly-built, cocoa man whose eyes were never harsh. Rising on his toes with each step, he walked with a springy boxer's gait. In the morning, on his way to his automobile repair shop, he whistled a soft, breathy tune known only to him. Pa had a mixed gray mustache. He always made me think of Santa Claus. Pa Johnston was a powerful, peaceable man.

I said, "Your brothers were mostly like Pa. They never gave Ma any backtalk. They were quiet like Pa, with that same springy walk. Your biggest brother, Dean, had Pa's smile. The girls at Deerpath High adored his bodacious walk. They said he looked like 'a brown-skinned Clark Gable.'"

"I think Dean was confused by all that girl attention, so he japed and teased at them," Tally said.

"I had a crush on Dean." I felt shy, even as an adult, saying the words. "I liked his bushy, black eyebrows and long lashes. You're like your mother, gobs of energy, a sharp tongue, and a hot temper."

Tally turned to listen to the laughter coming from the front of the house. "You remember my brothers and I remember my sisters. The girls were my best friends," he added in a soft, smooth-as-a-down-comforter voice.

"I knew that," I said. "The twins were as different physically and temperamentally as Pa and Ma. Tina had Pa's cocoa color, black hair, and melting brown eyes. Lele was fair-skinned, with gray eyes, and bright carrot-red hair, like Ma. People didn't want to believe they were sisters, let alone twins."

Tally stretched full-length on the bed. "Like book ends. Almost anything and everyone could hurt Lele's feelings. Ma said she was born tender-hearted. Tina protected and looked out for her. Folks said Tina was mean. I think she never felt pretty, that's all."

I said. "Baby Girl was the prettiest of all. Being pretty is especially important in the South."

"What's special about the South?" Tally asked.

"Living North, I've seen that the women in that part of the country prefer more sophisticated attire. A reporter made that remark about the way President Carter's wife, Roslyn, dressed."

"Yeah," Tally said. "Sleek and cool, up North. Cute and cuddly, down South."

Baby Girl grew into a shapely, bamboo-brown adolescent with Pa's dark, peaceable eyes. Men nearly ran their cars onto the sidewalk, almost into trees, when they spied her walking on Carolton's streets. Her salvation was, for sure, all those big brothers.

Janis and I were fascinated by our neighbors. None of our relatives lived in or near Carolton. My grandparents had died soon after I was born. The Johnstons became our extended family—southern style. Carolton was like a family with lots of "kin," some friendly and caring, others mean and remote. Even when our family had a live-in housekeeper, Jan and I lingered at the Johnstons as often as we could. Tally's house was more fun when Mother and Dad were not at home.

Tally said, "You guys grew up on our front porch."

"No," I said, "in your dining room, roasting sweet potatoes in the fireplace ashes."

After school began and daylight ran away too soon, Jan and I spent long evenings before that fireplace waiting for our parents to come from the office.

Jan loved to hear Pa tell stories. "Tell me 'bout the six men in one bed, Pa."

"It was six men in one room, Baby, not one bed," Pa would rumble.

Jan climbed on Pa's strong thighs and watched his mustache wag up and down as he talked.

"During the war, in 1918, I went to Philadelphia, Pennsylvania to work in a steel plant." Pa always said the whole thing—both words, Philadelphia, Pennsylvania. "I slaved fourteen hours, then I'd come home to an itty-bitty room I rented with five other men. We were all from down South. We paid a dollar a week for that itty-bitty room. We cooked on a coal stove that kept the room warm too. We slept three to a bed, in two big, iron beds. We didn't have but the beds, a table, and a stove—not even a chair. My partner was from Elberton, Georgia, name of Israel Pogue. His toenails scratched. We washed and strung out our clothes on a wire along one wall. Now, all of us didn't work the same time, shifts they call them, so somebody was always coming and going, and crawling in one of the beds, while the others tried to keep from waking up. In the winter weather, we took turns keeping the stove burning, but most times we'd be so tired, we'd forget to wake up and put in more coal. We don't have bone cold down here like they do in Philadelphia, Pennsylvania.

Pa pretended to shiver. He'd give Jan a powerful but gentle hug. Jan pretended to shiver and snuggled into his rumbling chest.

About that time, Ma would add, "Pa sent me every penny he didn't need for food and carfare. That's how we got the money together to build this house. Later on, we scrounged up what we needed to get Pa started in his car repair shop. It wasn't easy, but we always pull together. Takes a few years more, that's all."

Pa would put Jan down and walk his springy walk to the kitchen for a glass of water. On the way back, he would touch Ma's graying hair, his work-rough hand light as a leaf in a breeze.

Night was getting on. The kitchen team had run out of recruits. Pimiento strips on the wilting lettuce surrounding the potato salad were curling into dry slivers.

Louise and Nita reappeared in the bedroom door. "Come on, you two," Nita said. "There's someone up front who wants to see you before they leave."

Tally and I went to the front room. Maybe Tally had a tear or two. I did.

"I've a need to see Carolton the way we used to," Tally said. "How about we spend tomorrow doing some 'member this and 'member that?" Tally looked around at the few people still in the room at nearly midnight.

"I think that would be fun—but probably not for Nita." I said.

Tally caught up with Nita and Louise sitting with Mrs. Lowe. He said, "Gayla and I want to visit old haunts tomorrow. How about you?"

"I want to spend more time with Mother, we won't be here very long," Nita said. "You go ahead. You'll get a lot out of it."

"Thanks, you're a polished diamond," I said, giving her a kiss on the cheek.

The spirit of neighborhood included everyone with whom we shared common memories, time, and space. That was the character of Mrs. Lowe's home, the feeling of clan, of tribe, of nation. No one spoke of Mr. Lowe's absence, his pining away from unfound dreams, his dying earlier than he might have if he'd seen one of his inventions made real. Mrs. Lowe bore her buried loss in broad smiles and warm hugs. The event was a passing and a holding on.

George

"You told Gayla you want a divorce, didn't you?" George Tyner and Thalea Davison sat in her red convertible across from the fountain in Arbor Park. Icicles, melting from a slight warming, hung from the fingers, noses, and wings of cherubs.

"Whoa, Lady. You wouldn't have me spoil Christmas? My daughter was home."

"One minute please, Professor. You love me, you say. You want to spend every minute with me, you say. I don't understand."

George smiled a designed-to-disarm smile. "Sure, I love you, babe. You're a bright, new light in my life. But I didn't say anything about divorce."

"Not in so many words. You said that you didn't care if she came back or stayed in South Carolina."

George hesitated, said nothing, just followed the flight of a late, lost bird.

"George Tyner, I don't believe you have any intention of letting your wife go. You lied to me."

"Not me." George's hands moved upward as if to ward off a blow. "You heard what you wanted to hear. I said we belong together. I never said marriage."

George always told women, "I love you." He wasn't lying. He loved each one at the moment he said the words. Women were to be loved. They want to hear, "I love you."

"I'm sorry, George." Thalea's voice was subdued. "It's just that I haven't seen you in two weeks. You've become so much a part of my life. I must have misunderstood. I care for you very much."

George reached for and held Thalea's shoulders. "You're gorgeous. You laugh at my jokes. But, babe, face it, we've both been around long enough to know the story. You aren't naive about what's going on with us. I admit, Gayla's not the fun gal she used to be. She worries about her old parents, the kids, her work, even me. Sometimes she's downright boring. But, I'm not ready to let go, not yet."

Thalea lifted one hand from her lap. She traced the outline of his ear, down his face, around the neat mustache to his lower lip. George inhaled the aroma of her, now familiar, perfume. "Let's walk around the fountain three times for good luck," she said. Thalea opened her door and stepped out on the curb, her wide-legged stance poised like a racehorse at the starting gate. She waited for George to come to her side of the car. He was not as quick as she was unfolding from the low-slung space.

George heard, or felt—he wasn't sure which—"We're alike, very much alike. We both want what we want when we want it."

He counted off the circles, "One, two, three." Thalea held his hand as they walked back to her car. A half-hour later they were at her apartment building. They kissed. George got into his car and drove toward the freeway. He took his pipe from his jacket and lit it. "Gay's my steady rock. She'll be there for me," he said, holding the pipe firmly between his teeth.

CHAPTER 12

Gayla

THE COLD OF BIG JON'S funeral day was broken by "sweater weather" the next. Nita and Tally were staying at the Colonial Inn, overflow from the family in town for Jonathan's obsequies.

Tally came outside to meet me. "I'm going to catch my death of p-monia," he said. "I thought you knew everything, but I learned that "newmonia" starts with 'p' before you, ha. Hartford is cold until spring decides to come on stage, not this yo-yo stuff."

"I was just about used to the sudden changes in the weather, but Christmas back in Michigan closed my pores," I said, unbuttoning my light jacket. I changed my mind when the chill hit me.

"Nita's at her mother's. We've got all morning to play our game," Tally said.

We trouble buddies found our way to a wooded area north of the old cemetery—the place where Westminster Academy once stood.

Henry Lee and Myrtle Lee

Myrtle Lee had a ritual she followed only when she was sober. Putting fresh flowers on the graves of her parents every month was a promise she made to herself and kept. She replayed two memories together, the day of the week she last saw Henry Lee and her parents. "They roll over in my mind every month," she told the taxi driver who brought her regular bourbon supply. Except for going to the grocery and filling her gas tank, Myrtle Lee's world had moved almost nowhere in thirty years.

With her offering, a container of foliage and chrysanthemums, she waited for traffic to clear before she made her left turn between the marble pillars. Tally and Gayla were in the last car that passed. I don't know that man with her, Myrtle Lee thought. Guess it's her husband. Some people have all the luck, she thought. Myrtle Lee had bought a lacy, wrought-iron bench for her parents' grave, so she could sit and think. It was almost the only time Myrtle Lee didn't have the cut-glass tumbler in her hand.

Henry picks up his car from the repair shop. He washes and polishes it. He refuses to think about why he is going to drive past Mrs. Myrtle Lee Urmann's house before dark. It doesn't occur to him that he drives past her house before he calls Andrena, the woman he plans to marry at Christmas. Henry Lee doesn't stop his car; he just slows down a bit.

Ten minutes later, at home, Henry Lee answers the telephone. It is Myrtle Lee. "I saw you. You got your car. It looks real good. Now you won't be walking by my house anymore."

Henry's mother is in the kitchen singing, "My Lord, what a morning, when the stars begin to fall."

"Lord have mercy, Miss Myrtle Lee, how'd you know my number? You know this is not right—you calling me."

Myrtle Lee laughs. She sounds a little tipsy. "Don't call on the Lord, Henry. He hasn't got a thing to do with my call. I wanted to tell you I saw you, that's all. Your number's in the telephone book, so's mine."

"I appreciate you remembering me Miss Myrtle Lee. I honestly do." Henry Lee lowers his voice, just in case his mother can hear. "I'm going to miss our talks, but it's best we don't have any more. Carolton is a small town and people see and talk—you know. Things may be changing, but not that fast, Miss Myrtle Lee."

"Of course I know that, Henry. My family's been in Carolton County for nine generations. My mama says I've always been strange, as if I'm from some place else." She laughs, a high childlike sound. "I like people. Makes no difference who they are—as long as they're nice. You're nice, Henry Lee." She gives a hic-cough. "Excuse me," she laughs. "Bye, see you around."

Henry Lee holds the receiver for a long time. His mother calls,

"Supper, Henry." Henry slowly puts the phone down, his head spinning.

Myrtle Lee left the cemetery. She was glad traffic had dropped off. No tears, she thought; looks like I might be getting cataracts like Mama did.

Gayla

Tally turned his head one way then another, searching for familiar landmarks despite thirty years of change. "This is where I went for first grade. Pa and Ma scrimped to get fifty cents a week to send all us kids to school at Westminster. When Baby Girl and I came along it wasn't so rough. But the previous ones before us, some weeks Ma and Pa didn't have the money and they did without coffee or butter to make the fee.

"I attended only one year before it closed. I remember Westminster because it was like a family," he said. "The principal and his wife and children lived on the top floor. The teachers lived in a house next door. That's all gone, now."

Westminster Academy had stood two stories over its basement. Tally paced a line on the side of the house near one corner. "Some mornings the principal's son came down to class with his shoes in his hand. I didn't see why he couldn't get up and dress on time. Hell, I had to walk a mile to get here."

Westminster Academy was a Presbyterian day school, one of many that Northern churches came South to start for the freedmen after the Civil War. My grandparents, parents, and their friends attended those parochial day schools and boarding schools. The teaching was New England-style morals and Protestant, middle-class values. Southern, white school boards would only pay for reading, writing, figuring, and courses in wood shop, cooking, and sewing, which were called practical arts. Negro public schools were handed down old books from the white schools, and the school boards didn't care whether colored teachers were "prepared," my parents said. "White boards would rather have colored teachers who didn't know much," Dad said.

Families, mostly Baptist, Methodist, or Pentecostal, went to their churches on Sunday and to Wednesday-night prayer meetings. They sent their children to the Academy during the week. There weren't any Negro Catholics in Carolton, and there was only one white Catholic church. Catholics were in Charleston, down on the coast.

Tally sat on a large stone that had a bronze marker bolted to one side. The marker was tarnished. Rubbing his hand across it, Tally traced the date, 1890.

"Damn," he said, "poor Booker." He kicked a divot of grass into the street.

We held hands and looked across the overgrown space. It is possible for two people to have the same feeling at the same time. Tally and I did.

Tally's eldest brother, Booker Junior, works at the Carolton Building and Loan after school and during summers. Mr. Loveton, the manager, depends on Booker to run errands, stock the desks and the teller's cage, sweep up, and be available when he wants him. Booker watches Dennis, the other high school stock boy. Booker tells his friends, "I'm a better worker than that guy any day. I'm smarter too." One Friday afternoon in April, Booker taps on Mr. Loveton's office door.

"Mr. Loveton, I really like working here. You say you like my work. Would you want me to stay on full-time when I graduate from Westminster next month?" He hopes that mentioning the Academy will remind Mr. Loveton that he is getting a first-rate education.

Loveton looks at the eager boy before his desk, his watery blue eyes lost in a gaunt-faced smile. "Why Booker, I sure would. You're the smartest boy I've got here. The way you can figure in your head, why it's almost as fast as my adding machine."

"Do you think I can work up to being a teller in two or three years?" Booker is heartened by Loveton's words. He advances closer to the desk from his respectful six feet.

The older man's face turns blood red. "Booker, boy, you know no nigra can work up front like that. White people in this town won't stand for it, you working with white ladies that way. You've lived here all your life. You know better. What kinda uppity ways they teaching you at that Academy?"

"Oh no, Mr. Loveton. I hoped you'd give me a chance, seeing as

how you know my family, and I've been with you more than two years."
Rushing ahead, youthful energy overriding caution, he blurts, "You
know my work; I'm as good as Dennis."

Loveton gets up from his chair and walks to the front of his desk,
straight up to the seventeen-year-old face. "Look here, boy, you're out of
your place. You know better than to think you're as good as white, boy
or man. If I didn't know your ma and pa I'd whip your ass, right this
minute."

Booker hears the blood in his ears clearer than he does when he dives
to the bottom of the quarry. He can't move forward, and he will not move
backward. He stares at Mr. Loveton's nose, it is like a light bulb. But he
is Booker T. Johnston, Sr.'s son, and this is Carolton, South Carolina,
and it is 1936. He gets ahold of himself, as he's been taught. "I'm sorry,
Mr. Loveton, sir. I didn't mean anything. I just thought . . ."

"Niggers don't think." Loveton's words cut through the soft-spoken
voice. He rushes out his office door, leaving Booker Junior glaring down
at the desktop, quietly opening and closing his right hand, behind the
dust pan he holds in his left.

Booker initiates the out movement to Philadelphia.

Tally and I were gripping hands so tightly, our fingers were
numb. We let go and shook our wrists. Tally pulled his lips
together. He looked down at his hands, both of which kept
opening and closing of their own volition.

In Philly the choices were almost as limited as down home.
When there was work, pay was higher than in Carolton. Once
the grown Johnston children found jobs, they sent money and
gifts back home, just as they knew Pa had done when they were
babies and he worked in Philadelphia, Pennsylvania during
World War I.

Until the Depression closed Westminster and similar schools
all over the South, separate and unequal public schools exist-
ed—sometimes only one or two blocks apart—receiving
dependable but inadequate support from their community
fathers. It took courage for parents to send their children, aged
eleven or twelve, away from home to boarding schools and
courage for children to leave. Discrimination was the one sure

thing at home. Steady movement out was possible with ten- to fifteen-dollar sacrifices each month for tuition, room, board, and a dollar once in awhile for extras.

Tally's parents were shrewd and frugal. Rearing the last of ten children, their living standard was modest in a time and place where deprivation for most colored people was absolute.

We Hughes were comfortable. I never heard the word "Depression." Jan and I knew that some people had more money than others. We didn't know any more than that. A few times I heard the words "nigger rich" when I wore a new outfit to school or rode a new bicycle.

"Crabs in a barrel," Daddy said when I asked him what "nigger rich" meant. "Jealousy, that's all. People who say words like that think, 'If I can't get out, I don't want you to get above me.'"

My trouble buddy and I wove our way around childhood haunts. "Stop. Here's where I saw the lynched man," Tally exclaimed. I stopped the car. We did not get out. I felt a damp chill in that curve of the road, where only a moment before it was comfortably warm.

In an overgrown field at the bend of a sharp curve, Tally pointed and said, "The house was right here, hidden by bushes. My sisters fussed at me. They said I was too slow, I was making them late for school. 'Come on brat, we're gonna light a fire under your bed,' stuff like that." Grabbing a mouthful of air, Tally turned his head to one side and let his tongue hang out of one corner of his mouth. "A man was hanging from the rafters of that old, run-down house. I saw him inside the open door. His body swayed from side to side, like in the movies. A white washbasin sat on a table by the man's bed. The twins held my suspenders to stop me from running back home. Mr. Fleming, the undertaker, lifted the limp and wiggly man down and brought him out in a fishnet. I wet my pants I was so scared."

In the rising dew of the deserted field, the outline of the house and its dead man took shape in my mind. "You never told me that story before," I whispered.

"I was scared. I guess I buried it," Tally whispered back. "From that day on, I couldn't look at fishing nets."

"Why was he hanged?"

"Two tales edged around town. One was that the colored man was a bootlegger who had an argument with his white partners. They strung him up. They knew they wouldn't be punished for killing a Negro. The other story was that white bootleggers resented the money the colored man made. He brewed better moonshine and sold more than they did."

"We hear different stories and different reasons, depending on who's doing the telling—white or black, friend or enemy," I said. Luckily, my breakfast was fully digested. I guided the car through narrow, hilly streets. Older people waved as we passed them. Younger ones paid us no attention. Carolton was not a small, Southern town any longer.

I had often ridden Folly, my pinto horse, around Tally's dead-man curve. If I had known the story Tally had just told me, I would have galloped at that point or taken a different route. "I thought we didn't have lynching in this part of the state, that we had pretty good race relations," I said. "One or a thousand, it makes no difference."

"No doubt about it," Tally said. "The old folks knew about everything. They told us enough to keep us careful. They didn't want to kill our spirits."

"God, what a morbid conversation," I shuddered.

"Not really," Tally said. "We're talking about what we survived, if you please. We're alive ain't we? Hang on to that, girl."

"You're so heavy, Tal. You should have been a preacher. My kids think my life was as normal as theirs. George and I have tried to protect them. We didn't want them to hear or know the bad things; then they wouldn't have the fears that were bred into us, no matter how our families protected us."

"Same here. People don't want their kids to suffer. Our kids have had it pretty cool. They don't believe us. They think things are a bitch if it rains on dance night." Tally wiped condensed breath from the windshield, crumbled the tissue, and slammed it into the litter holder. "Nice place for kids to grow up, ain't it? And we did, lady, we did."

CHAPTER 13

Gayla

"COME IN, COME IN. Great God Almighty, it's been a long time." Daddy grabbed Tally's hand, shook it up and down and side to side, and pounded him on his back. "Boy, you look good. Mother," he called toward the interior of the house, "come see who's here." His smile broadened when he saw Juanita. "Young lady, I delivered you. You're one of my pretty ones." Dad loved to boast, especially as he drove around town. He'd point first to one, then another child. "I delivered that one." He'd add, "And that one's not paid for yet."

Mother hugged Tally and Nita. Holding Nita's hands, she said, "When are you coming back home? You know the air's cleaner and the weather's nicer. It's cheaper to live here, too"

Nita said, "Mrs. Hughes, we've lived in Connecticut lots longer than we ever lived in Carolton."

"Be doggoned," Dad said, "I hadn't thought of that. Let's see, you left here to go to college, then you went North for work, right? I guess you have lived up there longer. Be doggoned."

"All this 'back to your roots' stuff is overrated," Tally said.

Nita agreed. "After the humiliation we put up with in Carolton, I don't have happy reasons to return. Times have changed, but if I let myself remember, I get a bad taste in my mouth. My brother moved back home because he was sick. Big Jon was a happy-type guy, always looking on the bright side. I'm not as forgiving as he was."

"Wait a minute. Your hometown isn't that bad." Dad said.

"Look at me. I'm fine. Carolton's been good to me."

"Dad, have you forgotten how you were treated?" I ignored his disapproving glare. "You had to turn your patients over to white doctors because you weren't allowed to admit them to The County Hospital."

"Yes, yes," he growled, "the head administrator told me to come in the back door, so I didn't go there anymore." He brightened. "But I joined the American Medical Association, then I could wait on my own patients in the hospital."

"That was twenty-five years after we opened our practice, J. C.," Mother said.

Dad rushed past Mother's comment. "I always said the South would be a fine place for Negroes, uh, uh—I can't say "blacks" the way you young people do—when that segregation thing was finished. And I'm right. It is."

"Doc," Tally said, looking directly into my father's eyes, "you missed your prime years. And don't forget the moolah—the money you didn't make."

Nita said, "Seems to me much more needs to be worked out. My nieces say black people in Carolton don't have any power. They think colored people are going backwards—is that a word that's okay with you, Dr. Hughes?"

Mother, swallowed in her huge chair, tried to soothe impending harsh words. "Now, now, we don't need any arguments, young people. Everything depends on a person's perspective, that's what. To be ungrammatical, my dears, it's where you're at."

My father avoided controversy unless he knew he could win. "Something smells good in the kitchen," he said, sniffing a lemon fragrance snaking around the corner. "Alice, do you have something good for us?" he asked.

Alice entered, holding a tray of lemon squares and a pot of tea. "After all that talk, you need fresh energy. I made sweets this morning. I love that microwave. It speeds things. Life keeps getting easier."

Mother introduced Alice to Tally and Nita. "Alice is positively the best housekeeper we've ever had."

"Now who's forgetting, Mrs. Hughes?" Tally said. "You used

to have all kinds of trouble getting someone to work for you."
Tally took the tray from Alice, thanked her, and set it on the
coffee table. "Even when you went to work, and y'all could
afford to pay for help." He passed the tray to Mother.

Mother poured tea for all of us. Her hand trembled a little as
she handed the cups around. "We paid more than a few whites,
but some colored felt it was beneath them to work for their own
kind. It's a hand-me-down from slavery times."

Alice frowned. "That was before black pride. I don't understand it. Plain stupid to me. Those old-timey people had a
messed up attitude." She hovered near Mother. Alice seemed
genuinely fond of my parents. That felt good to me.

Alice folded her arms and wrapped the room in her composed view. "I wasn't the best student in school. Reading didn't
come easy. I figure if the English can have their nannies, and
upstairs and downstairs maids, there's nothing wrong with me
earning my bread with my own people."

I put one arm around Alice, the other across my mother's
shoulders. "I'm glad you feel that way, Alice. Thank you. Janis
and I spent many evenings at the Johnston's house when Dad
and Mother worked late. I think some of our help were crabby
with Jan and me because they resented the white children they
had to care for and took it out where they could. Leaving their
own children alone had to hurt."

"Always something I don't know," Nita said. "My mother did
domestic work, housework she called it, when times were hard.
Mama worked for a family in the biggest colonial mansion on
Whiston Drive. They talked down to her and worked her six
days a week for little to nothing. I don't know if she would have
worked for a black, uh, colored family."

Holding her arms against her sides to keep her from swatting
him, Tally said, "Knowing your Mama, she wouldn't. Hey, sweetheart, it's time for us to get along. Doc, Mrs. Hughes, it's good
seeing y'all. Keep on looking good. We'll be back in a few
months to check on Mama Lowe."

On his way out, Tally stopped to touch an old violin mounted
on the wall above Mother's desk. He said, "Gay, you kept this
thing? I thought you'd have thrown it away."

"Mother hung it there," I said. "It belonged to her brother."

"Does it have a dark ages tale?" Nita asked.

"Seems as if we have an endless supply," I said, "like *The Arabian Nights*. I wanted violin lessons and there was no colored teacher in Carolton."

Tally said, "I apologize. I didn't know it was a family treasure. Sorry."

"That's okay." I took the cherry wood instrument from the wall, strummed the dry brittle strings, and winced at the flat tones. "I found a white woman who taught music; somebody told me about her. She said she'd teach me. She'd taught a colored girl once before, a girl brought to her by one of the colored teachers. After the first lesson, the woman told me the next time I should come in the back door. 'That's what the other girl did,' she said. Tally was waiting outside, on his bike, for me."

Tally frowned, "It was the 'ho's kitchen door. We saw her cook through a window, with a white cap on—on Saturday, too. Every day that next week, our little gang argued about, well discussed, if Gay should go in that back door."

Nita didn't look too bored.

"My friends said different things," I said. "One said I should go because I wanted to play the violin. Somebody else said, because we lived in the South, we had to 'take low.' Around and around we talked. The next Saturday I took my dollar to the music teacher's front door." I gestured at Tally. "You waited for me, all sweaty, looking like you'd run if she'd come to the door with a gun."

Tally raised a hand. "Don't shake your finger at me. You look like your father when you do that." Everybody laughed except my daddy.

"The woman said, 'Oh, you're not going to take anymore?' I lied. I said, 'My mother doesn't want me to take lessons if I have to come in your back door.' She closed the door in my face. I waited. A minute later she opened the door a crack. Her face was flushed. She dropped my quarter change in my hand and slammed the door. Mother and Dad didn't know what I'd done, did you?"

"No indeed." Mother said, "That night when you told us,

J. C. said you were going to get him run out of town with your wild ways. You and he didn't speak for a week."

"Should have come to me," Dad said. "I knew how to smooth things over."

"Dad, you said I came into the world fighting. And you're still in town. I had to stand up for myself, didn't I? Anyway, I didn't know what I was going to do until I woke up that Saturday morning—and I didn't tell Janis, Tally, or anyone."

Daddy took off his glasses and wagged his finger at the five of us. "I fought the problem the right way. I was friendly with the good white people. They listened to me. Don't you forget I headed the local NAACP and ran for public office in this city when the chance came and no one else would do it."

Mother nearly bounded from her deep chair. "Now, now, everybody does what's right for them. J. C. was out there when no one else could take the risk. Teachers couldn't; they'd be fired. Some educated person had to go out on the limb."

Tally bowed before my parents. "Yes, ma'am, yes, sir. You are absotively, posilutely correct. Don't let Hot Temper Tally get carried away. Hooray for you, Doc." He imitated Sinatra, "We do it our way."

Juanita held her hands in a peace-making gesture. We were all laughing—even Dad. "I bet some folks are glad a number of us did leave this town." She moved toward the door. "We have to go now. Mama's expecting us for dinner."

"Wait a minute, young people," Daddy said. "I still say you ought to move back home one day."

Dad and Mother were umpteenth generation Carolinians. Neither of them could believe that any sane person would be willing to die anywhere but where they were born, where family lived. They didn't understand how George and I had our babies where we happened to be living when nature called. I should have "come home." When George Junior was born, Mother said, "Whoever heard of a baby being born in Michigan?"

Tally said, "We'll give your proposition serious thought, Doc."

Another round of good-byes and I took Tally and Nita to

their motel. Approaching a building identical to dozens from Connecticut to South Carolina and back again I said, "After dredging up dark ages tales, I wonder why anybody comes back home. But we had good times, too. Once, at the Christmas Parade, Jan, Mother, and I couldn't see over the crowd and a woman came out of a store where Mother shopped and took us to the second floor. One of the men held Jan so she could see. They made places for Mother and me. The owner and clerks were white, but they treated us like real people. Sometimes people forgot the rules and their humanity came through."

Tally was quiet. "I think the good times hung on how well-known you were. My mother's white half-brother gave her tips on buying tax delinquent property. Your folks moved to the house on Lowell because your dad's white cousin put out the word to the Klan to leave y'all alone. It was who knew you and how they knew you that counted."

"Exceptions, right?" Nita said. "Like Mrs. Hughes says, it's where you're standing, your perspective. If a colored person had status and the right connections, he could escape some of the pressure. "I don't remember privileges—none at all. My father was an inventor, a good one people said. He couldn't get anybody to back him. No venture capitalists in those days, at least not for him." Nita nodded vigorously. "And we all know who's got the moolah."

"Juanita, I've never seen you so passionate," I said. "You've been keeping things inside too long,"

Nita relaxed into the rear seat. She said, "Child, if I didn't keep that stuff on the back of a shelf, I'd have ulcers—or hurt someone."

"Privileges or not, I couldn't not see the signs—WHITE,COL-ORED—hemming us in. Maybe I didn't suffer enough," I said. "Our parents wouldn't let us ride the city buses. I couldn't avoid seeing Negroes on the back seat—the long seat we called it—or standing, hot and sweating in the aisle. Drivers deliberately turned sharp at corners, to send their black passengers stumbling into one another and dropping shopping bags filled with food and giveaways from the houses and jobs they worked." I heard *I'm sorry* inside my head. I was ashamed of my "privileges."

Nita said, "I rode the bus, had to if I needed to go any distance. One driver yelled at me. 'Hurry up, get to the back.' I looked at his tight, ugly face, and before I knew what was coming out of me, I said, 'White face don't scare me. My daddy's got a white face.' He could have caused me big trouble. Maybe I shocked him. He didn't say another word to me. I was lucky. You remember, my Daddy was nearly as white-looking as a white man. If he'd decided to move away and 'pass' he might have gotten someone to back his inventions. But he loved Mama and stayed in this Hell for us.

I let my friends off in the near dark. Standing in the open door, Tally said, "I can never understand white people. Carolton had Greeks and Jews who were darker than many of us. Foreigners were "treated white" no matter how colored they looked. We were the aliens. That's the schizophrenia."

"We spend too damn much time talking color, race, and junk when we're down here." Nita's voice was forced. "It's an addiction, always dredging up the fears, the old hurts. It's a pain in the behind. I'm sick of it."

Tally reached a calming hand to his wife, a gesture that his earlier words didn't match. "They talk race just as much as we do, maybe more. They're the ones keeping the thing going. This part of the country is obsessed with the Race Problem."

With a half smile, Nita said, "Let's get out of here, back home to normalcy, whatever that is. If we're honest, we know there's not much difference for us, anywhere."

"Tally, do you want to do one more little cruise before you and Nita go home?" I asked.

"You all are on your own, pals. I've had as much good-ole-boy talk as I want," Nita said.

"I've no problem, Gay." Tally said. I'll be ready after I take Nita to her Mama's."

Later, I called Louise at her job. "Can I take a peek at the Atlanta import? Does it work the way you expected?"

"I love it and Atlanta's not a foreign land." Louise was amused. "Come by after two?"

Our timing was perfect. Louise and I arrived at her house within seconds of one another. I recognized the new table and chairs she had bought in Atlanta. "You're right, it's perfect. You have beautiful taste. You'd make a fine interior decorator. You can do my house anytime, except I can't afford you. Everything you have is top quality, as well as handsome." I knew that the cost of living in Carolton was less than in Ann Arbor, but were the topline items cheaper in Atlanta?

Louise heard my questioning. "Sit down, lady. I'll get the Reingau."

"Lady, yourself. You've learned about good wines and things that don't fit the old Carolton." I crooked a pinkie and pretended to be a grande dame.

"I'm going to tell you something I've wanted to say for a long time." Louise's words were measured, her voice quieter than usual. She pulled one of the new chairs away from the table and placed wineglasses and napkins on the kitchen counter. She sat down and closed her eyes.

"You look as if you're going to confess a lifetime of crime. I'm no priest. I can't handle the heavy stuff," I said.

"It's not bad, it's personal." Louise wiped a smidgen of water left on the counter by one of the glasses. Sun through the blinds made light and dark bars across her face. "Lloyd left me with very little when he died. After our first tough years, we were beginning to make it, but we weren't over the hump. Lloyd made magic with fabric and color. He loved Carolton, but Carolton wasn't ready for a black designer. We should have gone North like the others. When he died, I went to work for a government agency. There weren't black secretaries in private businesses around here. One businessman volunteered to be a consultant to the Black Business Alliance when it started. He wanted to help improve the racial scene."

"You mean a white businessman?"

"Uh huh. He and I have been friends for almost ten years." She looked over the rim of her glass. Louise took another breath, then relaxed on another long exhale. "Yes, he's married. He and his wife have lived apart for nearly thirteen years. She lives in Columbia with her parents. He says she could never cut the umbilical cord."

"Why aren't they divorced?"

"Divorce isn't the reason. You know better."

"I'm trying not to think what is." I felt a lump in my chest.

"Interracial marriages aren't taboo in Carolton. Walk around town and you'll see mixed couples and children."

"I've seen." I covered my friend's hand, surprised to find it trembling. "Do you and this man love each other?"

"I wouldn't be in the relationship if we didn't, if it weren't absolutely mutual. We've traveled to Hawaii, Mexico, the Caribbean. Here's the rub. Nobody from one of the respected, old-line families has married one of us yet. I'm not bold enough to defy the old system."

"Has he asked you to marry him?"

"He has. But I won't agree. His business is here. He'd be ruined."

"So, you live on the proverbial crumbs?" I put both hands on my friend's clenched hand.

"I have much more than crumbs," she said. Her trembling quieted. "I have my work. I have friends, a lover, my mother and sister. I won't take as much from him as he'd like. He insisted on helping me buy this house. As far as I know, my mother and sister are the only others who know. No doubt people wonder and talk, but in this town they'd talk about Jesus Christ. A. J.'s lawyer knows. He's made some kind of legal arrangement for me and for the house, if anything happens to A. J. I'm happy, most of the time."

Louise leaned away from the table, her eyes in a faraway haze. I could feel the magic for her, regardless of obstacles.

"When we were kids everybody knew the interracial liaisons around here," I said. "We saw light-skinned children, a few blondes around."

She shrugged. "What we didn't figure out for ourselves, the older kids told us. Adults let things slip. When a man and a woman are attracted to each other, that's life." Louise shrugged, "I've heard that love makes the world go around."

Louise went to the refrigerator and poured second glasses. "I'm glad I talked to you. Sometimes I think I'm going to burst, holding it all in. I apologize for putting you off on our first date for Atlanta. All of a sudden, A. J. needed my help on a project. He asks my opinion, and usually we work out solutions together. Early on, I wasn't ready to tell you."

"Our generation is caught between the devil and the deep blue sea, my Dad would say. You're too smart for the old, casual, white-black sex scene, too scared to risk marriage, and born too soon for the more easygoing racial attitude of the younger generation."

"Come on, let's get out of here and do something fun." Louise put down her glass, picked up her keys, and started for the door.

"Thanks for confiding in me. I admire your courage. I believe it's important to take risks to make your own happiness. You say he's from an old family. Is it one that I know?"

"I don't know. I want to save that for another day, okay?" Louise put the wine on its side in the refrigerator.

"Sure," I agreed.

As we neared the front door, Louise and I caught our images in the mirror over the hall table. We stuck out our tongues at one another and laughed.

Henry Lee and Myrtle Lee

Myrtle Lee glared at herself in the smudged bathroom mirror. Even though Carolton had grown, the heart of the city was small. The same streets were thoroughfares from one place to another. Myrtle Lee thought a lot about Gayla since she first recognized her. "I know she drives all over town, soaking up stories, atmosphere, writers say.

"I can do the same," she said to her reflection. Myrtle Lee wasn't the pretty young woman that Henry Lee knew, but she was recognizable in spite of the puffy eyes. "Henry said I have a pretty smile. I've got it still, and I know the story—the true, real story that neither she nor anybody else can tell."

At first Henry and Myrtle Lee take the back roads to Lake Dillard in the dark. The Lake is ten miles beyond the edge of town. He can't stay away, despite fear and the talk about lynching he's heard from grownups since he was a small boy. Things are changing in the South since the war—opening up some. Also, everyone says that Carolton is not as hard a place for colored to live as downstate. When he brings Myrtle Lee home, he is relieved that her house is on the outskirts of Carolton, across from the cemetery. He can stop his car in a lonely spot without being seen, and there are plenty of trees and bushes, too.

At first, Myrtle Lee sits in the back, as if a taxi has come to take her to town. Even then, Henry coasts down the hill. He puts the car in gear and lets the motor take hold yards beyond her house. Then, he turns on his lights.

It is weeks before Myrtle lee says, "Henry, it makes no sense at all for me to sit in the back just to talk. I'm sitting up-front from now on. Heavenly bananas, we're just friends, aren't we?"

"You and I can't ever be just friends, you know that. Our talking is a sin and a crime around here—and lots of other places, too." Henry sounds strong, like a preacher telling his flock the gospel, but inside he is shaking when Myrtle Lee climbs in the front seat the first time.

Fall had arrived. No one comes to Lake Dillard so close to Thanksgiving.

"Are you sure your husband doesn't know that you're gone—or something," Henry says. "It doesn't make sense that a man would ignore, or wouldn't care about, where his wife was even for an hour, especially you, Myrtle Lee."

"He couldn't care less. Stu's fifteen years older than I am. We married when I was nineteen. I wouldn't say this to another soul, but I don't think my Stuart's the man others take him to be. I don't know for sure, but something's not right."

"Huh?" Henry says, watching his new friend lower her head, then look up at him with puzzlement on her face.

"Anyway, I go to my parents' house anytime I want. He knows that," Myrtle Lee says. Her eyes met Henry's with a mischievous gleam.

CHAPTER 14

Gayla

DURING THE DAYS OF MUDDY walks to the wagon, houses had been built to the very end of lot lines. Abruptly, gray-white concrete, rough-lined from recent paving, widened the old road. A low, many-windowed brick building sprawled where square, wooden, old Deerpath School had stood. The spacious playground was filled with colorful, expensive playground equipment. Children were tearing around and letting go of classroom confinement. A slim, blonde woman held the hand of a black child on one side, a white child one on the other. I sensed the ghosts of Negro children in that yard when there was no fancy equipment, no blonde teachers, and no white classmates.

"See that little girl all by herself against that tree, Tal?" I pointed outside the car window to a thick trunked pine. "I stood right there when that tree was a sapling, a few inches around. We didn't know one another, yet."

"Uh huh, Westminster had closed, but I was in another class," Tally frowned, struggling to remember so far back.

A petite, umber-colored woman wearing red slacks and a red scarf around her hair bent down, put her arm around a tiny unyielding body, and began to talk, coaxing a smile from the pensive face. She led the child to a make-believe log cabin, one built of plastic, not real, logs. A larger girl reached her hand to the smaller one. The teacher left them, tiny black hand in the larger white one.

Tally whistled. "Lots different from our days, huh?"

We left the car and walked along the sidewalk beside the school fence.

"Sure enough. My first day, there weren't any teachers out here and helpers were nonexistent. At recess, I stood beside that same tree. Kids were playing, chasing one another. A half-dozen girls circled in a corner of the yard, singing:

> Little Sally Walker, sitting in a saucer
> Rise Sally rise. Wipe your weeping eyes.
> Fly to the East. Fly to the West,
> Fly to the very one that you love best."

Tally sang with me.

> "Put your hands on your hips and let your back bone slip.
> Shake it to the East. Shake it to the West,
> Shake it to the very one that you love best."

Four decades reached forward and enveloped a friendly circle and I was outside, cut off from anything familiar. Gasping for air, I ran to the car, opened the door, and fell into the seat. Tally ran after me, "What's the matter, Gay?" he asked.

"Those girls stared at me as the circle went around and around. My hand clutched the metal handle of my Little Orphan Annie lunch box. My fingernails dug into my palms."

"What's happening, girl?" Tally asked. He looked puzzled.

My head's playing tricks with me. "It was my first day at this school. After what seemed like forever, I heard a small voice ask, 'Ain't you gonna ask her to play?' A tall girl looked through half-closed, mean eyes and said, loud enough for me to hear, 'Ain't gon' ask her nothing, old yellow thing.'"

Tally's voice was slow, not his normal staccato, "I read that scientists can touch a part of our brain and we hear music and smell odors just like they happened years ago."

"We don't need brain probes." I said. "I call growing up in Carolton, growing up schizophrenic. Some of it sure was crazy." I didn't know if I should cry or laugh.

"Mrs. Professor, up in Hartford the young bloods have no idea of what we went through, the color crap—outside and inside. Ignorance isn't good for anybody." Tally yanked a tissue from the holder between the seats and blew his nose.

"So this is what getting older does to you?" I pulled myself together, like the old people told us to do when we lost our tempers or cried. "There is a Chinese curse that says that your enemy will live in interesting times. We've sure lived in interesting times: segregation, wars, civil rights, and moon walks with white faces in white suits."

I felt better so we left the car, again, and walked alongside the fence.Lacing his fingers in the octagonal wire fence, a runny-nosed boy with inquisitive eyes followed us. I gave him a tissue. Tally held a stick of gum through the wire. The tyke stuffed the gum in his pocket, grinned, and continued to follow us, the fence vibrating under his fingers. A teacher's aide wearing bright blue pants called to him; he sniffed, grinned, and ran to the ragged line moving into the school.

"I've been here three months and I still don't know what to call this time," I said. "There's tension I can't touch, as if I'm waiting for earthquake aftershocks."

"Hasn't this little corner of the world improved?" Tally asked. "Blacks can do things in Carolton that Negroes couldn't."

"I've met whites who have moved South." I looked behind me to see if anyone was close enough to hear. "When I hear a different accent, not Southern, I'll say something like, 'Where's home?' One of my new acquaintances, from Wisconsin, said she's surprised by the way whites talk about blacks behind their backs. She didn't say anything specific, and I couldn't bring myself to ask. Guess I don't want to hear the 'facts.'"

A man, not very tall, portly, and puffing a little, was hurrying across the schoolyard. He signaled and called, "Tally, Gay, wait up."

We recognized Marvin Townsend from East Carolton.

"I missed y'all last night at Miz Lowe," he said. "Won't you come in? I want to show you my building."

"Right, man, you're the principal." Tally clapped him on the back. "Glad to see you, man."

Marvin took us inside. He gave us a tour, from computer terminals to the double gym. "They used to practice basketball on the side yard at old Deerpath," he said "Quite a difference, isn't it?" Marvin Townsend was clearly proud of the changes.

"What do you mean they practiced? You're as old as we are," I teased. "We played in that dirt. If a shower came up during a game, the teams and coaches ran inside, and people outside without umbrellas suffered in the muggy heat until the rain stopped. Then our team would come out and beat the devil out of the other team. Avondale laughed at us because they had a real gym. We had to win."

In Townsend's office, awards and plaques lined the walls and filled showcases. "I always wanted to be a principal, like Professor Ellis," he said. "The way things have turned out, I can hardly believe it. Man, when white parents and black parents are sitting together, and when my white teachers ask the black ones for help, it's a dream come true. I'm not knocking it one little bit, and it has been hard work." In the Principal's Office we drank sodas. The sound of children was audible in the background.

Tally said, "My brothers and I were talking about the Frankenstein monster at family reunion last summer."

Townsend frowned, "I'd forgotten him, a World War I veteran with a scarred face and a limp, right?"

"Right," Tally said. "The Board of Education traveled around town to all the schools once a year, late in the spring, near graduation. The colored schools were the last of the day. Professor Ellis, the teachers, and students had to sit in the hot assembly and wait for them to show. We never knew exactly when they'd get there."

"Yes, yes," Townsend warmed to the story, "one by one the line of tight-lipped men, no women, would parade to the podium, stiff smiles on their pale or ruddy red faces. It was their job to give the students a pep talk. The head guy always said, 'Y'all getting a fine education under your fine principal, *Professor* Ellis. I see Erma over there. She's been with us more than twenty years.' He'd point to Miss Flanders. 'You're doin' a fine job, Erma.' Sometimes one of them would talk about how the mother or father of one of the teachers had been his "mammy.""

"The board member we all hated most of all was the

Frankenstein Monster, a cracker in a too-tight seersucker suit.
He'd wipe sweat from his face with a red-and-white-checkered,
wrinkled handkerchief, push his little round glasses up on his
bumpy nose, and start the same way, every year. 'Now, I got this
old darky down on my plantation . . .' I don't remember what
came next. We'd stare death wishes at him."

Marvin went to the cooler for water. "The story goes, one year
something happened. The Monster began his, 'Now, I got this
old darky . . .'when feet started scraping against the floor. The
noise of heels tapping and growling noises behind closed
mouths got louder. It was a snowball rolling downhill. Even the
youngest kids knew what was going on. The Monster got redder.
His neck puffed over his curled-up collar like a turkey gobbler.
He couldn't believe it, neither could any of the grownups. All
those peckerwoods turned mean-looking. Mr. Ellis was already
standing; he wasn't allowed to sit on the same level as the whites.
The kids knew what he had to take, so they quieted down. After
the board left, mad as a dog with bees in its ears, Mr. Ellis said,
"You know how things are down here. We have to take it."

Tally said, "My big brother told me that Alvin Rutledge got
up and spoke out, 'It's about time we stop taking it. Our
grandparents took it. Our parents took it. Nothing's changed.'
Alvin was the football captain and the first boy from our community to be killed in the Pacific."

"Things are different—better—for you than they were for
Ellis, aren't they?" I asked. I was disappointed that I had no
older brothers or sisters to pass on stories to me.

"Different, yes. Better, somewhat." Marvin said. "All our
schools had black administrators back then, grammar and high
schools. I'm one of three in Carolton today, and we're all in elementary schools. Our kids don't see many of their own kind to
look up to anymore. Folks say the handwriting is on the wall.
Every time a black leaves, the board brings in a white. Our young
ones think that, because they wear a shirt and tie instead of overalls and the signs don't label water fountains, they have it made."

The closing buzzer sounded. Tally and I jumped. Marvin
Townsend laughed, "How could you forget that sound? It's
time to go home."

"Talking about assembly and Prof Ellis, it could be I thought it meant I have to run to my next class." I pressed my hands to my ears. "You've a fine operation, Marvin. Hang in there." I shook Marvin Townsend's hand.

Tally put his hands on Townsend's shoulders, almost—but not quite—a hug. "Thanks for the tour, man."

Outside, we watched children stream onto the sidewalk and climb into the line of yellow buses. We searched for our runny-nosed friend, but he was swallowed in the mass of children.

"Say, Gay, I mean Gayla—I know, you like your whole grown-up name now—what would The Monster do if he saw this mixed up bunch of school children?"

"Croak on the spot, for sure."

"Amen." Laughing to tears, we pulled tissues from the box between the seats.

"Let me drive," Tally said when his eyes were dry. "I'll rest you a bit and show you sights I'll bet you've forgotten."

"Watch out for one-way signs. Little Carolton isn't a one-horse town anymore. Do you think our feelings about Carolton are odd? Marvin isn't unhappy with his situation."

"Could be. He may be denying it, to keep from crying. You and I are independent cusses. That's why we're trouble buddies, scandalizing folks with outrageous doings. Creative, I call it."

"Maybe you're right. For us, being a boy and a girl made no difference. We didn't like to be pushed around or see anyone else pushed around."

Tally eased into traffic. "Some of our feelings have gotta be genetic. Look at our mothers; feisty heifers, aren't they? I don't worry about how we got the way we are; we just are. Gee-Gee," that was his special name for me, "don't you wish Janis was with us? I do."

"Yeah. I wonder what she would have made of her life if not for that accident?"

In her junior year at college, only nineteen, Janis and two coeds were struck by a car that ran a stop sign. Jan died, one girl was permanently crippled, the third was barely hurt. The driver, a prominent white farmer, paid a modest fine. I did not want to open that wound, didn't want to see the drunk cracker I imagined in every pickup truck, didn't want to hear him in every Southern accent, even a friendly 'y'all come again.' I didn't want to think they're all awful. No, Billy Joe Taylor's family are decent folk, I thought.

"Here's the Star Movie Theater, the one Jan closed us out of." Tally said, stopping at the curb in a nearly deserted area of the oldest part of downtown.

"Some joke. We egged her into it," I said.

Faded paint on raised plaster, stars, suns, and moons betrayed the origin of what was once a movie theatre. It had become Fall's Secondhand Furniture Store, a long slide from its days of fantasy and glamour.

A Saturday-morning half-hour quiz show is broadcasting on WBJL, Carolton's only radio station, before the cartoons, Westerns, and serials begin at ten o'clock. Young white patrons sit downstairs. Six of them are chosen to come on stage for the quiz. Colored kids fill the balcony, mute as they watch the downstairs crowd win coupons for ice cream, movie tickets, and pens from local businessmen. The patrons upstairs, who paid their dimes to get in and nickels for Baby Ruth and Butterfinger candy bars, aren't allowed a try. Week by week, frustration builds.

One Saturday, Janis mutters an answer to a question that is missed. Her balcony friends encourage her, "Louder, say it louder."

Janis squeaks, "The Suez Canal!" Heads look up in disbelief. The announcer glares.

Gay calls out, loud enough to carry below, "And she's only in the third grade." The announcer had said it was a fifth-grade question. Janis is actually in the fourth grade.

Week by week, the balcony becomes more restless and offers more answers. One Saturday at 9:25 A.M., the colored children are outside the balcony entrance. There is a CLOSED sign on the locked door. From now on, Negro children will arrive at ten o'clock, when the cartoons begin. Gay and Tally try to get their friends to boycott the theater. Older kids tell them to forget it; they'll stir up trouble.

No one takes the problem to the adults. Gradually the balcony fills again. There's nothing else to do on Saturday mornings in Carolton.

Cartoons, Westerns, and serials are glimpses into another world, even if Tarzan is a white African, and the "natives" look like relatives and friends we see daily, but without clothes or humanity. Bob Steele is Gay and Jan's favorite cowboy. He has black hair and a swarthy complexion. And they've never seen a white mouse. Mickey has to be "colored."

"We put stuff over on them. We escaped, worked, and found some of the goodies," I said.

"You're right. Still, I resent being forced into exile." Tally bit his lower lip, the merest tremble controlled. "I have my roots in this red clay. This is my home, too," he said.

Tally was animated. "We can thank the ones who came before us, the ancestors, our African foreparents. Mr. Ellis was intimidated; he had to follow rules, with watered down doses of everything," he said. "Our teachers knew how to be subversive, even if they never knew the word."

"Right on, fellow," I said. "They were making twentieth-century Harriet Tubmans and Denmark Veseys, right under the massas' noses."

"Second-rate schools be damned, our teachers gave us poetry and art from faded sepia copies of Reynolds' and Gainsborough's, even after the private church schools closed," Tally added. "It wasn't only European culture either. Our grownups knew African history. They taught us that we weren't always slaves or clowns, the way the movies played us."

I sat forward. "I don't remember seeing pictures of black heroes on the school walls today. When an assembly speaker was dull, I'd look at portraits the PTA gave the school: Du Bois, Bethune, Douglass, Banneker. We knew who we were."

"I saw Martin Luther King, Jr. and sports celebrities in some of the classrooms," Tally said.

"I guess I'm a snob. I don't put a ballplayer or rock musician in the category of Paul Robeson. That man was somethin'— athlete, scholar *and* artist."

"If you're not a snob, you're an old fogey," my buddy said.

"Never. I want kids—young'uns the grandma's said—to be aware, that's all."

Suddenly serious, Tally said, "They're aware, aren't they? They do Black History Week."

"It's Black History Month now, friend, in February, when everybody's home with strep throat."

We stopped by the lake to watch the ducks. Ducks, swans, and frogs let one another be.

The best black minds are forced to teach or preach. Medicine is a limited, expensive option. Neither white juries nor judges will pay attention to a Negro lawyer.

The history teacher at Deerpath, Mr. Stockton, uses radio quiz shows to encourage his students. "How many questions did you answer on Dr. I.Q. last night?" he challenges. He even tells which ones he missed, strange teacher.

Miss Cross has a treat for her algebra classes, if they finish early. She was a manager for a traveling musical show, before she chose the security of teaching. Miss Cross tells them about exotic places: St. Louis; Kansas City, Kansas; Kansas City, Missouri; Detroit; Oklahoma City; and New Orleans. She knows Louis Armstrong, the Deep River Boys, Cab Calloway, and Ella Fitzgerald.

Every summer Miss Wanda Lane goes to Northwestern University, way up in Evanston, Illinois. Not many second grade teachers are scholars like Miss Lane. She doesn't have scholarships or grants. She pays her own way.

Negro, Colored, African American . . . black children of old Carolton have their secret weapons.

Tally turned my face so he could see my eyes. "I'm enjoying this 'member trip, but we haven't talked about why you're spending so much time back here, alone."

"I came to help Dad and Mother manage business that they're confused about. I also wanted a break from teaching, and I was due a sabbatical. Those Michigan winters . . ."

Tally put one hand on my shoulder. "I know all that. But you and I are too close for too long. Something's going on inside you. Trouble with you and George?"

"Not really, maybe, I'm not sure." I couldn't fool my almost twin even when I fooled myself. "It could be that midlife crisis stuff that's on the talk shows. Experts yakety-yakking on TV is enough to flip a person into a crisis, whether you need one or not. No, friend, the change of space and time will give George and me time to think about our relationship." I paused. "George has a sort of wandering eye."

"Come on, not George? Must be women hitting on him."

Tally and I shared a lot as kids. We were adults now. How much could I say? "I hope you're right. I've called home several times, late at night, and he's not in. Hell, it's cold in Ann Arbor. He can't be out walking."

"It's not cold here," Tally said. He got out and waited for me, "Let's feed the birds. It's time for a stretch." We got out of the car. Tally clasped his hands behind his back as we walked for a few minutes. "George has got to know that he has a true-blue woman. I say, throw it out of your feeble brain. That's how your mother says it, isn't it? She used to say that to both of us whenever we were upset. If George is messin' around, you're better off not to know."

"I don't know, Tal. When Mother says that feeble brain stuff, I don't know if the emphasis is on the adjective or the noun. When you married Juanita, and George and I got married, expectations were different. Not just for marriage, but for being black and all the crap that was hung on us for that fact of nature." Tally didn't say anything else, so I went on.

"We married knowing we, Colored women, would help with bills and getting the good things. You and Nita both had to work to buy the house you wanted in a good neighborhood. I've worked, same as George. White women demand the right to work outside their home. They knock down doors to join corporate America. Black women have done double duty forever. I sometimes resent not having options, like being able to stay home with my kids like a 'Miss Ann.' Maybe Nita feels the same. I don't know. We did what we knew we had to do to survive and 'make it.'"

Tally spun around and glared at me. "Are you blaming George and me, black men? I don't believe what I'm hearing, Gay Hughes."

I wasn't seeing my trouble buddy, my longtime and best friend. I saw male energy, grown-up different. "No, no, you know better. You never used to misunderstand me. You're my 'long-timiest' ally," I said, using an old word to make him laugh, I hoped. "I've missed something important to me, I guess. I don't blame you or any old amorphous thing called black men, but something's wrong. I am a feminist, but not the stuff in white women's books. My perspective is different, broader."

"You sound like your mother, talking perspective."

"Good, I hope so. She knows things I don't seem to know about men and how to understand them."

We got back in the car. Glad that he was driving, I leaned against the headrest. Tally said nothing more about George, so I didn't. I wondered, how old is too old to change?

Tally was quiet for a long time. "I'm thinking, Gee-Gee. It would be a good thing if boys and girls could grow up together equal, like us. It takes doing it the way we did to be fair to the male and female."

"I've run on too long." I covered his hand on the steering wheel. "Please forgive me, but you opened the gate."

Kissing me on the cheek, Tally steered with one hand. "We have war stories and our scars."

"Can we say this is a settling in time?"

"Or settling out." Tally looked as if he wasn't sure of what he meant.

"Old buddy," I said, "you and I have been honest with each other from the beginning, since we were 'real little,' Gramma Ann would say. You're my brother. George is my husband."

Silent for several blocks to the outskirts of the city, we were soon at the motel. Tally leaned on the door as he got out, "Come on in," he said, "Nita's back.

Vaguely aware of how Tally and I would not have been welcome at this motel when we were growing up, I noticed a white couple leaving the adjacent room. They smiled.

"I think Nita's had enough of my tagging with you. I'll pass. Until next time, trouble buddy," I said.

Tally and Nita returned to Hartford. The Lowes who remained in Carolton settled into life without Big Jon.

CHAPTER 15

George

THE HOTEL ATTENDANT BROUGHT A morning paper to George's room. George hated being alone in hotels. "All headlines look alike. The news is the same. The rooms are alike. The food is the same," he said as he handed the attendant the money for the paper and a tip. He threw the Cleveland newspaper to the floor beside a chair.

The young man touched his forehead with his finger and mumbled, "Yes sir," as he turned and closed the door.

The big shots at BB Corp had summoned George. They were interested in his fastener design, "a coupling" they insisted on calling it. He was scheduled to stay in Cleveland three days—two, if he could "bullet" what they wanted.

Restless, George went to the coffee shop for breakfast. He found a corner table, where he could observe the entire room. Three young women in airline-attendant outfits sat nearby and ate breakfast.

"The dumb computer fouled up my routing." A woman about twenty-five, leggy, with a modest bust beneath her blue jacket, stabbed a piece of melon. Her eyes were framed by the longest lashes George had ever seen. She was a coppery brown that glistened like buttered toast. Her hair was cut in a short 'fro, which molded a shapely oval head.

"You can find something to keep you busy for thirty-six hours, Val. Take in a symphony," her short, blond companion suggested.

"Val at a symphony? Val, do you know the difference between a violin and a tuba?" A third woman, not as pretty as the one named Val, sat across from her companions. Her jacket fit snugly, as if she had put on a few pounds.

"I know the difference between a violin and a viola, Miss Smarty. Can you spell bassoon?" Val made a punching motion at her teaser.

"Kidding, just kidding," tight jacket said. "See, you're into a better mood already."

The blond applied fresh lipstick. "We have to run. Our flight's on deck in twenty minutes. Whatever you do Val, chill. See you soon," she said, looking around to be sure she had everything she'd come with.

The women left money for their breakfasts and tugged their wheeled luggage toward the exit. A shuttle bus waited at the curb.

George had a direct view of Val. She looked above her coffee cup. He smiled with raised eyebrows and shrugged his shoulders to acknowledge her plight. She lowered her eyes to her coffee.

He opened his brief case and took out his laptop. She got up to leave. George caught her eye and stood as she came in his direction, toward the exit.

"Excuse me," he said, while keeping several feet between them. "You and I are in a similar situation. You have boring hours ahead. I have an equally boring time coming up." He gave her his card.

Val read his card, took in his appearance, and said. "I don't do pickups, Professor."

"I have nothing of the kind in mind. I merely hoped you'd be willing to have dinner with me after my appointment," George said. A mildly annoying nudge just under his ribs caught George's attention. He pushed it down. No harm, he thought. It's a public place.

She studied his card again. "I don't know." She hesitated. "Tell you what, if I'm at the bar when you get back, you'll know."

"Is 4:30 good?" George said.

"I don't know," she said. Her eyes signaled nothing.

At 4:25 George entered the pub near the front of the hotel dining room. Talking to the bartender, Val sat on a stool. She'd changed from her uniform to a canary, off-shoulder blouse and black miniskirt. No harm, George's head said, ignoring—as he often did—another tug that was already too far away.

Gayla

Houses listen. They converse with you when you're good to them, when you love them. The house on Lowell Avenue was a good house from the day Ephraim McGuire began to build it for his bride Euphronia, in 1895. The McGuires bred and bore six children in that home. It wasn't until the last baby was born that the house, like all the others from the area's farming days, was given a number, three-five-zero, three blocks south of Central Street. The older people continued to call the dwellings the "Neely house," the "Slayton place out by the water tank," or "Cowans on old Indian Way." Creaking walls and whooshing winds across the pitched, tin roof didn't frighten the McGuire children. They were lulled to sleep at nap time and at night by the singing and laughter of a house that knew its reason for being.

The house was sold to my parents by the last child of Ephraim and Euphronia. No children had run through its rooms in many years. The house liked the smell and noise of children. It forgave our anger when there was a fuss and a shoe was chucked against a wall. No one truly wanted to hurt a sister or brother. The house knew.

When the grownups were away, my pals and I would run up and down the tin slopes of our house. The house had been expanded several times during its long life. We would count seven gables. I had felt powerful as I created thundering echoes beneath my footsteps.

The day was warm for November. I circled the old house, stepping over branches, layers of decaying leaves, and debris that had blown into the yard during the years the house had been abandoned. Spilling dried leaves down the steep roof in the backyard, centenarian oak trees ringed and towered over the deserted space. Apple, pear, and peach trees were long gone, as well as the fig bush and sour cherry tree. Treading through the overgrowth, I bent to tug scraggly, dead limbs and tossed them into small, random piles. The side yard stretched toward the late afternoon sun. Large oak trees blocked heat away from the tall, narrow windows. The effect of the hill on where the house sat made it like a desert mesa. If you stood on the next hill you could see the one on which the old house rested high above McGuire Street, a curving tail hugging the red-clay rise close to itself, tying Lowell Avenue to McGuire Street. On top of the hill, the old garage tilted to the east. Prevailing, westerly winds had an effect on the man-made structure that the oak trees defied with audacity.

Dad and Mother moved out of the aging house years after the fire and several years after George and I were married. They left when a chemical plant was built three blocks away. The serene neighborhood of Colonial and Victorian homes was killed by odors and traffic that oozed like lava down the small hills when nearby streets were widened to allow workers and trucks access to the new factory. No longer in a "good neighborhood," the house was for sale for commercial use. The oak trees slowed the wind as they, unknowingly, waited for the bulldozers.

In the overgrown backyard, I peered beneath the crawl space, its door hanging by one broken hinge. Covered by darkness, eyes gleaming, two cats made their home. I didn't see kittens, but knew there would be some, soon. Other animals once lived in that space: squirrels, rabbits, raccoons, and thin black snakes that never lived long enough to grow to full size.

Gay's pinto horse, Folly, waiting for her ration of dried corn and alfalfa, shakes her head. Phlegm spurts left and right, settling on the rough, wooden wall of her stable—a converted chicken house. "Stupid horse, you spit on my blouse." Folly is Gay's eighth-year birthday present. Everyone for blocks comes to stare. The biggest boys are bold enough to act out cowboy fantasies on Folly's sturdy black-and-white flanks. There's no one to ride with. No colored friends have ponies or horses.

"I'm an old cowhand, from the Rio Grande." Saturday riding, alone, demands imagination. But the galloping sound of horses bearing down from the rear is no fantasy. Glancing into the dusty cloud, she sees several mounts come alongside. Frightened, Gay spurs Folly, bad guys on her tail.

A beautiful white stallion pulls alongside. A round-faced boy, his damp blond-brown hair falling in his face, grabs her reins and yells, "Whoa!" His stallion rears, just like The Lone Ranger. "We've been watching you," he says. "You ride pretty good. You want to join our gang?"

He's the biggest, the leader. He introduces her to two boys and two girls, riding Shetlands and Arabians in a mixture of sizes and colors.

"What's your name?" a girl with wavy auburn hair and familiar eyes asks. She says her name is Naomi. She is friendly. "We've got a place where we meet when we go riding. You want to come with us?"

They turn off the dusty road, through brush that closes behind them, to a secret cave in a cliff that can only be reached by climbing a rope and digging dusty toes into carved uneven holes. This is where they tell ghost stories, roast hot dogs, and create a world under their control.

"Next Saturday, you bring the marshmallows. Everyone takes turns," Naomi tells Gay.

The gang troops back to Gay's house. She lives closest to the cave. They decide her house will be the watering hole after a hard ride on the Carolton Prairie.

On a Friday after school, the leader's little brother comes, alone. He asks Gay to ride to their cave. They sit and talk for a while. He asks her if she knows what their parents do at night. She says, "No." Little Brother tells her to lie down on the worn thin rug laid on the cave floor. He lies on top of her and squirms around for a few seconds. On the ride home, Gay wonders why parents would do such a silly thing. Little Brother looks so serious; she can't ask.

Janis and I had unusual freedom in the Bible Belt. Our parents were more modern than many of our friends' parents. Mavis Jean and J. C. Hughes didn't subscribe to the belief that children should be seen and never heard. Neighbors and townspeople whispered that the Hughes girls were allowed to talk back to their parents. Girls in Carolton, Negro and white, were confined to ladylike pursuits—sewing, knitting, playing with dolls, household chores, and child care. Janis and I were allowed opportunity, and time, to follow our imaginations.

I tripped over an exposed root and balanced myself against the rickety steps that rose to the door of the old kitchen. The splintering wood felt very different from the wood in the days of summer baths for Lil' Roland. Four sun-bronzed children were shaded by the oaks and shielded from grownup's sight by the garage. Whose idea was it to bathe Roland? Tally's? Mine? It didn't matter. We sensed the beauty of the little boy's perfect body in contrast to the neediness in his environment. His head was regal with curly black hair, large and widely-spaced brown eyes, topped by long thick eyelashes. Roland Goode possessed a classically proportioned body with well-formed hands and feet. Despite a sure lack of pre-natal care, his legs and back were straight, his carriage as erect as if aligned by a plumb line. Without adequate nutrition, his belly was flat, his teeth sound. The odor of the cleansed Lil' Roland wafted, as real as the breeze that stirred the tall weeds around my legs more than thirty years later.

Every Saturday for one whole summer, Lil' Roland came to our backyard to get his bath. Janis, who was three years younger and four sizes smaller than I, helped haul pots of warm water from the kitchen, down the tall steps, to the yard.

"Be careful, don't slosh. The floor's just been scrubbed. Mother'll be mad," I said.

We were five and eight years old, shuffling unsteadily across the green and red linoleum floor. Outside we poured the water into a yellow-enameled tub, leftover from Jan's baby days.

"Wait 'til I get some soap." Jan sneaked a used bar of Lifebuoy, a worn washcloth, and a towel down the six stairsteps for our weekly good deed. One of Tally's tasks, that first time, was to help us coax Roland into our backyard.

The first Saturday, Roland wasn't sure what was going to happen to him. He was scared when Tally said, "Come over to Gay and Jan's, we're gonna give you a bath." Roland tried to run away.

Tally grabbed his shorts and ripped the snagged hole further. "We won't hurt you. Have we ever hurt you? You know
better. Don't you want to look good for Sunday?"

Jan added, "I take a bath every night. It doesn't hurt." She
was a few months older than the boy but more worldly.

"We'll give you two cookies," I said.

"Where the tookie?" the grimy-faced boy asked.

"Go get them, Jan," I said.

Jan handed me the towel, ran to the kitchen, and returned
with two Vanilla Wafers. She held one out to Roland.

Gazing warily, he ate it. "Gimme the two." He held out a
dirty hand.

"Not 'til you're clean," Tally, the only male in the conspiracy,
replied with authority.

Roland let us take off his dirty shorts. Tally and I scrubbed
his cashew-nut-brown body until dirt ringed the small tub.

"You wash his ding-a-ling, Tally. You're the boy," I said.

Jan held the drying towel and sporadically chased two fat
puppies away from the soapy water coursing down the side of
the tub.

Roland Goode, the youngest in a large family, lived on
short, unpaved Hunter Alley. He, like other poor kids in the
neighborhood, fulfilled our need to help out. We realized that
there was a difference in the way we lived and the lifestyles of
the children in Hunter Alley, McGuire Street, and much of
Carolton—colored and white. We adopted Roland; as if he
were a plaything, a toy, a game, a new pet.

After his bath and his second cookie, his clean body was
creamy soft and shining. We dressed our new pet in one of
Jan's old sunsuits, one that wasn't too girlish. Buckling on a
pair of Jan's outgrown sandals, grinning and proud, Roland
strode across Lowell into Hunter Alley. Neighbors and visitors
on porches and in yards greeted him:

"Look at Lil' Roland, don't he look grand?"

"Hey, boy, you sure sharp."

"Yeah man, fine as wine."

Day by day, until the next Saturday, Roland's sunsuit became
dirty and torn. He wore it night and day. About Wednesday,

the familiar fabric flashed up and down the street, with one shoulder button gone. By Thursday, an older sister might tie an old belt or cord around his middle to hold up the remnant. Often Roland streaked along, holding his outfit with one hand. His mother left every morning at 5:30 in her white uniform to cook for a far-removed, unseen, well-to-do family. If the "new" suit did not last the week, the old pair of shorts would do. Saturday, sandals in hand, Roland arrived. We conspirators returned to the backyard for the next bath. The ritual ended as we grew and interest waned.

The next good deed might be to nurse a stray pup or make a sandwich for one of the drifters who sometimes wandered from the nearby railroad tracks just before dusk when he wouldn't be easily seen. Helping people, a trait learned at church, was important to us. Missionary offerings were collected for "the starving heathen" in Africa and China, and through the conversations and actions of older people in the community and our families, we learned to "give." We did not imagine that our choices of the "poor and downtrodden" might not be the same as the grownups' choices.

One summer, back home from college, I heard, "You're Gay Hughes ain't you?" I looked into the face of a small, fair-skinned woman wearing new dentures. "Well, this here is Roland. You remember Roland. You used to give him baths."

A foot above my head, a handsome young man smiled. His khaki uniform was the same shade of tan as his face. Roland was not embarrassed by his mother's very audible words. More prosperous in later years, she was seeing Roland off to an army camp. Lil' Roland stayed in the army twenty years.

Hundreds and thousands went away for thirty or forty years, or never returned. What was this home, this Carolton, to them? Was it people like Lil' Roland or a friend allowing you to be called "nigger"? Privileges and insults were what made home; both were Carolton. A few minutes after we parted, I felt discomfort at the reminder of those bath Saturdays.

The pecan tree loomed as tall as the water tank behind the ugly chemical plant. Sweet corn had once grown in the black soil nestled against the furthermost slope; weeds randomly filled where Mr. McGuire's barn once stood and cows slept. Beans, tomatoes, and potatoes had rowed up the hill; cantaloupe and watermelon had dotted the flat that bordered McGuire Street. Why, if a body wanted and took the trouble, a garden could grow there next spring. I was tempted, ever so briefly, to take on the old house—rehab, remodel, redo. No, George would not leave the university. We'd have no way to support ourselves. I was living in my fancy, again.

The sense of a hologram, where everything appears complete and in full dimension, disappeared and dissolved into a shattered reflection. In the overgrown backyard, the warm air was not as sweet smelling as it had been. I looked down the hill that rolled away from the rise. The wind had shifted from west to south. The new factory expelled odors worse than the abattoir at the edge of town where cows and pigs were once slaughtered, pungent acrid burning my eyes, throat, and nose. I choked, coughed, went to my car, closed the windows, and left.

CHAPTER 16

Gayla

"GAYLA, CAN I COME BY for a few minutes?" Louise sounded breathless. "I have a question and it has to be in person."

"I'm here. Come on over. Hey, you've forgotten what Mrs. Grant pounded into us in English class. 'Can I means you're able, May I asks permission,' she'd drone endlessly. Seriously, I can hardly wait." Exactly seventeen minutes later, I opened the door. Louise bounced in, her eyes like fresh rain.

I said, "What's happening? You know I can't take suspense."

"You're invited to dinner Friday—the next Friday after this Friday night."

Expecting more, I waited. Louise grinned and chewed gum. She believed the gum would help her stop smoking. "What's the occasion? We have dinner lots of times," I said. Louise's agitation was unusual. She is definitely a "together" person.

"I'm having a celebration. You and my friend A. J. are invited to dinner." It was Louise's turn to hesitate. Her smile faltered.

"Are you sure you want to do this? I don't want to intrude in your privacy. Of course I'd love to, if you and he agree?"

"We have." She hugged me, almost a full-body hug.

Pleasure returned to her face as I returned her hug. Standing away from her, I said, "Stay for a while if you've time. I'm sorting things to pack. It's amazing how much garbage I have bundled in three months. I'll never call George a pack rat again."

I made a pot of tea, brought out honey and lemon and a plate of bakery cookies. "These are for guests," I said. "I try not to tempt myself."

Louise peered into one of the boxes I was packing. "Have you finished what you wanted to do here?" she asked.

"I think so. I made sure that the repairman didn't gyp Dad and Mother as they had been a couple of years ago, fleeced by a born-again storyteller. It's awful to get old and have folks take advantage of you. My poor daddy is no business man."

Louise pulled out a cigarette, then put it away. "Is the house in town sold?"

"No luck yet," I said, feeling that I had somehow failed. "The agent, Mr. Crutchen, with a mouthful of 'Yes ma'am,' says Carolton is not growing the way it was a few years ago."

Her face animated, Louise was in a playful mood. "I haven't seen the inside of your old house in years. Let's take a look." She bounced from her seat, reached for my hand, and started to my front door.

The front door was warped from neglect and many rains. A couple of hard shoves and it opened, dragging dust and wood shavings across the floor to reveal a moon shaped bare spot. The hall was a vacant expanse; four doors alternated right and left; faded frames bordered smoky, beige walls. In the corners of the cove ceiling, cobwebs undulated in the air blowing from the open door. We treaded through empty rooms, a musty odor nearly overpowering us in a back hall where a leak had soaked and rotted the floor.

I led Louise through a large room into a smaller one, lighted by the fading afternoon sun. "This was Jan's and my first bedroom, this tandem off our parent's room. Dad said that sisters ought to share the same bedroom, even when we had three empty ones."

I rubbed a spot on one wall, where the bedposts of twin beds once stood. "This is crazy," I said to Louise, "do you hear singing?"

"Only creaking floors, if you call that singing," Louise said. "Do you?

"Naw, just imagination," I said. "One night Jan and I were singing in bed. We didn't know Dad and his white cousin, Dr. Bob Hughes, heard us and were outside our door. I think we were singing 'Sweet Leilani.' We heard applause. We looked up and Dad and Dr. Bob were smiling at us. Jan and I hid our heads under the covers."

"Was he your dad's cousin, blood and stuff, actually? A white man? He honest-to-God admitted it?" Louise said.

"Yep. Dr. Bob Hughes' father was Dad's father's half cousin. You know that slave mix-up thing, African mother, Caucasian father? Grandfather and his cousin grew up playing together. They lived in the same house for a time. They were close friends and each one passed on to his children the fact that they were blood related—family. We never went to their house. Maybe Daddy did. Dr. Bob sometimes came to our home and to Daddy's office. Know what, he and Dad had the same smile."

Louise said, "My family is mixed-up same as yours, but we never talked about it. I told you I didn't have any relatives except my folks and sister." She looked above my head. I followed her gaze to a spider crawling in its web. "There was someone, a girl. I knew about her, but later for that," she said.

"I've a friend who says people are 'neither fish nor fowl nor good red herring.' She was German and Irish. Both sides of her family looked down on her," I said. "I feel like an alien, myself. My Dad is a half-breed. My Mother's a marble cake. What does that make me?"

"Not chopped liver, I'd say." Louise began humming and walked out of the old bedroom.

We went into a large, rectangular room. The musty space was linked to the dining room by a wide ark.

"Our party room," Louise practically gushed. Humming and moving, she lifted her arms as if she had a partner. "Oh, the dances we had here," she said. "Your parents were special grownups to me. There wasn't a large enough space in Carolton where we could dance. Your folks always said yes when we asked them."

"They love music and having a good time. They like to see people enjoying themselves." I began dancing alongside her—to Nat King Cole's "Nature Boy" wafting through my head and heart. "Mother said that she and Daddy danced their way through Meharry Medical College. She wore out shoes fast and her parents never knew why."

There was no electricity in the house. We left as the sunlight disappeared.

"There's Mr. Grant. He's Napoleon, and Mrs. Grant is Josephine. She's taller than he is. No wonder he's dressed like Napoleon."

Voices float up to the sisters, who peek under the bedroom shade to the sidewalk after they have been shooed to bed. Tonight is the Halloween Ball. Teachers, doctors, business people from towns as far as Avondale, fifty miles away, are out for dancing, good food, and good times.

"What happened to that boy who let the raccoon loose in the laboratory?" one principal asks another.

"He dropped out before I could suspend him." They laugh.

"I told her . . ."

"He said . . ."

"We found . . ."

"How's your . . ."

Laughter, small talk, complaints, and lies fill the air. "Miss Flanders, you get prettier every day."

"Look, there's Mr. Stockton." Janis pulls frantically on Gay's robe.

"What's he wearing? Let me see." Seven-year-old big sister topples little sister from her spot in the window.

Mr. and Mrs. Stockton disappear from sight. The girls, defying orders, run to peer through a crack in the kitchen door for a better view. Stockton removes his jacket. He pulls a cardboard placard from a brown paper bag and hangs it around his neck.

"What's on it? What's it say?" Jan begs. "I can't see."

The handsome teacher, the dreamboat of every girl over seven, turns to the party crowd. He wears khaki pants and shirt, and a black tie. He struts, goose-stepping around the room. When he passes the kitchen door, the girls, peering through the crack, read the sign: "To Hell with Hitler!"

Mrs. Stockton follows behind her husband. She wears a peasant blouse—white with tiny embroidered flowers—and a long, pink, blue, and white skirt. Her sign reads, "I Love Mein Fuehrer!"

Monday at school Gay pledges a few schoolmates to secrecy. The idea of a teacher wearing a sign saying "Hell" goes no further than those who are already members of a special group, those whose parents were at the party but who missed the scene. Jim Stockton is their "brown-skinned Tyrone Power." Every handsome Negro male is linked to a Hollywood star. So-and-so is a brown-skinned Clark Gable, a brown-skinned Errol Flynn. Stepin Fetchit and Mantan Moreland, eye-rolling, shaved-head colored comics, are not sex symbols.

Gay does not share how much liquor is drunk, who gets sick, who argues over how much attention one man pays to another man's wife. An unwritten code tells her that those matters are secret, only for those who were invited. She understands that when her parents' friends relax, they are entitled to "let loose," to lock out the other world—that crazy one. Jan doesn't go to school yet. She can't tell.

CHAPTER 17

Gayla

"AM I FASHIONABLY LATE?" I asked, handing a bouquet of flowers to Louise when the door opened.

"I've been waiting ten whole minutes. He'll be here shortly. You're so dressed up, I'd think you were going to the mayor's for dinner instead of over to the house of little ol' Louise Hendricks Brown."

"This is a treat." I twirled in my paisley skirt, rust-colored cowl-necked blouse, and rust-colored pumps. "You don't look bad yourself. Take off your apron so I can get the full effect."

"We're not competing are we? Set these flowers on the table, will you? Everything's ready."

Out in the driveway, a motor died. A car door closed. Louise raised her arms as if she were a game show hostess waiting to open the door to the prize hidden behind door number one.

Louise's A. J. came in from the garage. His shirt and hair were not rumpled as if he'd been at work all day. Maybe he'd gone home first, to change. Louise lingered beside me. His blue shirt matched his quizzing eyes. His dark gray slacks were well-fitted to a body that won against a mid-body's tendency to spread. He and I reached to shake hands at the same time.

"Hi, you're Gayla. I'm A. J. Of course you are and so am I. That was dumb." Louise's lover was as nervous as a teenager on his first date.

Louise grabbed a tray with three glasses of wine. Awkwardly, we each took one. I was glad to have something to hold.

"To friendship," Louise said, holding her glass toward us.

"To friendship," A. J. and I echoed.

"You're the man I've heard so little about." I gazed steadily at a boyish face that belied nearly fifty years. His curly, dark-blonde hair was thinning at the temples. He didn't look like the smooth-faced Scots-Irish in the Upstate. A. J's face was reminiscent of drawings of Vikings.

"You've been good for Lou this winter," he said. "She's needed the stimulation of someone more like herself. Thanks much, Miss Gayla."

Louise looked pleased. "Let's eat before we gab so much my house specials will be overdone."

When we finished Lou's super-good dinner, A. J. began to clear the table. "My compliments, ma'am. You're a great cook. Dinner was superb, as always," he said as he kissed her forehead.

Louise filled the dishwasher. I removed the tablecloth and replaced the flowers. Louise brought coffee into the living room.

"A. J., I've seen you somewhere. I feel as if I . . . I . . . know you. Is it ESP or a former life?" I kicked off my shoes, a terrible habit, and pulled my legs into the deep, velvety love seat.

Across the room, sitting close to Louise, A. J. blushed, his fair coloring no match to hide the rush of blood. He put his cup on the round glass table. He let out a low groan. "Can you guess what my initials, A. J. stand for?"

"I hadn't thought about it." Initials are a fact of life in the South. Everybody is C. T., L. N., E. F. or something.

"My name is Andrew." He emphasized the second syllable. "An*drew* Jackson Burroughs."

For a moment I thought, so what? His dramatics seemed out of place.

My feet shot out from under me and reached for the floor. "My God, Drew? Drew Burroughs? You can't be. You aren't?"

"I am," he said, his voice quiet and breaking on the last sylla- ble. "And you're Jaybird's sister, Gay."

My impulse, after surprise, was anger. My mind flashed to Drew and the boys who sat under an oak tree in the neighbor's yard yelling "nigger" that cool fall afternoon. I clenched my teeth and tried to gather my thoughts. I didn't want to hurt Louise.

A. J.'s—Drew's—color was no longer red; he was deathly pale. "Gay, I knew this was gonna happen tonight." His voice rose a bit in volume. "I didn't know how I'd handle it. I waited to see what . . . well . . . this had to come, sometime, had to be faced." He was pleading, "I can't make up for the years we stopped being friends."

"You know one another?" Louise moved away from beside him on the couch. "A. J., you never said a word. You knew Gayla was my friend." She stood by the end of the sofa, her face colorless.

"Excuse me, Lou, please . . . I should have cleared this up when you told me she was your friend. I was chicken. You said your friend was Gayla Tyner. I didn't put it together. By the time I figured everything out, I knew if I told you, I'd lose you."

Rushing, his words came in breathy gusts. "I've thought about you and I wanted to talk to you long before I met Louise. It was the older folks who made us stupid, forced us to think bad of colored—I mean blacks—when we knew better in our hearts."

Feeling taller than five-feet-four, without shoes, I stood up. "I never told you but I always thought you looked like Jackie Cooper. Every time I've seen Jackie Cooper in a movie or on TV, I remembered you," I said.

Louise broke in. "Will somebody fill me in, please?"

A. J. was nearly in tears. "It was a bunch of kids. They made fun of Gay and Jan. I went along with them. I did."

"Louise," I said, holding back anger, "he let his friends call Jan and me 'nigger' and 'coon.' We stopped talking to him." I wiped my eyes with the palm of my hand.Louise looked from one to the other to find sense in the weird conversation.

"The main thing was, we couldn't be friends once I went to junior high school," A. J. said.

Louise poured fresh coffee. We settled back into our seats, so quiet the refrigerator's humming was as loud in my ears as a jet. Louise did not pull out for a cigarette. She was making progress.

I was calmer the next time I spoke. "A. J., Drew, it wouldn't be kind of me to hold bad feelings against you after so long. You're right; it was the adults, your adults, who caused our breakup. Those bigoted kids did what they'd been taught. Jan and I didn't tell our parents. Even if we had, they were powerless."

Louise said, "A. J., you could have told me."

"I didn't want to hurt you. I wanted you to see my changed self. It's fate that Gayla has come back and we have the chance to make things right between us."

"Drew, if you hadn't volunteered to work with the Black Business Alliance, you wouldn't have met Louise. Things work out for the best, I'm sure. I want to believe that. I'm so very sorry that Janis isn't here. She liked you."

"I believe she knows." Drew looked upward and winked. "My work with the Alliance is my way of expressing my interest not my guilt. I learned better when I went to California for college and the Civil Rights movement opened my eyes. I'm not guilty of my ignorance. Don't get me wrong. I like what I'm doing. It's right and important." He got up from his spot on the couch, held out his arms, and said, "Can I have a forgiveness hug from two charming, wonderful ladies?"

Louise turned her back and began to walk to her bedroom. "Come on, Gay," she said. I followed her, not sure for what. A. J.'s jaw dropped. He looked like he'd been hit in the stomach by a heavyweight boxer. At the bedroom door Louise stopped, turned, and pulling me with her, she walked back toward Drew— A. J.

She held my hand in a strange way until I recognized our Twentieth Century Club secret handclasp. I caught her purpose, a set up for Mr. Burroughs. Louise glared at A. J. for a long minute before saying, "All right, your heart's in the right place, no matter how stupid you were. I forgive you. Gayla, do you forgive this crazy white man?"

"I'll do it," I said, "We can help stop the craziness, a little— maybe."

"You scared me spitless," A. J. said. "I thought I was being rejected." He kissed the tops of our heads. "As the old folks said, 'Praise the Lord.'"

We talked until after midnight. We parted friends. On my way home, I decided I had been good. Not once did what I wanted to ask pop out: "When are you going to make an honest woman of my friend?"

CHAPTER 18

Gayla

TWO FOOT-LONG TEARDROP GLOBES hung high above a terraced, brightly-lit waterfall. Glamorously-dressed, stylishly-coiffured couples lounged on the broad steps that enclosed the waterfall on two sides. Polished green foliage softened the marble and concrete walls that soared three stories from a polished tile floor, the tiles from a nearby quarry. Opposite this panorama, an expanse of tinted glass reflected muted buildings and car lights on Avondale Boulevard. Beautiful people glided proudly inside. Outside, drivers of expensive, late-model cars snaked, bumper-to-bumper, toward the entry. The doorman, in crimson jacket and black hat, snapped his fingers to summon young men in golden yellow coats to jockey the Jaguars, Mercedes, BMWs, Cadillacs, and top-of-the-line Toyotas and Hondas to the parking lot.

The man moving toward where I stood, surrounded by this fantasyland, wore a dark blue tuxedo, a lighter blue formal shirt, blue reptile-skin pumps with a gold chain gracefully draped across each instep. His taut skin and slim carriage did not betray a specific age. He could have been forty or sixty.

"Hi, Gay. Bet you don't remember me. I'm Sonny Freeman," he said.

Up close, he was nearer sixty. His face shuffled into aware memory; it was a certain way he held his head.

"I heard you were in town. Haven't seen you since I left to go into the navy." The man reached for my hand. His clasp was warm. "I haven't been back home since my mother passed, ten years ago. I'm retired now." he said.

157

"That's a regular litany in Carolton, isn't it?" I returned his handshake. "Everywhere I turn, somebody's back home. I ask myself why does everyone come back?"

"Everyone doesn't. I see you don't want to." He winked, then continued. "I'm pretty typical. After the service, I worked in the Norfolk, Virginia shipyards for a few years. I heard things were better for us on the West Coast, so I hauled myself out there, worked in San Francisco and Seattle until I decided to head back here six months ago."

Forgetting my vow to stop, I wrinkled my forehead. "Didn't you have close friends and family on the West—or somewhere other than Carolton—after all that time?"

"Yeah, sure, but early is better. Tell you what," we stepped out of the path of several exuberant high school students, "I found jobs easier to get outside the South. I made good money, real good money." Sonny touched and smoothed the velvet lapel of his tuxedo. "Strong unions, good pension. To tell the truth, the feeling in my bones was always the same. Whites don't like blacks, don't want us around unless they need us to work or during a war. Child, I may as well be back in big-foot country where I *know* how *they* feel. They ain't changed. Here, I know my way around, know folks, leastwise who's left. My money goes further. The climate's better on my old bones, too. Blacks aren't sopping gravy anywhere."

With a sinking knowing inside I replied, "I hear variations of that theme over and over. Must be truth in it. We have made progress but it's awfully slow."

Sonny raised his glass. "Lovely affair isn't it?"

I took in the fancy dresses and natty ensembles. The mix of perfumes flowed like a pleasant stream behind passersby. Mirrored walls shimmered the crowd, doubles and multiples of everyone. Champagne bottles and goblets were piled on red linen-covered tables outside each of two gigantic doors that led to the banquet hall. Amber liquid in stemmed glasses sloshed, occasional droplets spilling onto the dark maroon carpet. "Oops," "Watch it," "Sorry . . ." came from animated faces.

"There's nothing prettier than a roomful of us, all decked

out." Sonny's eyes roamed the room. "A flower garden with all the colors in the rainbow. Yes, ma'am."

"I'm not sure what this affair is all about. I brought my parents. Dad doesn't drive at night anymore. He said tonight is sponsored by his fraternity. That's all I know. Dad's never let go of Rho Nu. He's as pumped as a freshman pledge when it comes to his frat brothers."

The wide hall was lined with high-school-aged young men and women accompanied by parents. Young ladies were glowing in white formal gowns. The massive doors to the dining room opened to the sound of a string quartet playing "Eine Kleine Nachtmusik." Eight African-American boys, about six or seven years old, in white pantaloons led a procession. When the music stopped, teenagers, in tails, were presented to the assemblage by a master of ceremonies who wore a giant bronze medallion on a purple satin ribbon that bounced on his ruffled pink shirt.

Sonny's eyes followed the boys. "At least they don't have to worry about being chased out of town like Henry Lee. That's one of the things scared me out of here," he said.

"That was a chill on a lot of people," I said. "Nothing like that is going to happen to those babies, I hope."

Sonny sucked in his upper lip. "Damn well better not. Long as I'm kicking."

Sonny's resolve was plain. "You're right," I said. "We'll talk again." I left to join my parents in the evening festivities.

The ornately-garbed spokesman pounded a tall, ebony staff several times, "Ladies and gentlemen, we are here to witness the dawn of a new day, a harbinger of our future. Each of these young men is an outstanding student who has already been accepted into the college of his choice." He named each young man, twenty in all, and the college each would attend next fall. After each name he pounded the cane on the bare floor beside the podium.

I swallowed a gasp. A silver bird, like the one on Poppa's cane, perched at the top of the staff.

One by one, escorted by their parents, the eighteen-year-young guys strode proudly to the center of the room. Each young man then approached the dais with a young lady who led him to a seat of honor at a long table.

The pomp and ceremony were new to me. I recognized the ceremony as a kind of rite of passage, the presentation of a class of Kunte Kentes to their elders. I was enthralled by the jarring juxtaposition. The room had the modern trappings—air-conditioning, and covered plates of roast beef, mashed potatoes, and beans almondine stacked on trays at the perimeter of the room. Impassive, uniformed waiters and waitresses, white, black, and a few Hispanics, ringed the room at a semi-parade rest stance while the solemn ritual was played out. A collective memory for three hundred or so modern-day African Americans, an ancient, but new, liturgy stirred my blood.

Hubris was roused, along with new energy for the struggles ahead and acknowledgment of the struggles behind. It was so right and so sad. On this night, I could finally see that we, of a five-hundred-year-long diaspora, needed rituals that had been lost. I wondered about the energy needed to break new ground and learn new transitions. Faces showed determination and desire to make a fusion of ancient and new dreams. Can we do it? Of course we can.

"What did you think of it, girl? I bet you don't have anything to beat that up in Michigan?" my father said later, on our ride from Avondale to Carolton.

"It was wonderful, Daddy. A little long, but inspiring. Maybe something like it happens in Detroit and Chicago. There aren't enough professional or any other kind of blacks—oops—Negroes in most of the suburbs for a spectacle like that."

"Those young people are from all over Upstate," Mother said. "We don't have enough for a good show just in Carolton."

"It was too long," Daddy said. He didn't like long programs. He said, "This is Rho Nu's first time to honor the young boys this way. My boys," Dad said, by which he meant the men of the graduate chapter of his fraternity, "will learn by next year. I'll speak to them about it."

"What about the girls, the young women, Mother? They were beautiful, and their names were announced, but that was all."

"Oh, no," Mother said, "Beta Phi Sorority is having a gala for the girls month after next. Our young people need all the encouragement we can give them."

Daddy dozed in the rear seat of the Cadillac. He'd persuaded me to drive it rather than my little car. "Makes a better appearance," he insisted. In a few minutes, I noticed that Mother had fallen asleep too.

I drove the forty-five miles home, reliving the evening. Had my children missed something important growing up in a primarily white world? It hadn't been all white. Asians, Africans, Europeans from various countries, and South Americans were in the university community. George Junior, Tony, and Pam were comfortable with all kinds of people. Little George and a schoolmate from Iran once sat under our kitchen window— not knowing I could hear them—exchanging "dirty words," most of which had to do with body wastes, in Farsi and English.

George and I chose to live and rear our children in what we thought of as the "wider world." We wanted them to be able to know and deal with all kinds of people and not be afraid of differences. Our kids would have to make it in their own world, not the one in which we had lived.

I thought about Sonny Freeman. I remembered that he had always been well-dressed, even fastidious. When I was a kid, men who were extraordinarily neat were called "sissies." Making ugly smirks with their faces, people whispered and snickered. No one told us what sissies were. We were supposed to avoid them: Miss Wilson, Miss Price, John Boy Pickens, Early Weathers. I didn't know how women could be sissies. I heard church ladies call one another "Sister." Parents were not the ones who cautioned us. We picked up the taboos from the town by osmosis, from older kids. Probably, they learned from older kids, too. The men sissies were safe for girls. By the time I was ten, I was afraid of anyone about whom I heard the least bit of whispering, men and women. Sonny Freeman wasn't one of them—a sissy. I was sure I was right. I learned a lot after I left Carolton.

The men who frightened me most were the "uncles," good friends of my parents and respectable men in Carolton, who

reached, touched, and made oblique remarks when I began
to blossom.

*"Hey, Mr. Boyd." Gay says to the man sitting in a red and white
glider on the front porch of his house. He is coaxing a freshly-lit cigar,
the end glowing like a large firefly. She drops her bicycle in the driveway of the large brick house, on another hill in Carolton. She runs up
the front steps of the painted green concrete porch and into the front
hall. She glances at and admires the grandfather clock, snug in its
niche between the living and dining rooms. Walking briskly down the
center hall, she realizes that the house is strangely quiet. There is no
light in the kitchen. She stops at Anna Sue's bedroom door. The room
is empty. Gay begins to retrace her steps. Mr. Boyd smiles at her from
the dining room arch.*

*"I was riding my bike and stopped to say hi to Anna Sue," she says
to her friend's father. No one rings doorbells when they drop by in
Carolton, South Carolina. She's been in and out of the Boyd's house a
hundred times.*

*"Anna Sue and her mother went over to church early." Mr. Boyd
doesn't move from the archway between the living room and the hall.
"There's a meeting on the annual tea tonight, and they went to set out
the chairs and snacks." His large, dark body is outlined by the light
from the late evening sun, which shines through the window behind
him. He stretches one arm across the opening and leans against the
other side.*

*A funny feeling, a warning alertness surges inside Gay. She bolts to
her left, into the guest bedroom and out the door on the other side of the
room into the hall, bumps the grandfather clock, then dashes out the
front door. Dragging her bicycle, she looks over her shoulder and sees
Mr. Boyd standing in the front door. On her way home, the wind dries
perspiration from her face, neck, and arms, and the tears from her
cheeks. He's known her since she was a baby. He's seen her in her bath.*

*After that evening, when Gay goes to Anna Sue's she makes sure
Mrs. Boyd is home. She says nothing to her parents. She doesn't know
how. Older girls talk and laugh about the town men who they call
"chasers."*

"Here we are, good old home again." Dad's voice brought

me into the present. Dad had awakened, automatically, as we
made the slow turn into his driveway. His voice often grated in
my ear and sent tension traveling along my spine. Mother
awoke seconds later.

I thought about Pam, if she had to escape episodes like
mine with Mr. Boyd. Pam had never said anything. Come to
think of it, neither did I. Wimp, I thought.

"The way we raised you," Mom Dutch, Tempy, Ma Johnston
and Gramma Ann sang in ghostly four-part harmony.

CHAPTER 19

Naomi

"HERE'S YOUR CHANGE. FOUR DOLLARS and sixty-seven cents. Thank you very much," the clerk at the cosmetic counter said.

"Thank you." Louise took the package and change from the saleswoman and opened her purse to put the money in her wallet.

"Excuse me. I think I know you. Did you ever live on Spring Street, near Whiston Drive?" The saleslady was the ideal representative for Lancome: chic, sophisticated, with jewelry and a Giorgio Sant'Angelo dress.

Taken by surprise, Louise said, "Yes, I did." Not sure whether to be accepting or resentful, she waited.

Friendly eyes appreciatively appraised the well-groomed Louise. "My name was Naomi Tillman. It's Naomi Bradley now. I lived on Whiston. We drove past your house, on our way downtown."

"Colonel Jake Tillman. Oh, yes. I could see you when I was outdoors playing. I haven't noticed you in the store before."

"No, my husband is a naval officer. We moved to Carolton a few months ago to decide if we like it well enough to stay for his retirement. I'm working at the store two days a week to get away from Lake Dillard once in a while."

Louise Hendricks Brown and Naomi Tillman Bradley studied each other, unspoken feelings beneath the pleasant external exchange, as if they had always known one another. Neither voiced the questions that had run through them since they had first glimpsed each other. At six years old, the girls had seen the reflected image in their faces and somehow knew the question they must not ask. Naomi's hair was auburn, Louise's black, but the sharp chin and broad forehead were too alike for coincidence.

Naomi Tillman—in a beige camelhair coat with a red fox collar, an imported French beret, and wearing kid gloves—would sit and stare out the rear window of her father's three-seater limousine. In the yard of her family's gray, frame house, Louise Hendricks—in brown wool coat, tam, and knit gloves—would wait for her sister to join her for their walk to school.

Hours later, Naomi poured a martini for retired Rear Adm. Dennis Bradley and mineral water for herself.

"How was your first day on the new job?"

"It went smoothly," she said. "I ran into a woman I used to know. We talked a bit. Nothing earth-shattering."

"Why don't you invite her over?" the white-haired, clean-shaven, proper officer and gentleman asked. "You really haven't made an effort to look up people in your home town."

She looked into the bottom of her glass. "I don't have anything in common with her. Perhaps, soon, someone will come along." The crushed ice in the shaker made a familiar clatter. She walked across the room to pour him another.

The Admiral was Naomi's second husband. She'd met her first during college—she at Charleston's Women's, he at The Citadel. Too young, inexperienced, with too-high expectations, they remained married eighteen months. A daughter was the one positive outcome of the immature dream. She had reared her daughter alone with more-than-adequate support from her young husband, whose wealthy family saw to it. Naomi met Dennis Bradley, a friend of her daughter's in-laws.

The condominium on Lake Dillard was adequate until they decided whether to stay in Carolton or try New Mexico. There was a colony of retired military men in the mountains north of Albuquerque. The Admiral had friends there.

Naomi cleared away the glasses and started the dishwasher. Seeing Louise and talking with her had been like a resurrected dream. Long ago, she had wondered what might have happened had her mother let her continue to ride her horse with the colored girl, Gay Hughes. Maybe, she could have gotten to know Louise through Gay. And her parents didn't have to know.

Naomi turned out the lights, checked the doors, and went in to bed. Dennis was watching the late news. He soon fell asleep. Nearing sun-up she felt him reach for her.

The patio door opened then closed. Dennis left for golf. Naomi swallowed sensations of anger and betrayal. At first she had believed the emptiness she felt after Dennis made love to her was her fault, a result of her years of abstinence and inexperience, a condition that would improve in time. The man who spilled semen into her did not know that his ten-second foray into her body was an indignity, a pain more cutting than childbirth. In their coupling, his hasty release left a sadness that hovered about the face of the Colonel's daughter, which those who saw called pensive.

Black people were different, more satisfying, and more satisfactory lovers. Naomi had heard rumors interspersed with nervous laughter from women at her exercise club. She had also heard whispers that women like Louise, who had a touch of blackness, of Africa, received and responded to sexual gratification that was more than physical.

In the bathroom, Naomi drew warm water and added peach kernel bath beads. She slipped into its warmth, leaned against the moist beaded glaze, and relaxed. Louise's face floated before Naomi. Louise's grandfather and Naomi's grandfather were one, the source of their similar broad forehead and sharp chin. Naomi had heard whispers and laughter among the Colonel's servants when they talked about the remarkable resemblance between the two little girls who lived less than a mile apart. "Like peas in a pod," the cook, Zorine, had told the driver, Wade. Louise had probably heard this too—along with whispers of neighbors who called her "half-white."

Naomi heard stories in the kitchen and yard that differed from the one's her mother read to her at bedtime. The servants talked about a slave woman who had children by her owner, a man named Bachman. They would laugh about how the man's wife hated the slave woman's children, but she couldn't do or say anything.

Wade said the kind of match-up between a colored man and a white woman happened once in a dozen coon ages. The Negroes laughed long and loud at Wade's words. Zorine said "It was most often the other way 'round—'way 'round the side door,'" she'd said. The Negroes felt as if the child couldn't make sense of their talk. Yet, they seemed to want her to hear what they said. They seemed to like her. She liked them. They sang and smiled more often than the white people. None of the men and women who worked for her father and grandfather were afraid to put their arms around anyone who wasn't feeling good. Zorine could make Naomi's stomachache disappear just by holding Naomi on her warm lap.

CHAPTER 20

Dreamtime

CAROLTON SLEEPS AS IT HAS *for one hundred-fifty years. New England towns revel in their maturity. Carolton is an adolescent, not half their age. If one were to hover over the neat, complacent houses night into day, he or she would witness the joys and secrets of heritage and legacies, the same as Gloucester, Massachusetts; Derry, Ireland; and Zuchindor, Senegal and Trinidad, West Indies. Immigrants come from all over to the USA south, peopled, by blacks, whites, the remnant native Iroquois we know as Cherokee, Choctaw . . . and all sorts of 'dukes mixtures.' Carolton's new immigrants are from Vietnam, Indianapolis, Teheran, and Miami.*

Scattering dreams, memories, and wishes, night moves over the city. Gayla tosses and flings one arm onto the empty pillow beside hers. Her dreams reveal what is hidden in daylight. Time and the limitations of yesterday, now, and tomorrow are nowhere to be found.

Gayla dreams that Janis is on the stage of the Atlanta Coliseum. One hundred strong, the symphony orchestra is ringed behind her. Faces of Carolton friends smile from the closest seats. The conductor, Robert Shaw, raises his baton, catches the lift of her head in his left eye, and gives the downbeat for Rossini's "Una voce poco fa." *Her final aria is a favorite of the diva's fans. There will be only three encores tonight. Janis must rush to fly to Paris to sing Musetta in La Boheme.*

Louise lies in A. J.'s arms. She hears his husky whisper. She stirs and smiles. "My love, you're so good to me," he murmurs while drifting through dreams.

*Louise murmurs, "You are too," and moves nearer. Lloyd, a pro-
tecting spirit, is happy that Louise is happy. Morning will be
Saturday. A. J. does not have to leave until after Sunday breakfast.
The pendulum on the stark, geometric clock sways quietly, electronically.
Black, modeled ornamental hands point to a nonexistent* A.M. *hour.*

Shaundra dreams that her thick, black, crinkly braids blow in the wind
the way Elizabeth's blonde, straight bangs do as they sweep from front
to back when she runs.

Elizabeth sleeps in her narrow, pine, lower bunk; her brother tosses
above her. She dreams that the dark, metal bed has turned into a
canopied, white wood, prettier than Shaundra's, and that she sleeps in
a room all by herself.

Mavis Jean places her fingers, stretched open, across her stomach. She
pulls her slender, five-foot-four inches as tall as they will go. The sound
of Gershwin's "I've Got Rhythm" fills the living room. "Okay girls,"
she calls to Gay and Janis, "just like Eleanor Powell. Don't move anything above your hips. Keep your book balanced on your head. Now
dance." Mavis Jean tap dances out the front door and onto the stage
of Radio City Music Hall. The marquee flashes on and off; it reads:
The Rockettes, featuring Mavis Jean MacKay.

Mom Dutch climbs down from her high, hard bed. Her legs work just
fine. She picks up a dust cloth from the kitchen pantry and pours thick,
pungent lemon oil on it. She skips into the living room and polishes
each curved and carved table, chair, chest, and shelf, saying, "Now,
that's the way a house should smell." She rests her hands on her copi-
ous hips. A satisfied smile lights the room.

Talmadge is seventeen. It is prom night at Deerfield High School. He
dances up the steps to the Lowes' front porch, rings the bell, and waits
for Juanita to open the door. He twirls 'round, whistling "Satin Doll."
"I'm sorry Pa's feet hurt him. I can dance the night away," he tells the
moon.

With a noise and a sudden chill, something alters the mood of

Gayla's dream. Red introduces itself on green, slowly metamorphosing to brown. A wind catches a dozen or so dried leaves at the corner of a yellow brick building. They scratch across the pebbly, gray, concrete sidewalk, spiral against the wall, and crumble into parchment bits. No one walks on High Street at three o'clock in the morning.

The old ambulance, the one usually parked in the lot behind Fleming's Funeral Parlor, backs slowly to the alley door. Mr. Fleming's pajama bottom cord hangs over half-buttoned, hastily-pulled-on, blue slacks. Horatio, the night helper, pulls the gurney to the open door. Black rubber wheels swivel a few times before they straighten forward. Mr. Fleming guides the back end of the awkward, narrow, rolling cot.

"This kid's heavy," Horatio puffs. "Hell, they could have waited 'til morning. Didn't have to get up so early, Mr. F. I could have picked him up by myself. You've got old man Clarke's funeral at eleven this morning."

"All in the line of duty, my friend. I wonder how they'll explain this one." Fleming pants a little. "Not as young as I once was." The gurney rolls silently down the incline. The men close the ambulance door; the noise clangs down the block.

"I'll work on him after daybreak." Horatio motions to his boss. "Go get some shuteye. There's no hurry."

Fleming washes his hands and, patting Horatio's shoulder, thanks him. He heads home to finish his sleep.

The sun has cleared and dried the night world. "Come in Doc. I called you 'cause I want you to see this one." J. C., trailed by his daughter Gay, follows Fleming into the embalming room.

"Hey, put something over you know what." Fleming calls ahead. "The girl's with him." Horatio fumbles on a table—piled with steel pitchers, rubber tubing, and ugly, splotched, pink rubber gloves— untangles a flat, square, metal plate, and lays it over the genital area of a chubby, light-cream-colored eighteen year old, who looks as if he is sleeping on the stainless steel table. A yellowish tube runs from his armpit to the sink beside the table. A thin line of pink liquid trickles down the drain. Water runs steadily, merging and swirling the bloodied liquid clockwise down the drain.

The three men stand above the dead man's head. Fleming tells Dr. Hughes, "Four boys were sitting in a car out on Winthrop Road drinking beer, when the High Sheriff came on them, brought 'em into town and threw 'em in a cell. This one's cap fell off when he hit the wall. According to one of the boys, the sheriff's men saw this hair." Fleming runs his hand over thick, brown, "white" hair. "One of the sheriff's men said, 'This nigger's got white folks hair; let's fix him. We don't want our women making moon eyes over him.'"

Horatio touches a finger to the depression the size of a quarter on the right side of the boy's head. He traces the outline of a bruise beneath the right eyebrow. At the funeral, the defects will be hidden to the mourners. Horatio is an artist.

Dr. Hughes, Horatio, and Mr. Fleming talk in hushed tones for a few minutes and whisper something about "legal lynching." In the car on the way home, the doctor tells Gay, "Your mother's probably wondering why we're late. I hope Janis's sore throat is better."

A wind stirs then dies. A stray dog rolls in the leaves and crushes them into smaller and smaller fragments. Gay scrunches beside her father, her brown coat and face rubbing into the scratchy brown tweed upholstery.

The angel demon whiffs away in the morning breeze. A kiss drifts back to the sleeping. Not sure of what is real, dream, memory, or imagination, Gayla stirs. Asleep, everything is the same.

Henry Lee and Myrtle Lee

Across from the cemetery, a dozen blocks from Gayla's apartment, Myrtle Lee Urmann lies in a bed that has not been changed in a month. Her dreams are always the same, a serial rerun.

"Henry, I feel so lonesome. Would you hold my hand?" Myrtle Lee Urmann and Henry are parked on the side of Dillard Lake, a spot that only a few kids knew. Henry and his friends had played in the heavy woods when they were in elementary school. Henry and Myrtle Lee wear wool jackets. Henry feels warm. Looking carefully in the rear view mirror before he does, he takes her cold hand in his large, molasses-brown one.

"Lord, Myrtle. We're being double-dumb stupid."

"Told you not to bring the Lord into this—friendship," she scolds. "Do you know how I mean that?"

"*A joke on your part, isn't it?*" *He covers both her hands with his. His warmth quickly soothes her coldness.*

"*More than that,*" *she says,* "*all my life, I've gone to church, Sunday school, youth group, prayer service, regular service, and revivals when traveling preachers came and the tent was full of singing and praising. Preachers and members talked about love and loving your neighbor. Henry, you're my neighbor. You live four blocks away, yet I don't even know your family, and I wouldn't know you if your car hadn't been broken.*"

"*I don't think most people know what they ought to know about being neighbors or most of the lessons church is supposed to teach,*" *Henry says.* "*You talk a lot like I feel. I don't say to anyone how I feel. I'd be called sacrilegious and a heathen.*" *So taken by his words, he doesn't notice he's moved closer to Myrtle Lee.*

The two named Lee are quiet until the moon is high. Henry starts the car and takes Myrtle home, stopping around the corner before her house. They shake hands good-bye. Henry backs up, turns around, and goes home.

CHAPTER 21

Gayla

"EXCUSE ME MADAM, IF YOU please, would you have a modest sum of seventy-five cents for a cup of coffee or any fraction of that paltry sum?" The words rose from along my right side as I started to walk up the stairs to the county courthouse. The long flight of stairs to the county courthouse confronted me. I had paused to shift my purse to the other shoulder for the climb, when the derelict—with excellent diction and grammar—asked me for money.

I looked into the face of a thin, gray-haired man whose clothes had not been changed in months or eons. My nose caught a body stench mingled with stale alcohol.

Automatically opening my wallet, I caught the eye of the hopeless man at the foot of the scrubbed, marble stairs. Under the grime and decay, something in his face held my attention. I held out a dollar. His heavy, gray eyebrows meshed in puzzlement under my attention.

"You're Tommy Fleming, aren't you?" I said. His hand was inches away from the money.

The man pulled himself erect. His alcohol-husky voice was distinct, "Yes, madam, I am Thomas Paul Fleming, Jr. And who might you be, charming lady?" His rotted teeth were a caricature of a once handsome smile.

"I'm Gayla. Dr. Hughes' daughter," I said, hoping to hear recognition.

His eyes fogged. He struggled to remember. "You're the littlest one. The cute one . . ." His voice became inaudible.

"No, Tommy. I'm the oldest. You know, Gay, not Jan."

He closed a hand eagerly over the bill. "Thanks, thanks, good lady. May the gods go with you." He limped away.

Tommy Fleming was the only son of the well-to-do undertaker, T. A. Fleming, Sr. When I knew him as a young man, he was tall, good-looking—and knew it—with sleek, black hair and brown eyes with lashes any girl would envy. His full eyebrows had lent a brooding gaze that delighted the most attractive young women in Carolton, and more than a few older ladies also.

I told Louise about my encounter with Tommy Fleming. "At one time he was the most handsome colored man in town, successful too," I said.

"Uh huh." Louise mumbled from her kneeling pad in her garden. "He's at least ten years older than we are. His mother thought he was so perfect his spit could sterilize dirt."

Louise was coaching me in the fine points of backyard horticulture. She hoped to advance my recognition of flowers beyond the rose and gardenia.

"Did he ever marry?" I asked. "He inherited his father's business. Now he's a bum, a street drunk."

Louise passed several bulbs to me and showed me the depth to plant them in her terraced garden. "No, he never married. My mother said that his mother found fault with every friend he made, male and female. No one survived Mrs. Fleming's scrutiny. She doled out money and expensive clothes to him."

Being careful to point the growing end upward, I measured a four-inch depth and inserted a bulb. "He looks terrible. How can he have lasted this long?"

"Good stock and early care, I guess." Louise checked my progress. "You're getting the hang of it, but I don't believe you'll ever be a Luther Burbank. After Mr. Fleming died, Mrs. Fleming managed the business. She wouldn't let Tommy do anything to learn the ropes. When she had a stroke and couldn't do it any longer, people stopped calling the funeral home. No one trusted Tommy. He sold the business at a loss, kept on drinking, and you see how he is now."

Shedding our gardening gloves, we washed up and waited on the patio for A. J. We would drive to Avondale for a tennis tournament at the university sports arena.

Louise and I sat in the rear seat behind A. J. I said, "Do you have any idea, Lou, how many of our generation have become alcoholics?" It hurt to think of Tommy Fleming.

"I couldn't guess," she said. "You're the college professor. I know what you mean, though. Rumors get around. Why do people, who have so much going for them, get hooked that way?"

"Don't know for sure, but I've a feeling," I said. "I've watched my college friends waste their lives, women who are bright and talented. I think boredom has a lot do with it."

"What?" she asked. "Women from your kind of family had it easy." Louise sounded as if she couldn't believe what she'd heard. "I mean, they're educated; they marry doctors, dentists, professional types. They don't have to work."

A. J. looked in the rearview mirror and said, "Don't they have children to care for? Being a mother takes brains and time. For Christ's sake, being bored isn't silly; it's plain stupid-dumb."

I glared at the mirror image. "The stupidity is that those women had little to do after their kids were in school. They had nowhere else to put their abilities and energy, considerable energy I might say. They couldn't join the Junior League or hospital auxiliary the same as white women from their kind of background. Most times there were only one or two like them in Carolton or Feldon, a handful more in Columbia or Charleston. Their husbands didn't need them to work. Incidentally, teaching was the only job open to them, and how many underpaid teachers would these towns need?"

Louise said, "Yeah, some of the girls I met at college were raised like hothouse flowers. One of my friends from Mississippi said that what she remembered most about the black doctor's children in her hometown was that they smelled like Johnson's Baby Powder and their fingernails were always clean."

"You aren't making excuses for someone becoming alcoholic are you?" A. J. turned to stare at me.

"Of course not, Mr. Burroughs, and keep your eyes on the road, please. Alcoholism is an illness. It sneaks up on you. Starts with normal social drinking and worms in like a tapeworm. My roommate's father was a college professor. She married well, as you say, Lou. One hot day, we were sitting by her pool when her daughter's sandal came off. She called the maid to put the girl's shoe back on. She never moved. Sipped highballs all afternoon. When her husband came home, the first thing he did was to go to the bar and mix her a drink. Perfectly legal, socially approved."

Louise bit her lip. "My good luck, then, is that I had to work; my family wasn't well-off. I guess I can see how isolation and boredom might make for problems," she said. "If you're different from what's expected, you are very much alone."

The tennis tournament was disappointing. The star was out with a pulled hamstring.Looking for something to make the evening worth the ride, we left early. A. J. found a restaurant that featured nouvelle cuisine prepared by a Japanese chef.

"The world is finally coming to Upstate," he said. Holding the restaurant door, he touched my arm. "Say, Gayla, I didn't mean to rile you about your alcoholic friends. Maybe you have something in your boredom theory."

"I don't mean to be heavy, A. J." I said. "I know sad, hurting people that I really care about. Tommy Fleming is one of the unlucky ones."

At the courthouse the next day, I searched for Tommy. He wasn't there. Seeing him made me hurt, so I stopped thinking about him. I found that my Daddy's affairs required more than a talk or two with a real-estate agent and repairs to the house. Before I left Carolton, I needed to be sure that a misplaced deed was legally clear. I was becoming known at the courthouse. The little clerk, who looked as if he had been there for ages, recognized me when I arrived. And I was feeling pretty good about my ability to manage my parents affairs, despite Geoge's attitude about my practical side.

I dozed on my couch, then groped sleepily for the phone. "Geor . . ." I said.

"Not yet, girl. It's me, ol' Tally, back in God's country. I wanted to let you know my brother Booker Junior died," he said.

"Are you and Nita coming back for the funeral?" I asked.

"No, we're scattered all over Pennsylvania, New York, and Connecticut," Tally said. "Some of the family wanted to bring his body to Carolton. But Booker gave his wife and children firm directions. He did not want to be buried in Carolton. Booker said the only reason he ever came back to Carolton was to see Ma and Pa. After they died, he never went home again."

"I'll bet the family is upset," I said.

Tally sounded down. "Right. Booker was the oldest, and the sisters think he deserves his place in the family plot, a place of honor beside Ma and Pa."

"Did you know he felt that strongly?"

"Booker didn't talk about his feelings, but his experience with Mr. Loveton, with Carolton, cut deep," Tally said. "He asked to be buried in Arlington National Cemetery. Sergeant Booker T. Johnston, Jr. was a World War II vet. He said the only free soil for him was federal ground." Across the miles of telephone wires, my trouble buddy's voice sounded sad, and at the same time, proud.

CHAPTER 22

Naomi

IN THE NEW MALL OUTSIDE of the old city limits, an aged woman slowed; her eyes sought one way, then another. "Oh Lordy, where am I?" she mouthed.

Naomi Tillman Bradley left her spot behind the circle of creams, powders, lipsticks, and eye shadow. "Excuse me, may I help you?"

The gray-haired, henna-brown woman shifted her walking cane to the right hand. Her left hand gripped Naomi's arm. "Thank you, child. I'm trying to find linens. Have to get a wedding present. My daughter went to find a parking space. I guess I came in the wrong door."

Naomi glanced behind her toward her counter. There was no one waiting; she could take her break now. "Come with me. I'll show you."

Naomi led the way across the aisle, through jewelry, around a corner, and into a varicolored display of sheets, comforters, and country-styled window treatments.

"Your daughter should be here in a few minutes. She'll find you," Naomi turned to leave.

"Child, you look like I know ya." The woman gazed intently into Naomi's face. "Most like a little girl that used to live near me, name of Louise Hendricks. I'm name of Hettie Sims."

Naomi smiled. Like a grapevine with all its lives and parts, Carolton was a series of connections. "I was a Tillman. My name's Naomi. I've heard that Louise and I are related somewhere down the line, a way back."

181

"Hope I didn't embarrass you none, child." Hettie Sims nodded, sucking her teeth. She touched Naomi's arm apologetically. "Sometimes when a body gets old, things slip out without thinking, things better left alone."

"Don't worry." Naomi stroked the hand that balanced the cane. "We all have to grow up and learn how to hear truth. And times have changed, haven't they? Excuse me, I have to get back now."

The elderly woman smiled, "Thanks for your help. I'd have wandered 'round 'til my daughter found me or I starved to death in this big old place. You saved old Hettie a scare."

Back at her counter, a new customer approached. After two customers, business was not brisk. Mrs. Hettie Sims looked the way Naomi imagined Zorine might look, now. Zorine had meant a lot to Naomi. Once in a while, Wade took Naomi along for the ride on Friday after dinner when he drove Zorine home for her weekend off. Zorine lived down in the country. Naomi had listened in on their conversations from her seat between the two large, dark people, who talked differently when they weren't around her mother and father—soft talk about taking problems to "Uncle Hosea," an illness or a personal problem, like Zorine's wandering husband.

Carolton exerted its pull on Naomi. She muttered aloud, "Uncle Hosea is surely dead by now. I wonder if there is anyone who still has the old power to know what no one else does."

"There she is." The lost customer and her daughter—a darker-complexioned, taller image of her mother, wearing oversized, ornamented eyeglasses low on her nose—were loaded down by two bulky packages. "This is Colonel Jake Tillman's daughter. She's the one helped me when I was lost." Hettie Sims grinned and bobbed her head.

Mrs. Sims's daughter removed her glasses, revealing a friendly face. She repeated her mother's thanks. Impulsively, Naomi said, "Perhaps you all can help me. It's been a long time since I lived here and there are people I remember whom I'd like to find. Would you know Wade Hampton Brown and Zorine Hall and if they are still in Carolton?"

"Wade is in a nursing home." The older woman said. "Lost his sight to sugar diabetes. Zorine, I don't rightly know for sure.

She might still live on her family place out on Rodell Creek."

Naomi had time to attend to whatever she wanted. Dennis Bradley played golf, built model boats, and generally was self-sufficient. The Admiral was a quiet man who was easy to live with, in most ways.

Naomi had no way to know in which nursing home she might find Wade, but she remembered where Rodell Creek was. The next day, she found the little gray house she remembered. Two gnarled black walnut trees framed the front door. The gray tin roof reflected the leaves that dipped and tapped the eaves in the wind.

Zorine Hall was scattering chicken feed to a few Rhode Island Reds, black-and-white Dommernecker hens, and a ponderous white rooster that roamed freely but stayed close to home, like pet dogs do. She looked the same as she had on the days when she mixed and stirred in Colonel Tillman's kitchen. Her hair was white. There was a line or two in her face, but Naomi saw clearly that she was a woman in fine form, for more than seventy.

Zorine put her bucket on the ground and laced her fingers on her forehead to shade her eyes. She strained to see who was getting out of the unfamiliar, blue Lincoln Town Car.

Naomi hurried, nearly stumbling on a root, causing a few chickens to flutter from their meal. She called, "Zorrie, it's me, Naomi, Naomi Tillman." The tall, black woman and the shorter, white one hugged and cried. Questions and exclamations tumbled out. Inside, Zorine's house was an accumulation of overstuffed 1920s and 1930s furniture, among them an ancient pump organ, and plastic vases filled with red, white, and blue artificial flowers.

Zorine set a plate of homemade pound cake and a tall glass of iced tea in front of Naomi. "Here, eat child. It felt like a voice told me you was coming."

"Zorrie, I have to watch my weight," Naomi protested.

"No you don't. I'm sick and tired to death of seeing nothing but skinny women on my TV." She pulled a thick photo album from a pile beside the couch and put it on the seat beside Naomi. Naomi admired photographs of Zorine's son, nieces, nephews, and "grands."

"Look here." Zorine's arthritic fingers turned pages. "Here's you." She pointed to faded snapshots of Naomi sitting astride her horse, diving into the backyard pool, and hugging Zorine. "Remember when you'd come in all hot from riding your horse and jump in that cold water?" Zorine poked Naomi in the ribs.

In the images of her childhood, Naomi saw more than one little girl. "You're teasing me, like always," Naomi said. "Remember I told you I wanted that colored girl who lived down the road from us to come swim with me?"

"I remember, and I told you your folks wouldn't 'llow it. I told you don't talk 'bout it anymore."

"There was a colored girl who had a horse, like I did. I wanted to play with her too." Naomi said, closing the photo book.

Zorine looked into Naomi's eyes. "Things were different then, you understand."

Naomi said, "I know. We can't go back." She sighed and gazed at her hands. "Zorrie, do you live all by yourself? Where's your husband?"

"That wandering fool wandered away for good one day. I didn't send the old dog to sniff him out." Zorine made a face, then bent over in a loud laugh. "Don't fret over me. I'm fine. I'm so proud to see you, sweet child. Didn't know you was back home. Now if I lived in town, the grapevine would have told me. You had to look me up. Honey, I am real proud you remember me."

"How have you made it on your own?" Naomi said.

Zorine grinned. "It wasn't easy and it wasn't hard. When your daddy died and your mother moved in with her sister, I went to work as a cook at the Piedmont Hotel. Carolton was never home to me, just a place to work. I came home to the farm every weekend when I worked for your family and in town. This land has been in my family one hundred years. This is home," Zorine said.

Zorine went to her kitchen. She brought back a pan of blueberry cobbler wrapped in foil and handed it to Naomi. "Been cooking all my life. I can't stop," she said. "My neighbors depend on me for a little sweet bread now and then. I bake every week or two. What you eating is pound cake, real pound cake—a pound of butter, pound of sugar, pound of flour, pound of eggs."

Two hours passed like two minutes. Naomi got up to leave. Zorine walked up-close and looked her in the eye. "I know you're here to see me, but I feel a sadness inside you. It's as big as a goose egg. What's troubling you? You know your Zorrie. I care 'bout you. You can tell me."

"How you can pick up on feelings amazes me." Naomi stared at the ground then off beyond Zorine's shoulder at her big car waiting outside. "Um, ah, I'm surprised at what I'm going to say. At my age I shouldn't care, but I do. I'm not experienced in women's ways the way I would like to be. You know how early I married the first time and what happened. My husband is a good man. Don't get me wrong. No one could ask for better. It's—well, there's got to be more than, well, you know, than we have."

"Nobody ever too old to feel good and be happy. You got no cause to be ashamed," Zorine said, patting Naomi's arm. "I don't know what Zorrie can do to comfort you except listen."

Naomi said, "You used to talk to Wade about going to Uncle Hosea. I guess I could go to a psychologist, but down here we had our ways of working problems before psychology. Maybe there's help for me in the old ways, like Uncle Hosea."

"I'm 'mazed you remember so long ago," Zorine said. "You had all your fancy schooling. Uncle Hosea's been dead more than twenty years. Left a daughter, name of Lucille. He schooled her in his medicine. If you mean what I think you're saying, I can look her up, take you to her. I hear she's good, pretty much the same as her daddy."

Arm in arm, Zorine and Naomi walked to the car. Naomi leaned on the car door. "If you can find her, I'd be grateful. There are other people from those days I'd like to see, but I probably never will."

Two days later, the weather was as hot as any day could be in Carolton. Naomi drove up a narrow country drive lined with large trees. Zorine sat beside her. An imposing figure of a woman waited for the car to stop.

Sister Lucille was six feet tall. In an orange and red caftan, she favored an ebony replica of Queen Nefertiti that perched on top of an ancient, player piano in her sparsely-furnished shrine. Lucille had black hair, parted in the middle and twisted into a ball at the nape of her neck, black eyes and straight white teeth, which were seldom seen in her dignified, serene face.

Outside the door to Sister Lucille's living room, Zorine stopped. "I'll sit on the porch, Sister," she said. "You work with Naomi and she won't be shy to say her say."

"You don't need to do that," Naomi said.

Sister Lucille and Zorine bent their heads in agreement. They knew.

A round table, covered with white, fringed, linen balanced an arrangement of dried coconut shells. Each half shell cradled a carved animal figure: a turtle, a bear, a tiny bird poised as if ready to fly. White candles burned in an asymmetrical pattern. Running onto the cloth, wax flowed down the sides of the candles. Smoke wafted upward. Mixing with the candle odors, smoldering sage and sweet grass permeated the air.

A wall shelf, two tiers high, held photographs of the Giza pyramids and an African anthill, beneath which stood a broadly-smiling man. The anthill was twice his height. Lucille had cut the pictures from Sunday newspaper supplements and framed them.

Sister Lucille motioned Naomi to a chair at a second small round table and sat in another across from her. She shook a number of small, polished, triangular, dried shells from a red velvet pouch onto the table. Nine times she cast the five diviners on the table. Once in a while she smiled; other times she frowned.

Naomi sat across the table from Lucille in one of two straight-backed chairs that made the room feel crowded. The words Sister Lucille uttered didn't sound English. Naomi wondered if the words were from an African language. Nevertheless, she felt at ease, that whatever Sister Lucille did and said could be trusted. It felt right.

Chanting, casting her beads, sometimes somber, other times smiling, Sister Lucille did her work. In the midst of the chanting, Naomi heard "DB, Dennis Bradley, yes, yes." Some of Naomi's words were too soft to hear clearly. After what felt like hours but also like no time at all, Lucille stopped; perspiration covered her face. Her concentration had been intense. Candles flickered, burning low in the bottlenecks. Lucille extinguished the candles with her fingertips and opened the blinds. The contrast between the darkened room and the sunlight that banished the shadows made Naomi blink and rub her eyes. Naomi pursed her lips inside her teeth to make herself wait.

The long-legged, regal figure wiped her sweat with a purple towel. She carefully replaced the shells in the velvet drawstring pouch and looped it over the belt at her waist. "I'm a healer as well as a priestess of Vudon," sister Lucille said. "Vudon is the ancient religion of Nubia that was brought west across Africa maybe fifteen centuries ago. People think Vudon is black magic, that it's something evil. Not so. It's a religion just like any other and a powerful, healing medicine."

Sister Lucille's voice turned gentle. "You have a sizable problem, Naomi Tillman Bradley. I'm going to work on it for you the best I can. I'll pray to Olorun, The Unlimited All; that's the same as God in English or Yahweh in Hebrew.

"Your husband doesn't know, like many men, that a woman has to be pleased as well as him. He's scared. You're both scared. He never learned to talk to his woman and you never learned to talk to your man."

"We have good communication," Naomi said.

Sister Lucille's large, straight, white teeth broke her solemn face like the unexpected sunlight when the blinds were opened. "I don't mean word talk. I mean soul talk, feeling talk. You have gotta use your inside ears and eyes, your skin, nose, and mouth, and feel deep inside to know and show each other what you want, what feels good. Do you know what I mean?"

"I'm not sure. Not really, I suppose," Naomi hesitated.

"Let me tell you," Lucille said. "My daddy taught me the old ways, the mysteries. Then I studied psychology at college. For years I forgot what my father taught. I thought it was superstitious nonsense. To look at me you wouldn't know I taught school for ten years, but my ancestors called so strong, I had to listen. There's a lot that's the same in Vudon and psychology. Both tell us we've got to take time to love. Now, your mister, he's as frustrated as you. He feels something's not right, but he doesn't know how to fix it. He loves you, that's sure. The goddesses and gods tell me. You can help him and yourself. If you bring up the subject, he'll listen."

"I'll try. You're right," Naomi said. "Dennis is a good man. He'll listen. I think," Naomi opened her purse.

"No money." Sister Lucille waved away the gesture. "We'll see what clears for you, then we'll decide if you pay."

On the porch, Zorine was dozing. She awoke when Lucille and Naomi opened the screen door. She got up and stretched. The women walked to the car.

Sister Lucille leaned into Naomi's window. "It's a shame some people are raised so stiff, not knowing their feelings, keeping them hidden," she said. "Ain't just white men, it's black men, brown men, all kind of men. Some women, too. You remember what the good Lord said about burying your talents. You've got to let all your light shine. Show what you're feeling. Ask your mister to do the same, and say it with love. Look for people you dream about, Naomi Tillman, the ones you think about from long time ago. It'll be good. I feel you want to know the woman, Louise and make up with the horse rider. You're all connected at the soul level. Everybody is. We all just have to wake up to that truth. I'll work special for you. I'll light beeswax candles and say prayers." Sister Lucille stepped away from the car window.

Naomi gripped the steering wheel and her eyes widened. "Oh, thank you," she said.

Naomi started the motor. Sister Lucille beamed her magnificent smile, grand because it was seldom seen. "Y'all come back when you feel the urge," she said. "This town, like every little place where folks have congregated on this earth, is full of stories—just too many hurting ones."

Driving away, Naomi asked, "How can she know things I didn't tell her, names I didn't even think myself?"

Zorine answered, "I don't question God's mysteries, child. I'm grateful for 'em.

CHAPTER 23

Gayla

I AWAKENED WHEN A CROW cawed loudly outside my apartment. I glanced at the clock beside the bed to see that I was awake a half-hour earlier than usual. I lay back on my pillow and fell into a brief, uncomfortable sleep. I dreamed of George, hundreds of miles away. I felt his hand stroke my neck. He whispered, "My dear Gay." Waking fully, my hand touched my throat; it burned.

"Mother . . .," I whispered through scratchy vocals.

"Goodness, child, you sound like Marlon Brando in *The Godfather*." Mother said. "Did last night's storm damage anything where you are?"

"No, no damage," I said. "It began to rain when I was on my walk and my old quinsy throat's got me. May I come stay with you overnight?"

"Alice and I will come to get you."

"No, don't trouble yourself. I can drive," I said, straining to speak from a throat nearly closed down.

Mother and Alice had the guest room bed turned down when I arrived. The bedside table held several of Mother's books. Daddy had a thermometer and medicine bottles. I asked for hot water with lots of lemon and handed Alice a box of herbal tea. A bottle of vitamin C was tucked in my purse, but I didn't argue with Daddy and his medicines.

"It might be an allergy and not the rain or maybe some of the fancy food I ate in Avondale," I croaked.

"Everybody's a doctor these days. You take these, two every four hours with water." Daddy put a brown bottle by the lamp. "Doesn't seem to be anything that'll need a shot. I'll look in later, just in case," he said. He placed the hypodermic paraphernalia back in the pouch. "Ring the bell if you need me."

He put a tiny brass bell on the table. Its handle was fastened with adhesive tape, the old-fashioned, pull-and-cut kind. I had helped cut hundreds of strips, sticking them along the edge of the examining table and watching the narrow, rippled lengths crisscross gauze-bandaged wounds.

"Oh Daddy, you kept our caller," I said, almost crying with the memory and meaning of the ancient little bell. I picked up the bell and gazed at the carved pattern worn and encrusted in a blue-green patina. It lay familiar in my palm. One hand covered it easily. Once, I had needed two hands to hold it. The tinkle was as delicate as wind chimes.

"I keep it in my top dresser drawer. Once in a while I ring up your mother or Alice when I'm under the weather," he said. He tentatively patted my shoulder, turned, and left.

Mother looked in on me as I—feeling like a little girl struggling not to cry—drifted into sleep.

In fitful sleep, Gay sees Tally and herself crawling through the warm, dry, grass behind the hedge and wiggling like puppies on their bellies until they slither around a corner of the big white house across the street. Letting them hear her admonition, "God don't love ugly," Gramma Ann can no longer spy them.

Gramma Ann sits in her cane-backed rocking chair on her front porch, next door to the Johnston's. Rusty nail heads poke above the unpainted plank floor that wobble every time Gramma Ann scoots back against the faded-yellow, wide-lapped outside wall of her house. Somebody has tacked a piece of an old tire to the wall behind her chair so she won't bang and scrape the long-gone paint every time her chair rocks.

When Gramma Ann's practiced hips pull the rocking chair to the edge of the porch, the floor boards squeak a wood-on-wood noise, which tightens the ears of those who pass on the street when no dogs, cars, or people move in the hot, quiet South Carolina summer day.

The old woman, as old as anybody could imagine, tells her story to whomever would give her a listen. "I'm born a slave 'bout time it was near over, but I do 'member some." She rocks a slow rhythm that echoes her heartbeat. She grips a corncob pipe between her gums. A few remaining teeth show as dark as her pipe when she calls out to miscreant children, "Stop it, I say."

All night and into the next morning, I lay in bed, except for trips to the bathroom. I flushed Dad's pills. Caught in a familiar pain, I was visited by odd scraps of dreams of Louise, Big John, Miss Sanders, McGuire Street, Lowell Avenue, my kids, my neighbors, Ann Arbor, college, and Carolton. I gulped handfuls of vitamin C with herbal tea and lemon water. I had—graciously, I hoped—declined an injection of a murky liquid in a squat, rubber-stoppered container that had a name ending in "-icin," preceded by a bunch of syllables.

Nearing eight o'clock in the morning, Alice tiptoed in with a cup of fresh tea.

"Morning, Alice," I mumbled.

The cup rattled in the saucer as Alice came near. "I thought it was too early for you to be awake. You scared me a little."

Poking my head above the covers, I squeaked, "Mr. Quinsy is almost gone. I'm famished, must be time for chicken soup."

Daddy stood in the door. "Heard you talking. Are you feeling better?" he asked.

Mother arrived with a breakfast tray.

"Your timing is excellent; I'm eternally in your debt," I said. It felt good to be pampered. I showered, dressed, and spent the morning helping Alice and Mother re-arrange kitchen shelves.

"Are you sure you feel up to this?" Alice said.

"I feel great." I tried a little dance step as I cut and laid new shelf paper.

Dad opened the refrigerator to get a glass of milk. "She's strong as an ox," he said.

"Go on, Dr. Hughes." Mother called Daddy "Doctor" around everyone except family and close friends, or when she joked. "Gayla, I want you to stay tonight, to be sure you have your strength back."

"I think I will." George doesn't believe in being sick. I don't think Daddy does either. He never admits to being ill. Only his patients are allowed to be sick.

My second night, the blue digital clock display snapped to 12:22 A.M. The nearly imperceptible click was enough to open my eyes. Turning the pillow, I buried my head in the cool side. Pillows smell differently in someone else's bed. At home, George's and mine each had a familiar odor of hair and body scents. My parents' guest bed smelled of rose sachet.

The night was quieter than in my in-town apartment. Footsteps in the hall went to the kitchen and returned to the master bedroom. I heard voices beyond a partially-open door.

"I'm almost sorry Gayla is better. Having her here, taking care of her, it's like old times." Mother's light voice carried in the stillness.

"She always was a bit of a hypochondriac," my father's voice cut through the quietness.

I lay in the dark, shaken with an inner urging to go to their room and confront him. I didn't.

Mother's voice deepened. "J. C., I'm exasperated with you. That child can't even be sick without your criticizing her. It would be wonderful if you could make real peace with your child before you go to meet your Maker." I heard Daddy pacing.

"Mavis, it's not anything I want to do. The words jumped out of me before I knew it. Since she came home, I've thought about the longtime hard feelings between us. I can't make sense of it," he said. "It's nothing Gay has done. She's gone out of her way to look out for us. Maybe I need one of those psychiatrists. 'Course, I don't believe in that mumbo jumbo."

"Come back to bed or you'll catch a cold, J. C. I decided long time ago that you and Gayla fight because there's so much of you in her," Mother said. "It would please me to no end and make us all happier if you would clear up your puzzle. Come on, lie down now."

The bed creaked. "It's never been easy for us to talk without having a difference of opinion," he said. The light went out.

Holding back tears, I squeezed my eyes tight. My whole lifetime

I didn't know how to resolve our differences or how to forget them. Every time I came to Carolton, I felt like an incompetent child. I long ago accepted that Janis was Dad's favorite. Parents can love all their children but feel closer to one. I loved every one of mine, but Pam was my girl, my ally. Jan was the youngest. Dad was the youngest in his family. Maybe that was why Jan was his favorite. I pulled the blanket over my head and murmured into my pillow, "He means well."

"Daddy, are you sure we're doctor's kids?" Jan's velvety brown eyes are clouded, her long lashes graze firm, round cheeks.

"Of course you're doctor's children. What foolishness are you talking about?"

Jan moves into the space between his knees. Janis is soft velvet and shining satin. Sable braids shimmer when she runs in the sunlight. Janis stands, subdued. Red ribbons at the end of each braid fall gracefully, one in front, one behind her shoulders. Her taupe brown face shows ruby-red downy-smooth cheeks. She plays with the red bow at her waist. "All the doctors that come to visit, no matter how dark-skinned the daddy is, the wives look white or near white, and their children look almost white. Gay and I don't look white; we're plain brown, so we wonder if we're really doctor's kids or did you adopt us?"

J. C.'s amused smile disappears. "I see." He reaches an arm around Jan's tiny waist. Perhaps he's never thought that his girls would be sensitive to the subtle gradations in skin color that make up American Negroes. He hugs his baby daughter. When they are out together, people tell Janis she is pretty. Jan is browner than Dr. J. C. or Mavis. Mavis Jean's mother was a coffee-colored woman with a heart-shaped face like Jan's. Jan inherited her grandmother's color with a dollop of cream to dilute the coffee. A child like Jan is labeled a throwback, because she is darker than both parents.

From generations of mixing African, European and Native Indian, Negro parents produce a variety of complexions ranging from European to Asian to African. Any African ancestor, no matter how removed, gives their offspring the privilege of being Colored, Negro, African American, or black.

"Look, sweetheart. It's this way. When I was growing up, some people thought it was a boost up the social ladder if a colored doctor had

*a fair-skinned wife. During slavery everything white, like the master,
was considered better. After slavery, it was what everybody had learned,
so it seemed right. I am the first in my set to marry a brown-skinned
woman, your beautiful mother." He brusquely pulls Jan closer to him.
"It's not the outside, baby, it's the inside that counts. You're as pretty
and smart as anyone in the world. You're my chocolate ice cream cone.
That's my favorite, you know." He holds her at arm's length, his green-
eyed, sandy-haired, barely tan, bright face reassuring his baby daughter.*

*Gay waits, saying nothing. People often say she looks Oriental,
Chinese or Japanese. She has a secret name that she calls herself in private, pretend games. She is Jade. She does not understand what is
important about the outside, when people say it's the inside that counts.*

*The visiting boy knocks at the playroom door. "I was looking for
you." He comes into the room unaware that his round, near-white face
with its straight brown hair and hazel eyes has been the subject of conversation. "Come on, we want to ride your horse."*

*Yesterday the girls had stared up the street for hours, waiting for the
visitors' car. The father, Dr. Green, had written to Dr. Hughes from
Boston, asking if his family "can break our trip with you on our drive
home to New Orleans."*

*A large maroon Cadillac turns into the drive at precisely 2:18 P.M.
on a hot June day. Gay is sure. She checks her watch.*

*Mrs. Hughes calls their Carolton home an underground railway
station. Negroes who grew up in Mobile, Montgomery, Atlanta, New
Orleans, and as far away as Houston, or almost anywhere cannot stay
in hotels and tourist homes along the nation's highways when they
visit "home." Sometimes, most often not, they find a clean rooming
house. There aren't enough colored traveling the highways to support
their own hotels and definitely not enough with money to spend on
hotels. Families with space in their homes give lodging and meals during the North-South pilgrimage of colleagues who drive to visit family
and home. Summers are peppered with overnight visitors. After breakfast, the cars drive on. No money changes hands. The unwritten code
is that guests leave a tip for the cook under the breakfast plate.*

*Janis and Gay and the Boston visitor find his sister standing by the
fenced paddock watching Folly nibble grass.*

"Can you ride?" Jan asks.

*"I took lessons at camp last summer." The hazel-eyed girl pulls her
hands through Spanish-dark hair.*

Northern visitors often talk in ways that show they feel they are superior to Southerners. On a trip to New York, a cousin asks if Gay and Jan have indoor toilets down South. In Chicago, a new friend gives Gay directions to wait at a red light and cross the street when the green light comes on. Gay doesn't tell her that Carolton has traffic lights and she knows perfectly well when to cross the street. It isn't polite.

Tiring of riding in the small corral, the children go inside to the playroom.

"I had my tonsils taken out last month. Wanna see?" the boy throws back his head. "I was dressed in a white shirt and cap. They took me to an operating room and gave me a smelly gas to put me to sleep. Afterwards I couldn't swallow, had to spit all the time."

"Did you have a room by yourself? Was it a big hospital?" Jan says.

"I was in the children's ward," the visitor says. "I made a new friend, Salvatore Ben-dri-ali. He said to call him Sal, but he's a boy, not a girl. Boston Children's is one of the best. My dad says it's the seventh biggest in the country."

His sister adds, "We've been lots of places. Have you been to the Petrified Forest? That's in Arizona where the Grand Canyon is."

"Not yet," Gay answers. "But I met W. E. B. Du Bois in Nashville, Tennessee."

The visiting mother, gray-eyed, auburn-haired, calls the children outside for photographs. "We always take pictures to remember our new friends," she tells the sisters.

Her husband—years older than his wife, with teeth sharply and white in a caramel smile—removes the camera cover. "Come on, smile pretty," he beckons to the children.

Jan runs to her father. She pulls his ear down to her mouth and whispers, "Daddy, I don't want to take pictures with them. I'll come out black as coal."

"No, you won't. See, the daddy is brown and so is Helen." Helen is the teenage girl who travels as nursemaid. "Come on, you'll embarrass our guests." He leads Janis to the rose arbor. Jan goes, reluctantly.

"Let's load up. We've got to get moving if we expect to make Montgomery today." The Boston doctor herds his family into the car. They pull away waving, laughing, and calling out to new friends. It is 9:30 A.M. according to Gay's watch. The family wanted to be "on the road" by eight o'clock.

"Good-bye. Come to Boston to see us."

"Okay. We will. Hurry back."

"We will."

Across Lowell, the Burroughs family watches the good-byes. The Hughes' obviously interracial guests are, at first, disturbing to the neighbors. Drew asks, "Who were those white people at your house yesterday?" His family is relieved to learn that the white visitors are colored.

Overnight bag on the bed, I was dressed and ready to go back to my own abode when Mother came into the room. "You don't have to go." Mother laid a frail but firm hand on my arm. "It's good having you here; I'm sorry that you decided to take the apartment in town."

"M-m-mother, I'm tempted." I almost said, "Mummy," the name I used until I was three, when I decided I was too big to call her by a baby name.

"I'm being selfish, but that's a mother's prerogative. Alice has been whistling since you've been here. She enjoys having someone around other than old folk."

"You are not old. You'll never be old. You have the spirit of a sixteen year old." I laughed. "Alice is whistling, huh? Gramma Ann used to say, 'A whistling woman and a crowing hen never come to no good end.' I didn't know what a crowing hen was, but I'd stop whistling. Thanks for wanting me, even if Dad does think I'm a hypochondriac."

"Dear, dear, you heard him." Mother caressed my hand. "He doesn't mean it. There's something in him he can't get beyond." Mother looked as if she were going to cry.

"Don't worry, Mother. That just popped out. I'm sorry. I'm not too upset. He and I are always spouting off, like whales. Whales do it to live; it's their breath. Why do we do it? Way down deep inside me I get this tugging feeling. It tells me: if we black women don't hold together, the bottom will fall out. I'm not making sense I suppose, but something is not right."

"No, no bottom's going to fall, no top or middle either." Mother moved closer. "We won't fall, child. I have it better; you have it better. Just look from all the way back up to now. Your children, they're having it better. Gayla Marie, it's worth holding on. I promise." Our arms and bones grinding into one another, like they hadn't in a long time, we rocked, hands circling, rubbing shoulder spasms. Vibrating way down inside and out, Mother hummed.

Letting go, relaxing against my mother's small bosom. I whispered, "There's a song we sang in Friday assembly. Professor Ellis always started. I thought it was a dumb, slow thing." I began to sing. "We are climbing Jacob's Ladder . . . Every round gets higher, higher." Mother's off-pitch humming joined me. The meaning of the words traveled, like a wave, down my chest. I stroked her arms with my hands.

Mother flinched in sudden pain. "Excuse me." I apologized. "I didn't know I was hurting you."

She shrugged and patted my cheek. "How many times have I told you, throw it out of your feeble mind?"

"Yeah, well I don't know about that feeble bit."

"Oh honey, it's a figure of speech. It means, don't try so damn hard. Your mind is stronger that you think."

We stood together, her familiar odor, of soap and lotion, soothing and sure. Over Mother's shoulder, Daddy stood in the door. Holding back, wanting to say something unkind or scream at him, I simply said, "Thank you for being so good to me."

Outside, wagging their tails and sniffing my legs, the dogs came to my car door. I didn't have to drive around Brownie this time.

It was dark when I reached my apartment. Staring across the courtyard, listening to faint laughter from Shaundra's apartment, I sat quietly. From somewhere in my mind came the face of a tall woman who I could not recall. She called herself Sister. "Everything is going to be just fine," a deep voice, I didn't recognize, said. Oddly, I believed her.

CHAPTER 24

Gayla

SPRING IS EARLY AND CHARMED in the upcountry. Trees bud and the grass is tender-fresh. Evergreens regain their sharp, dark color. Gardens exhibit their first array of purple, pink, yellow, and orange. The tapestry varies from month to month for seasons onward.

In Michigan the earth is frozen hard for six weeks more. Life is stretched out, slower, in the South. Here, warmth spurs organic, gradual unfoldment that is not as visible or exciting to natives as to visitors and those who have returned. People who belong to the land echo the patient languor. A resistance to push or pressure is evident in movement and manners (someone holds open a door until you reach it even if you're twenty-five feet away.) This is the way spring should be.

Aside from Louise, and then A. J., my social life had been low and quiet. Tally's brief visit had faded to pleasant thoughts. After remembering, sharing pride in children and family, and remembrances of "where is . . .?" with those I knew who remained in Carolton, conversations lagged, then died. Caroltonians have an easy rhythm: work, family, church. For me, up North was a constant push of family, work, administrative bureaucracy, faculty in-fighting, and George's private world of work to which I had no entry.

At Upstate University, in nearby Avondale, I found a tiny, aware enclave of similar-minded people amidst the bastion of Southern conservatism. Occasionally, I went to the university

199

for plays, music, or lectures. One speaker said that in these changing times people must learn to make friendships and let go quickly. He said everyone has to learn to live with ambiguity. Maybe he's onto something.

Mary Michaels, an anthropologist, and her husband, a poet and humanities professor at Upstate, were uneasy migrants from New York City. We met at a reception for a visiting lecturer. Just as things went in Michigan academic environments, we were drawn to one another because there were few African Americans on faculty or in the social circle. It wasn't that we had things in common. Other people assumed we did because we looked the way we did—dark skinned. Mary made her imprint early and loudly. She wore a bouffant, sixties-style afro and confided, in her most professional accent, "The poorer class, farm and factory workers in this area, are conditioned to a status that shows itself in what appears to be mental retardation. They've accepted that they're dumb. I believe it a result of the humbling process."

A few guests moved away from our little gathering beside the shrimp cocktail tray. Mary's husband was accustomed to Mary's proclamations. He draped an arm over her shoulder and sipped his drink "Do you want a refill, sweetheart?" he said.

She handed him her glass. Raising eyebrows at the public display, he kissed her and walked away.

I said, "Why don't you do a study? Perhaps it's merely your impression. Perhaps it's an observation worth doing the numbers." Being married to an engineer had taught me a second language.

In her brash, New York accent Mary replied, "The administration wouldn't give me research time. Besides, we're looking for appointments nearer home."

"Everyone wants to go home," I said, with more than one degree of irritation.

Henry Lee and Myrtle Lee

Myrtle Lee seldom went out at night, especially now that she had told herself she was getting cataracts. Her eye doctor had not told her she had a problem. She couldn't sleep. She drove, after midnight, to places she and Henry had gone.

Henry doesn't like his dream. The woman he is making love to doesn't have his fiancée's face, or her dark brown eyes. In his dream, Henry tries to run away from the petite woman with rosy skin and red hair. He moves a few feet away, then an invisible force pulls him close to her. When he awakes, he knows he has to tell Myrtle Lee about the dream. A sadness holds him, like a rope around his chest, a foreboding. He knows that Myrtle Lee means more to him than a friend to talk to on occasion.

They don't meet on any regular schedule. No need to give nosy people a routine to notice. Sometimes it is Monday about seven o'clock at night. Other times it can be any day, except Saturday or Sunday. Myrtle's husband, Stu, is home all day Saturday, and church and her parents take her whole Sunday. Chores for his mother, increasingly uncomfortable visits to Andrena, his church, and family take Henry's weekends as well. The time Henry visits Myrtle Lee varies from after seven to nearly nine. Days are getting shorter. It is always dark.

Henry's first embrace surprises him. He never would have imagined that Myrtle Lee's body has a shape and softness the same as other women he's held, including Andrena. He thought a white woman would feel different. He recalled stories he'd heard from guys who fought in the war in the Pacific. They'd imagined that Asian women would be built differently because their eyes were slanted instead of round, their private parts left to right instead of front to back. Henry laughs to himself. Even he knows human beings have the same anatomy.

"Henry, I want you to get in the back seat with me," Myrtle Lee says matter-of-factly, while looking straight into Henry Lee's eyes.

"Myrtle Lee, it's dangerous we're sitting here, hugging and kissing. I don't want to go any further, though Lord knows I feel it. One of us has got to show some common sense." He groans, remembering where he was at that moment.

"Both of us have sense enough to know how we feel. What do you want me to do, act like some kind of slave mistress to get you to do what you know you want? Better judgment or no judgment we've gone too far to stop, don't you think?"

"But I'm the one that'll be dead," Henry says.

She sits away from him, suddenly sobered. "I apologize; I'm being selfish, thinking only of myself. You're right, Henry."

They drive silently into town. Preoccupied, Henry Lee is deep in thought. He forgets to turn off his lights to coast to a spot between her house and the corner. When he realizes where he is, he sees a man's body outlined behind the living room curtain. "If he asks who drove you home, think of something quick."

"I already have," Myrtle says. She gets out of the car and turns, as if to pay a taxi.

Gayla

George called. "I have to go to the Cape to demonstrate my coupling. I'll be in Florida three days, then I'll run up to spend my returning weekend with you."

"Great," I said, "You can help me pack for home."

"Babe, you wouldn't believe the precautions I have to go through to make my little presentation, the cloak-and-dagger arrangements to get me through airports."

"I know it is tiresome, but you're accustomed to it," I said.

"I should be, but I never will," George said. "I'll see you, soon."

I made a shopping list. Louise could tell me where to find George's favorite wine. I hoped Carolton had a good brisket, somewhere.

George

In the campus bookstore, George accidentally bumps into Gayla, then picks up her scattered books. His apology becomes an invitation to hot chocolate. Few Negro students attend Pennsylvania State in the 1950s. Gayla Hughes is the first attractive colored woman—the only colored woman—George Tyner has seen on campus during the two years he has been a student. She is intelligent, fun, and she likes him.

Buckling his seat belt, tuning out the attendant droning in the background, George leaned back and closed his eyes. He had adjusted to Gayla's absence. Gayla was usually busy with the children, cultural and political things, and her students. He loved her. She loved him. They had been together almost twenty-five years. He was eagerly occupied with his work. To him, Gayla lived in a foreign world, one of nonspecifics: words—literature and poetry. "That stuff is intangible," he told a colleague during a rare discussion of things personal. "I prefer precise, factual work."

Nodding in agreement, his fellow engineer said, "Aeroelasticity and flutter are functions I can calculate. Calculus can be counted on. They are precise, concrete."

George buckled into his seat. He was relaxed ever since the escort who had ushered him past the security system said, "Have a nice trip."

George knew that life had treated him well. He was particularly pleased with George Junior. The boy had inherited his analytical mind. He'll go somewhere, he thought. He kept his feelings about Antony to himself. Antony, that Tony. He'd get himself together someday, find a way to use that art stuff in business, maybe in marketing, he hoped. Pamela resembled him on the outside; she was her mother inside. Those two could look at each other and talk without words. Were men supposed to know what went on in women's heads?

George settled into his flight to Orlando. He opened his briefcase. Its hidden compartment was undetectable. He checked the pad of graph paper, laptop, and foolscap filled with notations. An alarm would disintegrate the interior compartment if he were separated from the case by more than five feet. The two-and-one-half-hour flight to Orlando did not require that he visit the men's room. George shut the deliberately-worn-looking cover and opened a magazine. Minutes later, it seemed to him, the plane landed.

George strode toward a tall, uniformed figure at the far end of the Jetway.

"Dr. Tyner, Dr. Tyner," a crisp voice called from George's right side.

He turned away from the man in uniform, whom he had assumed was waiting for him. A few inches below his six-foot-two height, a bronze, oval face smiled.

"I'm Major Brocton," she said. She extended a firm, sure handshake. "We're driving to the Cape on the Bee Line Express, sir." Hanging-bags over their shoulders, two men flanked her. "Meet Drs. Hayes and Esterholdt. They are here for your presentation," the major said.

George shook hands with the men. "Glad to see you again," he nodded to Hayes who, like himself, was one of the first African American engineers in corporate aerospace. Esterholdt—red-haired, freckled, eager, young, and new to NASA—with no success, tried to appear blasé on his first assignment.

Major Brocton and the men entered a black limousine for the hour-long drive to Cape Canaveral. "This limo looks like any airport livery," she explained, "but it's bulletproof, and our driver is Special Services. We prefer not to take unnecessary risks. That's why you gentlemen arrived separately." George wasn't surprised. He regularly worked with governmental agencies, but this time he felt they were going overboard. His latest invention wasn't contributing anything to international intrigue.

Major Brocton was a happy change from his usual escort. She wasn't stiff, with the robotlike manner affected by some military personnel. She spent much of the drive describing the sights to young Esterholdt. George found himself examining her more often than he talked with Hayes, whom he considered brilliant, but a self-important bore."Tiresome journeys, aren't they?" Hayes leaned wearily into the limo seat.

"I try to cut the boredom as much as I can," George said. "I can usually find something to divert my attention."

Hayes' laughter shook his side of the limo. A smoker and beginning to gain weight, he coughed from the exertion. "I know what you mean. I've cut out the little diversions, myself."

George knew what Hayes meant. He filed it away for later. Someday he'd get the pompous ass. "The coupling I've developed takes less space and weighs considerably less than the current one. I'm looking forward to this conference," George said.

"I read your précis on the plane. Looks interesting," Hayes said.

"Thanks," George said, hearing envy in the remark.

"The university gets the credit, of course," Hayes said, taking a magazine from the seat pocket and thumbing through it.

"I'm happy for the opportunity to do my work. That's enough for me," George said. "The process is quite simple, in fact. Anyone could do it, if they can see through the garbage."

NASA and the contractor's representatives were impressed

with George's design. At the close of the two scheduled days, it was agreed that a second meeting was needed, a few more calculations to be done. They made plans to return in three weeks.

Major Brocton and George made the drive back to Orlando alone. Hayes was taking a later flight to Houston. Esterholdt was flying piggyback, behind the pilot, in an Air Force jet to Denver.

"Lucky me," George said. "I haven't seen much of you. Are you from around here?"

"Philadelphia," she said.

"Me too. Thought I recognized the brogue. What's your school?"

"Penn State, class of 1974."

"Same here." He didn't say class of 1959.

The major let him off at his terminal. His flight to Carolton would not leave for two hours.

Gayla

The day after he arrived, George and I were on our way to meet Louise and A. J. for lunch. He surveyed downtown Carolton. "This town is dullsville. I can't imagine staying here unless I was too ill or too old to do anything else."

"We are close to Atlanta." Surprised by my feeling of loyalty, I defended Carolton. "And Charleston has the Spoleto Festival. There's much to see in this state."

"But, Carolton, babe," George cringed.

I could see that Carolton and my old house would be an uphill sell with George.

The Chalet was an inviting restaurant on Lake Dillard. Carolton and the surrounding upstate had become a retirement haven for wealthy Northerners who shied from humid, overcrowded Miami. The anonymity of the Chalet's patrons made the spot appropriate for Louise and A. J. Farm-grown trout and catfish, and the owner's herb garden, attracted lovers of fresh catch.

A. J. asked the host for a table in the massive, tinted window that cantilevered over the lake.

"Spectacular view," George said. "You must have tipped the maître d' a bundle."

"It is great, isn't it?" A.J. seemed delighted that his choice was appreciated. "Makes you want to take to sea and never come back. We can't see the far shore, the lake is so large."

The men were not at all similar. A. J.'s solid blondness and George's wiry darkness were distinct contrasts. Heads turned as we went to our table. I saw our reflections in a curve of the mirrored wall opposite the window. I said, "I hope I'm not too vain, but I think we look pretty good for a bunch of near mid-century folks."

"Vanity or pride, if you don't think highly of yourself, who else will? You've done fine for a stringbean, ol' girl," A. J. defused my joking concern.

George glanced at our reflections in the mirrored wall. "It's in the genes," he said. "Choose your ancestors well and enjoy the results."

"Happy to know you all, I'm sure." Louise emphasized a Southern accent for George's benefit.

"I wish we had more time together, but Lou and I are leaving for Mexico in the morning," A. J. said.

"I'm ecstatic about seeing La Pascua Florida Fiesta," Louise said. "We've missed it on our trips before."

"Business or fun," George said.

"Both," A. J. said.

Louise coughed and A. J. turned to offer her a glass of water. When A. J. turned back to George he said, "I wanted to be an engineer. But Daddy hinted strongly, twisted my arm in fact, that the family needed an accountant. He said it was best to have one of our own on the inside. I was good at math and the family property was growing by the time I finished high school, so I was dubbed the old family bookkeeper."

I wasn't sure if it was my imagination or if Louise's cough had turned the conversation away from Mexico.

A. J. gave our orders to the waiter. "We have peach and pecan farms and grandfather's original construction firm, thanks to my lawyer sister," he said.

"Carolinians are raised on FAM-I-LY and guilt." I spelled the first word into the tablecloth.

A. J. held Louise's hand. "I used to wonder if I missed something by going along with the program, but if I'd moved away, I wouldn't have met this lovely lady. She's worth every bit of it." He kissed her hand.

"I don't know if I'm happy because of how you feel about me or sorry that you missed out on your destiny. A little of both, I suppose," Louise said.

"In my case, it was hands-off." I said. "I wonder if I'd been a boy would my dad have encouraged me into medicine. He allowed me to help him in his office when I was a kid. The patient would ask me, 'Lil' Doc, you gonna be a doctor like Big Doc when you grow up?' I'd grin and say 'Yes.' But he didn't ever suggest any dreams or plans for me." I jabbed a large, peeled shrimp into low-cal dressing. "I'd probably have made a lousy doctor," I said. I was beginning to comprehend the source of the tightness I felt in my gut and my throat whenever I was around my father.

Louise said, "No such problem for me. My folks weren't able to make demands or grand plans. I went to college in Columbia for one year, then Lloyd and I married." She stirred tea that she had stirred moments ago. "I've added computer and accounting classes at County Tech. If not for that, I'd have missed A. J. Fate is strange."

George said little during our conversation. Acknowledging comments with nods and little smiles, he looked at each one of us. Between mouthfuls of sautéed catfish, he finally said, "You Southerners are a distinct breed. I grew up in a working class neighborhood in Philly. My father worked construction. He couldn't get into a union. You're familiar with the history, I suppose?" He grimaced toward A. J. "College was my open sesame. I worked summers and on campus after classes during the year. Louise, you may be right about fate. I'd add that being in the right place at the right time helps, along with hard work."

A. J. said, "Yeah, right time and place. I met the black lawyer who won the South Carolina NAACP case that ended up being

part of the big one, the Brown versus Board of Education decision. He told us at a seminar that the first time he took the Bar
in this state, *they* failed him. He received a letter from the state
licensing board three years later, stating he could sit for the
exam again. He said, 'This time *they* passed me.' The only
black lawyer in the state had died and they were ready for the
next token. Lawyer Boulware said he was in the right place at
the right time."

I did not know that A. J. knew anything about African-
American history, especially something as obscure as the story
of Attorney Harold Boulware. I reached over and squeezed his
hand.

"Two-thirty, too soon. We'll have to dash." Louise looked at
her watch. "I'd love to stay all day but we have to catch the
plane to Monterey."

"I clean forgot," A. J. exclaimed.

"I know; that's why I remembered." Draping her purse on
her shoulder, Louise turned to George. "When you and Gayla
move back home, we'll have mucho fun."

A. J. claimed as lunch his treat.

Standing on the lakeshore after our good-byes, I reached
for George's hand. "Let's walk. It's lovely here."

We followed the shore's curved, gravel walk bordered with
manicured grass for nearly a mile. Returning, George said,
"Where does your pal, Louise, get the idea that we're moving
down here? I couldn't live in Carolton. It's an intellectual waste-
land. Are you entertaining the possibility, babe?"

"Not at all." I was taken aback by the strength of his rejection.
"A number of former Caroltonians are retired here. Lou and I
were talking about why so many come back home, that's all."

An elderly couple met us on the path. The man stopped in
front of George. "Would you ask the lady back at the restaurant
to send my jacket out to me? It's colder than I thought. Tell her
it's for Mr. Wright." The man pulled a handful of bills from his
pants pocket.

George stared at the man.

"We're guests here, not servants," I snapped in my strongest
Middle Western accent. Quickly starting toward my car, I

pulled George's arm. My hand shook as I unlocked the door. "It's still here," I said through clenched teeth. "Only when they all die will it stop," I groaned. I accelerated faster than the posted limit of thirty-five miles per hour

"Whoa, watch it, babe. I don't want to give the police any blood money. What was that all about?" George asked.

"The old crackers don't understand that every Negro, uh black person, isn't their servant, waiting to do their bidding for a quarter."

George's eyes widened. "Oh—OH—I didn't catch it right away." George almost yelled, "And you want to live here? That's nuts."

"George, we've had fun, a great lunch, a lovely walk. I had forgotten my first visit to Lake Dillard."

He looked behind at two buildings set amid luxuriant landscaping. "The restaurant looks brand new. When were you here?"

"The restaurant and condominiums are new, but the lake has been a local recreation spot for a long time." I shuddered. "Everything came back the minute I opened the car door. The summer this lake was opened to the public for boating, fishing, and swimming, someone sold my dad tickets to the opening ceremony. Somebody who wasn't thinking, I guess. Once in a while, people forgot the race thing and acted human. Daddy, Mother, Jan, and I came out here.

"Young guys were taking tickets in the middle of the highway. One of them took our tickets. 'Howdy, Doc. Come on in,' he said."

"Everybody was having a good time. Jan and I kicked sand and watched speedboats with their noses in the air, all red and blue and green and yellow. After a while, we sat on a bench to rest and watch. A man appeared beside me and mumbled something I didn't hear clearly. I looked up into the angry eyes of a short, white man, his face wrinkled from years in the sun. He had on baggy wash pants, suspenders, a red bow tie, and a brown fedora hat, like Humphrey Bogart. 'Huh?' I asked, 'cause I hadn't heard what he said. I did the next time."

"Breathing onion odor in my face, he grabbed my arm and

yanked me to my feet. 'I said these benches for white folks.' I see his angry face right this minute. I can't stand for anyone to breathe in my face."

"Dad jumped up and told the man we had tickets for the show. I was confused and scared. Jan ran, crying to Mother."

"Obviously you got out fast. Nobody put you in jail," were George's first words after my long tale.

"No, no," my voice strangled, "about that time a regular policeman came along. He knew Daddy. He asked, 'What's the trouble, Doc?' The men went off to one side. We couldn't hear what was said. After a few minutes, Daddy came back and said the policeman explained to the cracker, who was deputy for a day, who we were. But the fun was gone so we went home. Funny, I didn't remember this was the same place. Assuming you were a servant. Damn," I said a second time.

The steering wheel calmed my shaking arms. I feel in control when I'm driving my car.

CHAPTER 25

Gayla

WESTMINSTER PRESBYTERIAN CHURCH NEEDED A COAT of fresh paint on its modest steeple and wood trim. The parking lot could hold three times the amount of cars that actually filled it at the eleven o'clock Sunday morning service. I helped Mother from the El Dorado. George held Daddy's elbow. Dad planted his ebony cane on the ground for a firm footing.

"Take it easy Papa Doc, this battleship is a long way from terra firma," George joked.

Inside, George whispered to me, "Where are the people?"

Dad overheard, "Boy, people have a notion around these parts that if a colored man isn't Baptist or Methodist, some white man's been messing with his religion. Show's how little history they know."

Mother turned both hands palms-up indicating, 'it's no big deal.' "We Presbyterians are a shade too quiet for many of our people."

The young minister compared Jesus' crucifixion and resurrection to the world today, how people need to "rise from the crucifixion of innocence in the ghettos, Central America, and war everywhere." All in all, the sermon was in the spirit of Mother and Daddy's familiar Presbyterian enlightenment.

"Intelligent sermon," Mother said as we left the church. She rubbed her hands together with a prayerful gesture. She touched George's sleeve. George didn't attend church. "Son," Mother cajoled and instructed, "our ministers have to have seven years of college, like a lawyer does. They study Hebrew, Latin, and Greek. Most people take their religion purely on emotion, not us," Mother said with an emphatic rise in her voice. She read books that she said had been left out of the Bible. "There's more to religion than most people want to know," Mother said, pursing her lips and nodding with conviction.

Despite empty seats, the service was heartfelt. On our way to the restaurant that Dad had chosen for dinner, Mother shook her head sorrowfully when a carful of youngsters roared around us, music doppling. "No discipline on Sunday or any other day. That's why we can't leave our doors open the way we used to do."

The popular cafeteria-style restaurant dining room was nearly filled, the racial split about equal. Sunday dresses and suits graced children, mothers in spring hats, men and women in dress-up clothes.

"People around here love to eat and lots of it," George said in amazement as he bumped into me. "Everybody's here, from couples with babies to three generation families."

I had that feeling of being watched and when I turned to see who it might be, I saw only an unkempt woman, in a corner of the cafeteria, hunched over her food. Her demeanor indicated she didn't want anyone to intrude in her space, and despite a full clientele, no one sat at the table directly across from her. She seemed familiar but today was no time to play good Samaritan.

Henry Lee and Myrtle Lee

Myrtle Lee forgot it was Sunday. She didn't like crowds. When she did venture away from home to eat, she went after the lunch rush and usually on Monday or Tuesday, when few people would be out after a big Sunday. Recognizing Gayla, she put her head down when Gayla turned in her direction. Myrtle Lee thought, she doesn't remember me. I lived on McGuire Street, played with her and her sister before my daddy got his big promotion and we moved to a good neighborhood. That's another man with her, not the one who was in the car the last time I saw her. Guess Miss Hughes, or whatever her name is now, has a lover too. The one you marry never is the right one.

"Why are you looking in the rearview mirror so often? I was very careful. No one saw me—or you, I swear," Myrtle Lee says.

"I feel something's not right." Henry says. The chill of early spring does not reach him, he feels as hot as an August cotton field. "My mama is asking questions. She says I've been jumpy recently, as if something's chasing me. Myrtle, if I go to Pittsburgh, get a job, and send for you, would you come? You could get a divorce and we could get married."

"Colored and white can marry up North—legal? I didn't know." Myrtle is animated; her eyes sparkle; her shoulders straighten from the weighed-down shape they'd taken recently. "I'd do that, Henry. I would."

Henry makes a sudden turn onto a street he'd not taken before. A moment later, a tan sedan he's seen at Lake Dillard passes the corner. The driver doesn't see them because Henry turns into a driveway and quickly cut his lights and motor.

"Myrtle, we've got trouble. I thought we were being followed. I was right. We have to get out of here. In the morning, I'm going to get my money out of Liberty Savings and Loan. We'll leave as soon as dark." He lets her out behind the house of a neighbor and drives across a rough field behind another house and into his street.

Gayla

Dad smiled and spoke to everyone. Munching on food they had chosen from the overflowing salads and steam table, they smiled back. Pink-and-green-checked wallpaper formed a background for wood-framed prints of Southern mansions and gardens.

"How're you doing, Doc?"

"Beautiful day, this Lord's day, isn't it?"

"You're looking good, Doc."

Walking briskly, pulling back his shoulders, Dad insisted on carrying his own tray, although a waitress volunteered to take it to the table for him. Peering over the room with the air of a potentate holding court, Dad caught the eye of first one, then another of the brightly-dressed diners. "Glad to see you, young fellow," he said to a man who looked at least sixty. To a toddler he said, "Enjoying your meal, little lady?"

Lifting and jabbing his fork, a leathery-faced white man stopped our party. "Nice to see your whole family out today. The Virginia ham's mighty tender, Doc. Did you take it?"

"No sir. I took the turkey and dressing. Ham does look tasty. Can't eat everything at once," Daddy was dead serious. "I'll be back another Sunday. It'll be here."

We stopped several tables beyond the ham advocate. Daddy removed his dishes from the tray, took Mother's tray, and gave it to the waitress along with his. He pushed his napkin into his vest top and whispered conspiratorially. "That man who hailed me, he's forgotten that he didn't want me to run for city council. Said ugly things about me. He's nice as pie now." Dr. J. C. Hughes beamed like the canary swallowing the cat and lifted his cane in benediction.

A cute little girl, her hair in old-fashioned, Shirley Temple curls with ribbons, smiled at George over the back of her chair. George winked at her. Blinking both eyes, she tried to do the same.

Daddy ate his fill then leaned back in his chair and yawned. "I'm ready for a nap. Guess it's time I got on home." Once home, he did just that.

George asked, "Mother Mavis, is there anything I can do for you while I am here?"

"No, it's Sunday, and you're here such a short time. I enjoy seeing you, son," Mother said. "Gayla is taking care of us fine. I don't know what we'll do when she's gone."

"I appreciate what you say, Mother Mavis, but she belongs to me. She'll come back if you need her." George laced his long arms around me and bent to kiss my cheek.

"Alice is very capable. And you look so good you're going to outlast your grandchildren," he said.

George drove. I looked through the rear window at the figures of my parents growing tiny like people, cars, and trees dropping away under an airplane.

Later, in the apartment, George and I began to pack articles I would ship to Ann Arbor.

"Babe, is there anything more you want in this box before I seal it?" He waited for an answer.

"If there's anything left over after these are shipped, I'll toss it in the car. Let's rest. You have an early flight," I said.

"Getting my muscles into physical stuff is good, after all that mind work at the Cape." George took the glass of wine I brought to him.

I sat beside him, kicked off my shoes, and pulled my feet under my thighs. "You've been good to put up with my being away so long," I said. "This was something I had to do."

"Yes, that's what you said. I don't understand the urgency," George shrugged, "but since it's what you wanted, that's fine." George's father was dead. His sister had taken their mother to live with her family. George sent a check regularly.

"The new roof looks fine. I didn't know you were so good at overseeing contractors," he said.

"That's a put-down if I ever heard one," I said. "Who juggled three children, two moves, work, and you, and never dropped one baby?" I grabbed his ear and pinched it between my thumb and forefinger, but not too hard. I learned long ago that George did not see the managing that I did.

"George, you know how Dad and I have always sort of been at one another—in a gentle way I like to think." I was tentative but felt I had to try. "Well my dear, hear me out George, please? I now understand the anger I feel over my relationship with Daddy and the feelings I have about Carolton. At least I think I do."

George said, "I promise to interrupt only to refill my glass. Shoot."

"Being here this time, I studied Dad carefully and analytically, the way you would one of your engineering problems, George. I worried and cried, at first," I said, looking to see if he seemed interested. "Dad, and lots of colored like him, had to put up with denial of his work, what he valued, and had to swallow all kinds of crap in order to make it in this down South world."

George drained his glass. "Your father's done very well.

Better than anyone before me in my family. Look, babe, Pop
Hughes had educated parents. Even his grandparents owned
land." George drew a make-believe zipper across his mouth.
"Sorry, I meant to keep quiet, but I don't see where the good
Doctor had reason for any pain."

"Porgie, it's like the story I heard about the first licensed
Negro lawyer in the state. Can you imagine day after day going
to his office, waiting for clients who didn't show? They knew a
white judge wouldn't listen to him. I'll bet it was slow torture
inside. I understand his pining and his drinking himself to
death. He couldn't do what he knew and loved. Back in our
dark ages we were told, by our grownups, over and over, 'colored have to be twice as good to get half as much.'

"It's really no different from your father in Philadelphia. It's
just a matter of degree . . . relative, as Mother likes to say."

George got up to go to the small kitchen.

"Let me finish, please?" I said. "Saying it aloud helps clear my
feelings."

"Okay, babe, I'll try. Just one minute." George came back
with more Carl Graff Riesling Spatlese.

I curled into one corner of the sofa and watched him nod
appreciatively at the bouquet and taste of the wine. "I believe
my Dad saw me as a threat, I think, a kind of competitor. We're
alike—'stubborn as the day is long,' he says. Jan was smarter
than I was, particularly where Daddy was concerned. She
always let Dad believe he was right. I blow up. I argue, complain. On a deep level, I see how his life was controlled. He
couldn't do and be what he really was. Making a good living
wasn't enough. The money was secondary." I was aware I was
running on and on, but the words kept coming.

"Dad, poor blacks and whites were the same even if it didn't
look that way to the outside. Even A. J. was controlled. His dad
was like a massa. A. J. had to do what he was told. Most of us
do, somehow." I felt I finally had a grasp on something real,
something true.

"Come off it, sweetheart. A. J.? Damn, the man's *white*. He's
been free many thousands of years." George frowned.

"We don't see eye to eye," I said. George's frown was enough to stop me. "This is how I see it," I said, barely loud enough to be heard two feet away. "Something, somebody's always limiting, always saying no. Dad saw *himself* in my escapades and saw the limitations I faced. Pushing the system, like in my violin fiasco, I used his status to do what he couldn't do. I think Dad was afraid for me, for himself, for the fallout he'd get if I screwed up. He couldn't take the chances I did. It's fear and power, George. People of color get the more obvious crap." I paused. I was talking to myself.

"Excuse me, I'm trying, but I only hear generalizations," George said. He leaned into the opposite corner of the couch. "Give me a specific, a concrete example. If you're being analytical, like you say, excuse me, I don't see it."

Going down for the third time, I went on, "Let me think . . . maybe you'll get it from this story." I gritted my teeth. "One day Jan and I had an argument with a couple of our white neighbors, a girl and a boy who'd moved up the street. Kids fall out all the time and make up, no big deal. Well, their mother saw the *demon race*. She called the police—I still can't believe it. Dad and Mother were at the office, as usual. A cop was sent to investigate. He was a nice young fellow and told Jan and me to stay at our end of the street. I told him, 'No, we have to go to school, go downtown to our daddy's office. And we've lived on Lowell longer than they have. We won't stop walking on our own street.'"

"The policeman laughed. He knew it was kid's stuff. Some Negroes were walking down the sidewalk. They heard me and crossed to the other side of the street. I was 'talking back' to a white man. I knew for sure that I was *right*. The way we were treated in some places some of the time—like okay people—made me confident. I didn't know Dad couldn't do what I did. He played his role."

"You were a stone brat," George said. "You could have been in big trouble."

"George, please. That wasn't long before the Civil Rights movement erupted. The pot had been simmering all along," I said. "It took time for consciousness to rise. The rage is always inside." I got up from the couch. My knees were stiff. My head throbbed.

"Whoa," my husband said. "You're getting carried away. When you get like this, I'll bet it's the way you and your trouble buddy Tally acted when you got into mischief. Come on, give me a smooch."

I moved into his arms. He buried his mouth in my neck. His moustache tickled. I shifted and felt his lips on a pulse. Sharp hairs pressed smooth and flat against my skin. I wanted to scream. I couldn't.

Close to his ear, I heard myself whispering, "Georgie Porgie, I am the way I am, a brat, because I've been slow to understand the pressure Dad had to—I think the word is—sublimate his feelings. I didn't trust him to be in my corner. He couldn't trust himself to stand by me. The pain has been inside for a long time, for both of us, for all of us."

I pulled out of George's arms. I said, "I finally know why I came to Carolton: to deal with the pain in Daddy, in this place, and in me. Mother handled her pressure and frustration differently," I said, with a firm shake of my head. "And she let me be."

"Some philosopher-psychologist you are." George gazed up to the low ceiling of the little apartment, then nestled his lips in the curve of my collarbone. "Babe, now that you've solved your weighty problems with your Southern roots and your father, you can come home. We'll pick up where we left off."

"Thanks for the use of your ear, George." I felt cold. "I'll be home in three weeks." Talking with George was like talking with Daddy, except George humored me. He didn't hear me either. He made love to me.

CHAPTER 26

George

GEORGE RETURNED TO ANN ARBOR and entered his new calculations into the university's mainframe. He wasn't sure if he would have the student cleaning service give the house a going-over before Gayla came home or do it himself. He was feeling a little uncomfortable about his interest in Anne Brocton, the major. Thalea had stopped fishing for more. She was still fun. The graduate student last term didn't count. She went with him to a conference at Michigan State in Lansing and kept calling him "sir." Her score, zero. Yes, he would call the cleaning service. Gayla would like that.

Gayla

Days eased longer and warmer in Carolton. Louise and I left our last beauty shop appointment, at Casa Bella, together. "I'll miss you terribly," I said, pushing my hair behind my ears. "One day I'll let the gray show, but not yet." I dropped the receipt in my purse.

"When are we going to put our vanity on hold," Louise asked, "let nature be, the way our mothers do so beautifully?"

"Nevermore," I kidded. "We're the last of the Twentieth Century Club, la creme de la creme."

In the parking lot, we wandered, not remembering where we parked. Louise stopped. "I have been starved for female companionship. A. J. knew it. I didn't."

"We've been good for each other." I gave her hand a squeeze.

"Do you remember Colonel Tillman and his daughter?"

"Everybody in Carolton knew who they were. His daughter, Naomi, rode horseback with my Saturday pals." I said. "When her parents heard that I was riding with the group, they made her stop. What's up?"

"Naomi is back in Carolton and lives at Lake Dillard. She looked me up—really odd, huh? She wants to be friends, I think. We're to have lunch tomorrow. What do you think?"

"I'm flabbergasted. You have to know that everyone in Carolton—our Carolton, anyway—knew that you are related to that family. You looked alike, except you're prettier. That's it!" I snapped my fingers, my mouth open. "The picture of you, the one in your gallery, looks just like Naomi. What do you think?"

Louise shrugged. "I guess she's lonely. What else? I don't know. I'll let you know what happens, if anything."

"Maybe things do change. Tell her I say 'Hi,' if she remembers me. By the way, I don't want to stick my nose in your business. You know how I feel about you and Drew, I mean A. J." I felt weird trying to say what I meant to a good friend. I felt uncomfortable. I didn't want to hurt my friend's feelings.

"I know what you're thinking and I planned to tell you before you went back to Michigan. May as well do it now. A. J. has been offered a vice presidency with a Mexican firm, the one he was consulting with when we were in Monterey. We love Mexico. He's going to take it. And we're getting married."

I nearly blurted a 'Thank you, Lord'; I seldom prayed. I prayed when George Junior fell off his bicycle and was in a coma for two days. I prayed when Antony was lost at the beach when he was three. Mom Dutch says 'Thank you, Jesus,' over and over. That's not exactly Presbyterian. I just grinned. "You're going to get out of here, hooray! I'm happy for you. I want you to be happy."

Louise said, " I am happy. I've not seen you so bubbly since you came back. Since my plans make you so buoyant, I wish we'd done it when you first arrived."

"Lou, how wonderful it is that times have changed—have gotten better." An image of a sad face crossed my mind. "Lou, I wonder what happened to Henry Lee and the white woman who were in love and had to leave town? I remember Henry Lee."

"Oh, yes," Louise said, "They were both named Lee. I haven't any idea what happened to them."

"I hope they went far away and are living happily, ever after," I said.

Lou and I linked arms. She said, "Let's walk a spell, as the old folk say."

We found a secluded spot at the edge of the parking lot. Traffic funneled to a stop at the mall. I saw a bench around a curve and said, "Now let's set a spell, as the old folk also said. I'm beginning to like some of those homey sayings."

"I thank you for keeping your counsel about A. J. and me," Louise said. "Since you're leaving soon, I want to be a real friend before you go."

"'Scuse me, you mean you've been an imitation friend all this time?"

"Not that way, dummy," Lou slapped her forehead in mock dismay.

The bench was new. A brass plate hammered into the top board read, "In Memory of Evangeline Nancy Pettigrew-Lewis." Pink and white dogwood blossoms created a pleasant setting around the bench.

"I won't pussyfoot, Miss Gayla. Have you decided what you're going to do about that marriage of yours?"

"Funny, other folk see what's going down before the principals. George and I have been through a lot together. You know the cliché, 'Does he beat you?' No, Miss Louise, he doesn't. If George has any notion of how our relationship has changed, I don't know. Marriages like our parents aren't seen much these days. I can't say, right now, how I feel about us or how he feels about me—about us." An ant purposefully carried a fragment of food, larger than itself—tipping, zigging, zagging, but staying on course.

"I have a lot of nerve," Louise said.

I hesitantly touched her hand. "The pot can't call the kettle black."

Louise started to stand up, then sat back down, "Women, men, black, white, whatever, we're all needy."

"No." I stared at the ground. "If and when the time comes, I'll know what to do. And I'll do it. Einstein said he didn't believe God played dice with the universe. Sometimes, I think that's actually what the Big One does." The ant had disappeared. His crumb lingered, inches in front of my foot. I rubbed the morsel into the red dirt.

Our old playground tune came out of nowhere. I sang, "Little Sally Walker, sitting . . ." People driving into the mall lot turned to look; the little garden spot was usually empty. Louise joined me, all the way to ". . . the very one that you love the best."

George

George left his desk and went outside for fresh air. He paced and chewed his pipe for a few minutes. He went back inside and dialed the number Major Brocton had given him two weeks before. "I was hoping you'd be assigned to meet me when I come back to the Cape tomorrow," he fought down the caution that he wouldn't acknowledge. "We didn't have time to get acquainted. We could have dinner together, see the sights."

The major's Pennsylvania brogue cut through the earpiece, "I'm sure it can be arranged."

George hummed as he packed and activated the alarm on his briefcase. Images of Anne Brocton entered his mind. When she called him "sir," she didn't sound the same as his graduate assistant. No harm, he thought, while looking in his mirror then down at his watch.

Maj. Anne Brocton met George at the airport. Esterholdt and Hayes would fly in later. She drove him across the NASA Causeway and dropped him at the motel entrance. "I'll come back for you at six-thirty for dinner."

In his room, discomfort brought a shiver, a coolness that led George to check the thermostat. He considered phoning the young major and calling the whole thing off.

Gayla and he had a good thing. He'd taken his chances. Men are supposed to make conquests. That's the way the world is. He hadn't taken anything away from Gay. He would never hurt her. This will be the last time, he thought.

The desk rang. "Major Brocton is here, sir."

George ran his comb through his hair—three new grey strands—turned off the lights, and closed the door.

"Dr. Tyner? I'm Major Richard Brocton. Call me Rick. Anne's waiting for us in the car. We have reservations at the most fabulous seafood restaurant in southern Florida."

The younger man, by perhaps fifteen years, shook George's hand and held the door for him. Not as tall as George, he was ebony black with a thin moustache above full, chiseled lips. Major Anne smiled from the front car window. Maj. Richard Brocton opened the rear door for George. Sliding into the driver's seat beside his wife, he started the car and began the trip to the mainland to that fabulous restaurant.

Gayla

I asked Mother and Daddy if I could have a farewell party at their home on my last weekend in Carolton. Mother said, "You don't have to ask."

My little friends, Shaundra and Elizabeth, were invited. Several new friends came from Upstate University. There were no raised eyebrows when the mixed couple—Thai and Italian—arrived.

"See," I whispered to A. J., "there are other kinds of mixed couples. You're not so special." I noticed that Viking descendants seem to blush easily.

Shaundra's father came after we ate. I hugged the children good-bye. Elizabeth's new tooth was coming in fine. Shaundra said, "I'll never forget you, even if you don't like being called a teacher." I was surprised. She saw and understood my reaction the first day we met. She never gave it away.

The adults relaxed with after-dinner drinks. "Do you notice anything special about our gathering? And I don't mean anything as obvious as color," I said. I aimed my last remark at Ron

Michaels. Ron, jokingly and seriously, saw every event in the context of race. At the reception where I met Ron, he introduced himself, saying, "You look as if you are on familiar ground." There it was again. I must look like my occupation, just as Shaundra noticed the day we met.

His wife, Mary, prided herself on her rapid repartee. "We're from different parts of the country. That's it."

"I think it's our intellectual acumen," Ron said. "We're a bright group, if you'll pardon the pun." His mariney-light face turned redder.

"Does anyone have it correct?" A. J. asked me.

"You're all right, to a point. But I noticed that, except for Louise and A. J., you're all people I've met on this visit, and I didn't know I knew A. J. My childhood friends are shadows. They've left Carolton."

Bill Thomas and his wife had moved to Carolton two years earlier, their fourth corporate transfer in ten years. "Lots of people never leave home and stay exactly the same," he commented. "They think and act just as they always did, and their folks, and their folks. I see complacency, here and when I go home to Georgia."

Deep in the house, I heard the phone ring. Almost immediately, Mother, her face somber, beckoned from the dining room door.

"What is it? Are you okay? Is Daddy okay?"

"It's Miss King, 'Mom Dutch.' Young Dr. Porter called from the hospital. Robbers broke in on the poor old soul, beat her up, ransacked her home. She's asking for your father. The doctor wants J. C. to come to the hospital right away. I hate to spoil your party. Can one of your nice men friends drive him? It'll take a half-hour for a taxi to get out to us."

"No, I'll do it, Mother."

My guests understood. Following a fast drive into town, I left Dad with Dr. Porter. "Call me when you're ready to come home. I hope Mom Dutch isn't seriously hurt." The tall younger man and the short older one walked swiftly down the wide, buff corridor.

Within an hour, I was back at my party. I told what little I knew. The long drive back to Avondale loomed before Mary and Ron and the mixed couple who came with them. A. J. and Louise stayed until Daddy called and I went to bring him home.

I escorted my father to the car. He looked and moved like a man years older. He slumped into the seat beside me. His small body seemed to have no bones; his color was ashen, gray like the synthetic interior of my car. "She's dead, Janis. The low down dirty dogs beat that sweet woman because they thought she had money. She was no fool. Her valuables were in the bank, in her safe deposit box. What is this world coming to?"

I felt sick at the horrible way Mom Dutch had to die, and at hearing my father call me Janis. It would do no good to confront him. He could not understand my feeling of abandonment. Janis was dead more than twenty years and he called me by her name. At times, I've thought I had made my peace with my feelings toward my father. I understand a little more each time. One day all the hurt and sadness may disappear. I'll have to continue the Sisyphean task, like everyone else.

Agapé, agapé ran through my head. I wanted to forget, to forgive. I wanted to scream, LOOK AT ME, I AM GAYLA! I didn't.

I tried to comfort him. Daddy and Miss King went back to the beginning of his practice, fifty years. At home, he went straight to bed. Mother and Alice were clearing away the last of the remnants of the party.

"I asked you to leave that 'til morning and I'd do it." I wanted to call back the sharpness in my voice, but it was out before I realized it. Immediately, I apologized. "I'm sorry. I didn't mean to be short. It's just that I talked with Mom Dutch not long ago. She was a grand lady."

"Don't fret. We understand," Alice said. "Miss Mavis and I have to keep busy. We don't mind one little bit."

I left for my little apartment. Mother and Daddy needed to comfort one another.

Punk rockers with spiked, purple and green hair climb over Mom Dutch's carved furniture when the lion comes alive and chases them out of the house, across the cow pasture, and into the creek that meanders through it. Pouring rain overflows the narrow ditch and floods the field. Screaming obscenities, the creeps float away. The brown water runs purple and green. Mom Dutch stands on the bank; she shakes her floppy bonnet in triumph. She flings her wash pot stirring stick at the rascals.

In the morning, Louise and Mary called. They enjoyed the party. I was to let them know if they can help in any way.

The amateur thieves—murderers—were caught the day after Mom Dutch's funeral. Just teenagers—one black, one white, and both too young to be sentenced to the electric chair—they wanted money for drugs. They tried to sell two antique chairs. The dealer called the police. Carolton was still small enough.

The two-day drive to Ann Arbor was easy. I loved long, solitary drives, as I had enjoyed my solitary rides on Folly and reading in quiet, empty rooms. When our children were small, We'd load them in the car for trips to Chicago, Pittsburgh, New York, and the Grand Canyon. After games and gazing at scenery, they slept a lot—good kids, most of the time. Now, I escaped Country Western music overload with tapes and silence.

CHAPTER 27

Thalea

GEORGE AND THALEA JOGGED ON the path in the park across from her apartment. He puffed, "This physical stuff isn't too bad. I can't believe you talked me into running."

"This isn't running, George. It's jogging. You keep one foot on the ground all the time."

"I guess I can get used to it," he panted and dropped behind the lithe woman in the lavender and black running suit.

"If you want to keep up with me, Professor, you have to keep moving, in more ways than one."

"How's your little car behaving?" George said, as he caught up with her.

"You were right about the problem. The ground wire was shorting out. It's running great."

They stopped and stretched to cool down. Wisps of clouds blew slowly across an intense blue sky. The morning sun was bright and the air still cold. It would be a while longer before signs of coming spring.

"Come on up and shower," Thalea said. "You can get your wind back and you won't be tired driving home."

"Sounds good, thanks." George tied his jacket around his waist. "It's cool outside and I still worked up a sweat."

"Race you to the door." Thalea spurted away from him.

"No can do. I'll walk." He took his time getting to the entrance.

George went into the bathroom to shower. Thalea selected

a skirt and blouse. "Sorry, there's nothing for you to wear," she called from her bedroom.

"That's okay." Humming tunelessly, he turned on the water. "Hey, what's up?" he exclaimed when the shower door opened.

"Thought I'd join you." Thalea stepped into the stream of water. "Do my back, I love having my back washed. I'll return the favor."

George soaped and rubbed her back. The softness of her skin in the warm water led to a request in her ear, "Don't do this to me; I can't take it," he said.

"Yes, you can," she laughed, pulling away from his embrace. Rinsed, she stepped onto the mat.

A towel around his shoulders, he followed her into her room. He put his sweat suit back on and began to fasten his shoes. "Damn," George said. "I forgot something. Let me borrow your car. I have to dash to Central Campus to start up the final figures on my project so they will be finished by noon. The drive will give me a chance to see how your car sounds. I'll be back in thirty minutes. Gayla should be home before dark."

She tossed him her keys and he hurried out of the apartment. She watched from the window as he got into her car and sped away. The latest *Essence* lay on a table by the couch. She picked it up and slid into a deep, comfortable chair to read while she waited for him to return.

The grandmother clock in the kitchen chimed. She'd been engrossed in her reading. Thalea looked out the window. George's car was in her guest parking space. The early afternoon sun was obscured by light rain.

She picked up a phone and hit the speed dial button for George's number. She hung up after several rings. "Strange man," she said, "he won't get an answering machine for his office phone." Another half-hour passed. She tried again. "I have things to do, George Tyner. Where are you?" she said to the silent telephone.

Thalea paced from window to telephone. As she reached for the phone for the third time, her doorbell rang. She opened the door, quickly. "George, where—" Two police officers stood in the doorway.

A sober-faced young officer with an obviously well-rehearsed demeanor said, "Sorry to disturb you, lady. Do you own a red BMW convertible, license number TD 36?"

"Was it stolen?" a taller, thin, blond man asked.

"No, it wasn't. Is there a problem?" She felt a tightening in the bottom of her abdomen.

"Well, ma'am, there's been an accident. You need to come with us. Your husband's been hurt, Mrs. Davison."

"My husband? Oh God, what happened?"

"Try to remain calm, Mrs. Davison. We'll fill you in at the hospital. If you'll get your purse and coat, we'll drive you." The shorter, sober-faced officer took her arm. Thalea hesitated, her knees weak.

At Parkview Hospital, Thalea was taken into a pink-and-blue-wallpapered office. The medical director and a nurse waited in front of a large, metal, paper-piled desk. "We're sorry, Mrs. Davison." The director extended her hand. "Your car was broadsided by another car that ran a red light on Riverview Road. Your husband didn't survive the crash."

"He's not my husband!" Thalea blurted through clenched teeth. "He's . . . a friend, Dr. George Tyner. I let him drive my car, that's all."

"I'm sorry," the director said. "He didn't have his wallet on him. We use license plates for fast identification."

"So, that's why the officer asked if the car was stolen." Thalea was struggling to hold onto a semblance of rational thought. She recalled George putting his wallet on her nightstand before his shower.

"We couldn't save him," the doctor's voice was distinct, yet calm.

The doctor's words sank into Thalea's consciousness. Her thoughts jumped around, unlike her normal, controlled way of thinking with which she managed life with absolute control.

"How can we contact Mr. Tyner's family?" the nurse said.

She stammered, "Dr. Tyner and I, I'm Dr. Thalea Davison—

we're colleagues at the university. You can contact his dean. His family is not in town." She gave them the department number. She did not ask to see what remained of George.

Gayla

The garage door opened noisily and revealing an empty concrete floor. "He's not here," I mumbled. "I told him I'd be home today, probably about three or four." I went into the family room and dropped two suitcases. "I'll let him help me lug in all the stuff." I said to the silence.Glad to be in my own home again, I walked into every room. It was 4:20 P.M. by the grandfather clock in the living room, 4:22 by my watch.

I walked from room to room. "My, the house is clean. It smells fresh." The emptiness threw back a slight echo. "I wonder if George broke down and sprang for a cleaning service. Bless his bones." I ran my fingers over the sparkling mirror and tabletop in the dining room. Familiar furnishings, which I had chosen, were comforting.

I was jarred from the quiet of the empty house by the doorbell. Two women police officers greeted me, their legs apart the way military people stand. One was about my size, chocolate-brown with full lips, no makeup, and kind black—almost purple—eyes. The other was taller with a few freckles across her nose and cheeks, red hair tumbling to her shoulders when she removed her cap and stuck it under her arm. She could have been a rookie; she looked all of eighteen.

Kind eyes asked, "Are you Mrs. Tyner? We've been sort of watching for someone to arrive."

My chest filled with a heaviness that spread to the bottom of my feet. "Yes," I choked, "what has happened?"

Procedures followed in one timeless, noncomprehensible maze. I had been driving from Carolton to Ann Arbor and no one knew exactly where I was. Once there, I was numb with shock, surprise, pain, and the rising question of how.

George, Junior and Pamela rushed home. My parents flew up. We could not locate Antony until days after the funeral. He would come home as quickly as he could. Juanita and Tally flew from Hartford, and Louise and A. J. called daily during the numb days. The university community was supportive. No one in the family knew that George's accident held a huge question, only Louise and Tally and Juanita. My family was accustomed to George's always-busy, moving schedule. It was an easy lie to tell my parents and the children that he was checking out a friend's car when the accident occurred. Knowing George to be an engineer who loved to tinker, no one questioned. And as I was not there when it occurred, they accepted that I did not know all the details.

I could not tell if they accepted my explanation or not. We Presbyterian Hughes learn early to be "polite" and never stir the waves, or there might come a hurricane. We avoid hurricanes. I'm beginning to see that a hurricane is refreshing. It brings new life and growth to the surface. The lifelong habit of keeping problems to myself, of working through them in my own way, was my pattern—just as I had done with the violin teacher.

Tally, Juanita, and Louise received more of the real story, as much as I knew so soon after the accident. Louise did not say, as she had in Carolton, that I should not have left George for such a long time, but I remembered. Tally could only say, "My poor Gee-Gee." We did not talk as we had when we drove around Carolton. As always, we had lines of communication that did not need words.

George Junior was like his father. He was calm and composed, just as George would have wanted. He took back with him to Seattle George's oldest pipe and a painting of a tiger on blue silk that George bought on a trip to Japan. The painting had hung above George's desk. "I always wanted it," he said.

"Please let me stay with you, Mom. You need me," Pam pleaded.

I insisted that she finish her school year.

I knew Thalea Davison. I'd seen her, vivacious and glamorous at university functions. We were cordial out of necessity, for we were a scant handful of African-Americans on faculty.

She didn't call. Four weeks after George's funeral, she sent a note on lavender, scented notepaper, "May I come to talk, or would you care to come to my place? Perhaps, you'd like a neutral setting. Let me know."

The children, friends, and George's family were gone. Mother and Daddy were back in Carolton. I waited two weeks after the scented note before I called Thalea.

"Let's meet at the arboretum. We may not run into anyone we know there."

"Yes," she said. "This is the time of the year when school children are taking field trips."

I dressed in my prettiest outfit. It was April and spring had begun to come to Michigan. Plants in the arboretum greenhouse perfumed the moist air. For a moment, I was sorry that I'd chosen that spot. There were a number of large florals at George's funeral. Then, I felt reassured; these plants were living and growing.

She arrived, later than our agreed upon time. "Do you want to sit or walk?" she said. She towered over me. She wore purple and yellow.

"How tall are you?" I said.

"Five-nine."

"I thought George liked short women." I didn't care that I was rude.

Thalea Davison laughed, high and girlish, a pitch I didn't expect from her low, husky-speaking voice.

"George loved women, girl. Tall, short, light, dark, young, or a little mature. The only ladies George ignored were ugly ones."

I gestured toward a bench where we could sit, a long one. I felt my stomach churning. I had not put a roll of antacid in my purse.

Thalea's face and tone changed to one I took for sadness, even sorrow. "Thanks for meeting me," she said earnestly. "This has been an awful time for you, I know. I wanted to come to the funeral and the memorial, but gossip has got to be heavy."

"No one's said anything out of the ordinary to me," I said. My stomach didn't growl as much as before.

"They wouldn't," she said. "You and I know tongues are

flapping. I won't waste your time or insult your intelligence. George was driving my car because he was checking out whether the mechanic had really fixed it. The accident was a turn of fate."

"Then, you weren't having an affair?"

Thalea Davison surveyed the stone floor of the arboretum for many seconds. "We'd been seeing one another since shortly after you left. Frankly, I was trying to get him to leave you. He wouldn't."

"That should be a relief," I said. "I sensed that George was not being honest with me. He was away on business so often I couldn't be sure. After so many years, a woman ought to know."

"Sweetheart, for an educated woman, you are grossly naive," Thalea said, but not with meanness.

I moved from my seat beside her. Heart pounding, I walked to a display of fragrant exotic blooms, cupped a large red blossom in my hands, and inhaled its scent. Instances of suspicion that I denied would not stay away. I continued to smell the flower until its fragrance absorbed the images and feelings that wanted to overwhelm me.

Thalea remained in her seat. Her eyes were closed when I returned. "So," I said, "a conversation I overheard between my teaching assistant and her friend could have been about him."

"Teaching assistant, stewardess, cocktail waitress, whatever, whoever, George liked to play. I do, too. George and I understood each other. At least he was caring and careful to keep his playing away from you. Some don't." Thalea scrutinized me with what seemed to be respect or maybe wonder.

"We women are our own worst enemies. We allow men to have their freedom, and we claim ours only when it seems to serve them, not ourselves. Okay, so we've had centuries of maneuvering around our true feelings and best interests. Sure I'm angry with you. I'm angry with George. I'm angry with myself for being, as you say, 'naïve.' I'm going to be 'up-front' from now own. I'm going to take this catastrophe as the biggest and best lesson in my life. The older folk used to say 'be yourself.' They really meant, 'act how I want you to be.'

That's a cruel burden to place on a child. It's a wonder any of us have survived. I don't think I want to hear anymore. I need to digest today. We can talk another time, if you want to." I wanted to run, and fight, all at once.

Dr. Thalea Davison, svelte and tall, tentatively touched my shoulder. "I understand. I've hit you with a lot today. I am truly sorry. What's happened has opened my eyes to things about myself I don't like, important things. We're sisters and we need to be open with one another, even if we can't ever be friends."

She moved away quickly, high heels clicking on the stone floor. I sat for minutes more, then drove home where I began removing every reminder of George from our bedroom.

His pipe collection went into the trash. A new one, ceramic with a matching stand, which I didn't recognize, broke into small pieces when it crashed against the metal bottom of the dumpster. I aired my bedroom.

CHAPTER 28

Gayla

I SAT ON THE EDGE of a drab plastic seat in Detroit's Metropolitan Airport and licked my lips until the lipstick faded. The attendant announced the arrival of Flight 594. For what seemed like twice as long, but was nearer to ten minutes, I watched the stream of passengers. Exiting the Jetway, reddish-brown hair and beard towering above most heads, Tony's hazel eyes hunted. Good Lord! His moustache twisted out from his face, a twentieth century Franz Josef. White tints glistened with some kind of wax or oil. An amused, tolerant grin greeted me. Where was she? Circled in the crook of Antony's right arm was a striking woman with almond shaped black eyes and a lustrous copper complexion. She seemed to float just below his shoulder but slightly above the crowd.

Antony's deep baritone voice attracted attention. He spoke in a language that I didn't understand. Then, enjoying my consternation, he said, "Hi, Mom." He kissed me on both temples.

"Hello, son. You look, uh, spectacular." I never knew how my artist son would appear from one time to the next, what creative mood he would be exploring.

She had stepped aside while he greeted me. Antony reached to bring her close to us. She smiled, gazing steadily into my face.

"This is my bride, Khalda Mading-Tyner." Antony's voice was filled with pleasure and pride.

"How do you do, Mother Tyner? I am happy to meet you." She held my hand in a warm, firm clasp. Her English was pleasantly accented, somewhat like—but not really—British or Caribbean.

She's exquisite, I thought. When Antony wrote that he was bringing home an African wife, from Sudan, I fought unexpected prejudice, an ancient caricature: barefoot, bones in body parts, breasts bouncing in a dusty circle. Despite "knowing better," I contended with childhood indoctrination for a fraction of a second. (A pox on those Saturday, Tarzan movies.) "Hello, Khalda. I'm so happy to have you with us. Welcome." Antony's taste for abstract art was not reflected in his taste for his wife. "Let's get your luggage as quickly as we can. You've had a tiring trip."

"Mom, I'll drive. Let's see if I can remember to drive on the right side of the road," he said.

Outside, Antony called Khalda's attention to the terminal building. "This building is the largest post-tensioned concrete structure in the world. Beautiful, isn't it?" Khalda was appropriately appreciative. "My Dad impressed me with that fact when I was a little boy," Antony said, a slight break in his voice. We eased onto Edsel Ford Expressway.

Tired but excited to be home after ten months, and with much to tell, Antony talked during most of the drive to Ann Arbor. "I traded my bicycle to a man in Libya for a week's lodging, a wool blanket, and two chickens," he said.

He bantered with Khalda. "See those people over there? They're Detroit terrorists," he said, pointing to bicyclists in training for a race.

"Their guns look like water bottles to me," she said.

I was delighted to see her challenge her new husband.

"Mom, we can stop with you at home only as long as it takes to get my portfolio accepted at The Art Institute in Chicago," Tony said. "We haven't told you all our plans. Khalda will finish her last year in economics at the University of Chicago. Her Dad's made the arrangements."

"I am proud of Antony, his slides and sketches are already accepted for a scholarship." Despite the darkness, Khalda's smile lit the car.

Khalda's family had moved south in Sudan ahead of the drought when she was four, she said. She shared some of the intricate story of the Democratic Republic of Sudan, the first

African nation to wrest free of European colonialism.

"After years of being split by the English-controlled south and the Egyptian-controlled north, the struggle for nationhood and internal cohesion is not yet solved." Her happiness over Antony changed to sorrow for her home. "I am very sad about what is happening in many places in my home continent. Perhaps, here, I can learn how to help more."

"I am very definitely one of our new Sudanese women," Khalda said. "My mother's family moved from Ethiopia to settle at Wad Medani three generations ago. My father, Izz Mading, is a Christian from the Dinka and Beja nationalities. We know we were Nubian long ago, but hardly anyone thinks of it today," she said.

"It's fascinating to hear the real story from someone who has lived it." I hung on her words. "Books are good, but real life is exciting."

"Thank you." Khalda seemed pleased that I was interested. "My family is not a usual one. The only thing the Beja and Dinka have in common is our long legs, which I have inherited. My family is very close, and it seems we have always been adventurers."

"America is an adventure that will top all the others, I'll bet," Antony said as he maneuvered my car through expressway traffic.

"Antony says I will not be a curiosity in the U.S. I will be exotic. Is that so?" Khalda asked.

"He is absolutely correct," I said.

"Some in my family are Muslim, some are Christian, and others follow traditional ways. I wish to withhold my decision for some time to come. The U.S. has every kind of belief, doesn't it?" Khalda said.

I marveled at the enthusiasm and exuberance of my new daughter-in-law. "I think you'll find lots of far-out beliefs here."

"Far-out is fine." She smiled. "My father is a diplomat, so I have lived in London, Moscow, and Cairo. The American way of talking may not be as easy to learn. There is so much to understand before I make important decisions, except for Antony."

Khalda spoke Arabic, Dinka, English, and Russian. My poor French was no good testimony to my education. I surveyed my baby son and daughter-in-law. Tony disliked my, sometimes forgetfully, referring to him as my "baby son," so I only felt the words. "I want to go to Africa, beginning with Sudan," I said.

"I am not atypical of today's African women, although many men are unaware of it," my lovely new daughter said.

"Wonderful," I said.

Antony was not satisfied with my story of his father's death. He coaxed more. I asked him to take a walk with me as we talked.

"Antony, I don't want to bring disrespect to your father. I want you to always remember how much he loved you, loved us." I began this litany that I dreaded.

Antony shoved his hands into his jeans pockets and slowed his steps, his legs lopping along, reminding me of George.

"Your Dad really was testing her car. He'd given her advice on what was wrong with it. You know your dad, the tinkerer."

"Please Mom, let's cut to the bones. I can handle it."

"I will, I will. I'm trying. It isn't easy." I faltered. "They were having an affair, and he was with her that day, the same day I was on my way home from Carolton. Those are the bare bones, son. The woman and I have had a talk. She's not a bad person . . ."

"I don't need to know anymore," he said.

We had made a complete circle of our neighborhood. Antony grabbed me in a smothering hug, little boy to mother and man to friend.

We went into the house. I busied myself in the kitchen, when I heard the door close again. Antony had left. I heard Khalda moving around upstairs.

I would one day have to have a similar conversation with Pamela and George Junior-well maybe not George Junior. He looked more like his father, but I always sensed that he had a lot of me inside, holding in, keeping his own thoughts. I hoped I would be ready for whatever came when it was time.

Antony

Antony almost bounced across a quadrangle at the university where he had spent most of his life. He liked the campus. It was hometown to him. Students changed, but the faculty remained fairly constant. Some students were perennials, living off grants and jobs as waitpersons.

Professor Roth stopped him in a hallway that led to his father's office. "Antony, what's with the Fu Manchu?" The older man peered up, his eyes fixed on Tony's face.

"Howdy, Dr. Roth. Fu Manchu drooped. I soar." He lifted the ends of his mustache. "It's an experiment in antigravity." He twirled his facial hair and gave a mock leer.

"I'm awfully sorry about your father, my boy. Mrs. Roth and I visited your mother, Pamela, and George Junior when they were home on the sad occasion. I don't think you call it 'sitting shiva,' like my people do, but the meaning is the same, isn't it?" Right? But you're not serious are you, Antony, about antigravity?" The stereotypical college professor stared nearsightedly. Brown tweed jacket with suede elbow pads, gray flannels, and dirty "Dirty Bucks," he wasn't always sure when his leg was being pulled by the younger generation.

"Not serious, sir." Antony enjoyed teasing his neighbor, the Greek History scholar. I'm married now, Dr. Roth. My bride is from Sudan. I'll call Mrs. Roth to see when we can drop in.

"Sudan, eh? A civilization of which I know nothing. Can't know them all in one lifetime, you know." Smiling at his little joke, Professor Roth went down the hall, out the end door, and into the faculty parking lot.

Antony stood outside the door to his father's office. There was no one in the corridor. He spoke to the closed door. "I'm a married man. I choose Khalda and I'll never betray her."

He ran out of the Engineering Building, crossed Regents Plaza and paid no attention to the imposing Physics and Astronomy Building. He slowed to a walk, his long legs striding effortlessly.

Antony's tenth birthday is tomorrow. He goes to his father's office to remind him, for the last time, of the model car he wants. As he begins to push the door open, he hears his father's voice. Antony stops, politely, as he's been taught.

George's voice sounds different from the way he talks at home. He is telling someone on the phone that they will meet at the Kit-Kat at eight. Even at ten years old, coming tomorrow, Antony wonders, "How can Dad go to the Kit-Kat tonight? He has to get the basement ready for my party. He sounds like somebody in one of those mushy movies that Pam watches." Antony wonders if he'll get his new model for his birthday, after all.

Gayla

In the kitchen, Khalda showed me photographs of her parents and her sisters and brothers. "There are five Mading sisters and brothers. I am the fourth, the second daughter."

I saw the closeness Khalda felt for her family, and her homesickness. "I hope Pam can come home before you leave for Chicago. If she can't, we'll have to run over to Chicago to see you later. I know that you and Pam will like each other." Impulsively, I took both the young woman's hands. "I'm very happy to have a second daughter."

The front door opened and closed quickly. We heard footsteps on the stairs. Puzzled, Khalda said, "Excuse me, Mother Tyner," and ran lightly upstairs.

Like a sleepwalker, I followed her and stopped outside the door to the room. They did not see me in the hall.

Antony sat on the bed in the guestroom, not the old cluttered room that he had shared with his brother. He stared at the wall but turned when he heard Khalda. He raised his arms. She went to him. He buried his face in her breasts.

"We're going to love each other always, faithful and true," Antony breathed hoarsely.

"Always," she assured him.

I tiptoed downstairs. A half-hour later Antony and Khalda came into the kitchen, arms around each other.

"You, you shaved your beard and mustache." I quickly set the pot on the counter when I felt the heat.

"Yes, and he looks exactly like you, Mother Tyner," Khalda said.

"Facial hair doesn't make a man. Besides, I won't scratch Khalda." He rubbed his reddened cheeks with both hands. "She can see the real me, all of me."

"Oh, no, Antony." It always came out An-*tōny*. "I do not complain. The heart comes out; it shows no matter the hair, the face or clothes."

There would be no family reunion. Pam was in an intern program on Capitol Hill in D.C. The opportunity to work for the Black Caucus was too big to pass up, she said. George Junior would make a business trip to Chicago in a few weeks. He would see his brother and new sister at that time.

Antony and Khalda left in his Volkswagen Bug he had stored in the garage when he left a year before. He swore the old car would make it. "No problem, Mom. You know, American expressions are all across Africa. Everywhere I went, everyone said, 'No problem.'"

I crossed my fingers behind my back. "No problem, sweethearts." I held and hugged them.

I met with Dr. Dowd, my department head, to set my class schedule for the next term. I was glad my leave was over. I missed my students and the familiarity of routine. Reaching agreement with the department head, I stopped by my office for book order forms. The room could stand a dusting. I had plenty of time for that. Antony had said that the phrase, "No problem" is heard all over the world. There were problems to be met and issues to be sorted. I planned and hoped to take my changes one day at a time. But, I wished my children no problems—what a fantasy, but that is what mothers do: want for their children. No problem.

CHAPTER 29

Gayla

Dear Gayla,

I have not bought one pack of Belairs since you left. Does that mean that you shamed me? I know, you didn't say a word. Our plans to move have me so happy, I don't want a smoke. Whatever the reason, I have kicked the habit.

I miss you. I envy you and your daughter-in-law. Do you pronounce it Kahalda, KAlda, Kalda or are all of these wrong? She sounds like a gem.

Guess what? A. J.'s divorce is final. His ex is going to marry a man she met in Columbia. He goes to her church High Church Episcopal. La de da. A. J.'s sister is livid that he is leaving the business. He told her about us. She wasn't nearly as upset. She knew something was going on. I don't think she and I will make the effort to meet each other, at least not yet.

A. J. has to be in Monterey on the first of August. He managed to wrangle a position for me as well. I'd go bonkers with nothing to do. I'm studying Spanish at County Tech. Que Pasa?

You are invited as soon as we're settled. My mother and sister have given their blessing. Thank goodness we, colored-Negro-black-African Americans, have fewer hang-ups than other people. Why can't we settle for everybody being American?

My "cousin" Naomi and I met twice. Said she didn't have a sister or brother, hopes we can be like sisters. She remembers your "dark ages" and would like to see you again. I'm not sure we can be close, but I'm willing to try. Naomi and her Admiral Dennis are moving early next year, either to New Mexico or Arizona, as soon as the Admiral decides which one. Naomi says there are more people of "his kind" in those places. There are large numbers of military retirees around. Old Mexico and New Mexico are not too far apart.

Please don't be alarmed, but on impulse, I stopped by to see your folks yesterday. "Doc" looks fine. Your mother seemed a little peaked to me. I know she won't say anything to you, so I'm taking the liberty.
Write when you can. A. J. sends love.
From one creme to another,
Louise

I called. "Dad, how are you? Is Mother okay? Louise wrote that she wasn't looking well." I tried not to sound anxious.

"I'm fine, Gay. Yes, Mother has been a little under the weather. Alice is taking her to the doctor in the morning. There's nothing to be upset about."

"All right. Don't tell her I called; I don't want to worry her. I'll call tomorrow. Bye."

"Sure, stay in touch." Daddy did not sound worried.

George's death and the sudden, unexpected airline trips back and forth between Carolton and Ann Arbor for George's funeral were too much for Mother. Giving no hint of a serious heart condition, she had kept her fragile health well hidden. She died in her sleep before Dr. Porter could see her. I had expected Dad to leave first. How much more will show itself? The old ones said that "trouble always comes in three times." Mom Dutch, George, and now Mother, is that my rule of three? I can't be sure. Mom Dutch was a dear friend, but she wasn't family. I will not think of anything negative. I'm prepared for everything and I affirm that the cycle has turned for me.

As surely as if she were rocking on her rickety porch, I could hear Gramma Ann cackle: "The good Lord never gives nobody more than they can shoulder." Mother's ladylike cadence floated above the cackle, "It's all relative, my dear."

The funeral was over. Daddy, Antony, Khalda, George Junior, Pam, and I sat with two ancient, distant cousins, Mother's relatives, people of the old ways. People we didn't know closely, but who knew Mother, had left us to ourselves.

"Granddaddy, do you intend to stay in this big house by yourself?" George Junior asked.

"Not by myself. Alice will be with me. I want to stay in my own home. I'm not going to one of those rest homes. Your grandmother and I agreed, we wouldn't be caught dead in one of those dying places," he said. Then he laughed, wagged his finger at George Junior and said, "How do you like my little joke, boy?"

I saw Mother in every inch of the house and smelled and felt her presence inside each room. No one sat in her maroon chair with the matching ottoman. "When Daddy wants a change, he'll come to live with me," I told my children when he was not near enough to hear.

Alice called us for a light supper: homemade soup, cheese cornbread, cabbage, and carrot slaw with apples. No one ate.

I needed to get out of doors. I took Daddy's big car and went for a drive. A rough, raw clearing waited for the new strip-shopping plaza. Passing Deerpath High, I stopped at Westminster Church where Mother's funeral was held. Spattered at ground level by Carolina red clay, the red brick colonial structure was imposing in its small, solid way, proud with freshly-painted white window frames, doors, and steeple.

I went to the cemetery. Sitting alone, I felt calmer. I knew Mother was already somewhere else looking at me and saying, "Chill, Gayla. I'm fine."

A small woman, my age I guessed but looking older, was sitting on a filigree iron bench a distance away. She and I approached one another as if drawn by magnets.

"You don't remember me," she said in a soft monotone. "I'm Myrtle Lee Urmann. My name was Myrtle Lee Tolliver. We used to play together when I lived on McGuire Street and you lived on Lowell. I had a little sister. Her name was Allison. She died."

Scenes flicking before my eyes like an old-fashioned rolling television screen, I reached for her hand. "I remember," I said.

"You're going to write a book about coming back to Carolton, aren't you?" she asked.

"I haven't thought about doing anything like that at all," I said. "I came back for different reasons."

"You are. I know," she said. She squeezed my hand tightly, then dropped her hand to her side. "I want to tell you my story, my way. I don't know if it will fit with what you're going to say. I'm a teensy tiny part of Carolton, but what happened in my

life is like much of everything that's gone on in this town for
hundreds of years. In a way, things never change. Most things
are the same, today and for a long time to come."

Myrtle Lee Tolliver Urmann didn't wait for me to give permission. She told her story, her way.

"The man I loved and who loved me, we weren't allowed to
love in Carolton."

Henry Lee and Myrtle Lee

*Henry Lee answers his phone. A man's voice, a white voice, says,
"We don't want to cause trouble in town. You get yourself over to Mr.
Stuart Urmann's house right this minute. Talking's got to be done—a
lot of talking."*

Henry's mother asks him, "Where're you going so late."

"Business mama, insurance business. I'll be back soon," he assures her.

Only one light was on at the Urmanns', one light in a ten-room house.

*Stuart Urmann, Myrtle Lee's husband, opens the door when Henry
stepped up on the porch. A policeman called Big Pat and Mr. Dodson,
owner of the auto repair shop, are standing in front of a fireplace.
Henry wonders, where is Myrtle Lee? Has anybody hurt her? Stu
Urmann goes to his easy chair. He is about forty-five with medium
brown, thinning hair and going soft in the belly. The policeman and
Dodson are more formidable, men who have worked farms around
Carolton since they were children.*

*Something about each of their faces looks alike, even though they
aren't kin. It is their eyes that have bullets aimed for Henry's heart and
head. He forgets he is afraid. Whatever the outcome, it is his doing,
only his. That's the way a man operates.*

*The policeman, Big Pat, says, "No need to pretend and play games.
We know." He holds up a black notebook. "I can read you date, hour,
and place for every time you two have been together for the last three
months. Don't need to read it, I suppose?"*

*Dodson breaks in, "I found somethin' wrong when you brought your
car back for a checkup. My mechanic showed me a lipstick from your
back seat. You ain't no taxi, boy. That lipstick color ain't used by no
colored girls around here. None of 'em light enough."*

Henry tries. "I believe that lipstick belongs to my cousin from

Pittsburgh. She was here Christmas. She's real light," he says.

Big Pat laughs. "What Dodson told me was enough to get me to fol-lowing you. Dodson says he never trusts a colored boy who's been North. Hanging's no longer legal, but some of us don't like the new ways. We oughta be able to find a loophole in the law for you."

Henry thinks it odd that Mr. Stuart Urmann says nothing. Myrtle Lee walks out of the dark from another room to a space right between Dodson and Big Pat. She doesn't look at her husband. She holds a large manila envelope in her hand.

"I don't think you're going to do anything to Mr. Lee," she says in her soft, polite voice. "I've got letters between my husband—the upstanding vice president of Liberty Savings and Loan—and a man in Avondale. I've got nothing against a man loving a man, but most folks in Carolton do."

She turns to her husband and looks him in the eyes until he lowers his head. "For most of the last six years, almost since we were first mar-ried, I didn't understand why I had to beg you to make love to me. It was like thawing out an iceberg. I don't like snooping, but I had to set-tle my wondering." She locks eyes with Big Pat. "Don't get any ideas, Big Pat. I made copies. My mother's got the original ones in her safe deposit box and there's one in a place you'll never guess."

Henry doesn't move. The three men go out to the front porch, leaving Henry and Myrtle Lee alone, something they'd have never done if they weren't so flabbergasted.

Henry says, " Myrtle Lee, they're gonna do something to hurt you,"

"Don't think about it. White women don't get hurt unless they birth a black baby. They won't touch me," she says.

After a few minutes, the men come back. "All right boy . . .," Big Pat catches Myrtle's eye. "Mr. Lee," he says, "you got to leave town. Twenty-four hours at the most. Somebody else may be on to y'all. I can't be responsible for what they might do."

A half-hour later Henry calls Myrtle Lee. "I'm leaving as soon as I close my account at the savings and loan, first thing in the morning. I'll call you from Pittsburgh. My mother says you can be in touch with her. I told her everything. You'll come, won't you?"

Myrtle Lee straightened her shoulders with only the barest hint of a shudder. Her voice and face suddenly looked much younger. "Henry left the next morning. He didn't get any sleep and with the worriment he'd been under he got as far as Washington, Pennsylvania, driving straight through. He went off a bridge into the Monongahela River. You can use my story anyway you want."

Gayla

She let me hold her hand for barely a second or two. A smile shifted the corners of her mouth perceptibly upward. I watched Myrtle Lee Tolliver Urmann cross the street, her thin shoulders straight, and walk into the run-down house with its crumbling wall and wild hydrangea bushes. It looked as if it, too, had given up. I wandered around the cemetery looking for graves of my father's white relatives, buried before the cemetery was integrated.

A heaviness lifted, the clean, warm air moved my mind away from the death space. The colors inspired a sign of life. Friends and family could always visit, leave flowers, remember, and speak with people they can no longer touch. I left the cemetery and, with no memory of doing so, I pulled to the top of the hill at 9119 Laney Drive. I parked Dad's car in the garage.

It takes a lot of weight to break open the stones, keeping the door closed to the inner self, the soul. Seeing Myrtle Lee felt like the door was almost opening. She was a link to the schizophrenic childhood of colored and white, of comfortable and poor in my separated—segregated South land. I began to feel that there's not too much more before my door is wide-open. As children, we looked and listened. We didn't talk much. Old habits stick around. I don't believe in the rule of three. Every moment of my life is a stone to close or to open the heart. It is as painful to put a stone in place as to take one away. Some stones are small and some are large. Myrtle and Henry Lee aren't big stones, just to think of them. Daddy, Mother, George, Tally, Drew/A. J., Louise, my children, my work—there's not one second that's not part of becoming Gayla Marie Hughes Tyner. It just takes time to figure it out.

I knew the old house that whispered fanciful words and

conjured worlds far beyond Carolton was not my answer. My answer was not the city with its pride of nesting in the Piedmont, the foothills of the Appalachian Mountains. What I loved and what formed me, Gayla Hughes, was people—the grandmas, my parents, neighbors, and the children on Lowell Avenue and McGuire Street, friends and people—even the unkind ones. Nothing can wipe out the good feelings for those people and the gifts they freely and unknowingly gave. I didn't hate Carolton, white folks, or the South, as I had thought. I can take, ignore, or forget events and experiences. It is my choice. That's what those tired, retired, returning Caroltonians of many colors knew long before I did. Jane Austen was right-on, more than two hundred years ago. "One does not love a place less for having suffered in it." Her landed gentry had a life that never did exist in my Carolton. I want to believe that there are echoes across centuries, sort of "blowing in the wind," that is a link between the old and the new— almost new, anyway.

I leaned against the trunk of my father's "land yacht." I saw him above the house in his favorite spot among the pines. The silver top of his cane reflected in the moonlight. Brownie, stimulated by the evening coolness, chased Scruffy, who darted back close to Dad and watched out for him. I wondered what he was thinking, just staring into the sky. He'd done his best. I was sure.

J. C. Hughes

J. C. finds the pole star. He watches clouds come and go for a long moment. He thinks, Poppa, Mavis Jean is up there with you now. You know how long it'll be before I come to join you. I don't. You, Janis, and Mavis Jean are together. I'm the only one left.

"Calvin, you are as stubborn as anybody on God's green earth." Poppa's voice was commanding. Obedient, as always, J. C. stopped his mind chatter and turned his head so that one ear was cocked upward.

"Don't you think I've been through enough, losing Mavis Jean Poppa? What more can I do? I thanked Gay for her help."

"See, you call her by the childish name she doesn't want anymore.

You would feel better if you talked with her about things that matter to you. The same things matter to her too, Calvin."

Poppa's voice vanished when J. C. heard another voice—this one flesh and blood—from below the hill. He looked down to see Gayla standing at the edge of the mowed grass where the wild weeds took over.

Gayla

I savored the red clay and pine-cone-scented air. I breathed deeply, over and over, pulling and letting go, again and again.

I checked my watch and moved to the edge of the backyard. I called up the hill, "Daddy, it's time to come in from the night air. You don't want to get a quinsy throat." I thumped my forehead with the palm of my hand. I got it. Finally. That is another thing my father and I shared, those pesky sore throats.

He'll stay here, in his own home, as long as he wants. If he never wants to come to Ann Arbor, or wherever I may be, he'll be happy where he wants to be. I will, too.

My father, as bent and hollow as he was the night Mom Dutch died and the day I cam to Carolton for Mother's funeral, held on to each tree as he made his way down the hill.

"Can you get me a dish of butter pecan ice cream" were his first words.

"Sure Dad, don't you think I know your favorite flavor after all these years?"

"Come to think, I never thought about it. Your mother knew that kind of thing," he said, looking surprised.

Alice was in her room, the door closed, a faint TV sound was coming through the door. I dished out the ice cream, two scoops. Too much milk and he would have to get up and go to the bathroom, breaking his sleep. Mother had told me. I started to leave him to eat his ice cream alone, but changed my mind and sat across from him—not in Mother's chair, but one that was seldom used, at the far end of the kitchen table. He ate slowly, savoring each mouthful.

Suddenly, he laughed. "You don't know that your mother said I can have only one scoop. You gave me two."

I laughed, too. We gazed at one another for a long moment,

still laughing, when he stopped and his face became still and quizzical.

"Gayla," his voice sounded far away. "All your life people said you look like me. I never saw it." He got up. I sat, puzzled. He came close to me. The light was on a dimmer, sort of a half light, casing a shadow across his arm. My father put out his hand and touched my cheek.

"That's my face," he murmured. "I never saw it before. That's my face."

Tears gathered in my eyes and rolled down my face. Daddy wiped them with his palm. I reached up and did the same to him. I stood and folded my arms around the man whose shoulders I once could not reach, but which were now only a few inches above mine. We said the words at the same time. "I love you."

A half-hour later, ice cream dish washed and put away, I watched the elderly man, Dr. John Calvin. Hughes, my Daddy, gently pull the door to his bedroom almost closed. "Night-night, don't let the bedbugs bite," he said.

"Back atcha," I said, going to the bedroom down the hall to sleep well.

One individual's story can't be stripped away from the stories of those who breathed the nearby air, moved through the same spaces, and greeted one another with "Hey," before the Northern "Hi" invaded Carolton. I had reached a place inside myself where I understood my sense of ownership. The comfort of having a housekeeper-cook, a once-a-week gardener, a laundress, and a handyman-chauffeur were privileges that masked the screams of my sense of displacement. It was not unreal. Tally and I may, one day, have more talks about our down-home schizophrenia. In the interim, we somehow found spaces of sanity, allowing us to walk between the labels bestowed on us. Color, class, male, female, kids, as the grandmas told us, "It makes no nevermind."

Ghosts do not leave. They linger, an energy that cannot be destroyed, only changed in form. A shadow cluster of Negro children play on the sidewalk outside Westminster Church. Across the street, a troop of Boy Scouts stands in broken formation: khaki uniforms, red kerchiefs, ribbed knee socks, all matching the uniforms rising out of brown brogan oxfords. In a few minutes, they will march from the vacant lot, down the hill, to Central Street for the Confederate Day Parade. The lead boys, ones with the most merit badges, hold unfurled flags, windlessly limp. One scout—red-haired, freckled, and approaching teen age—holds the flag of the United States of America. Beside him, an older Eagle Scout balances the battle flag of The Confederate States of America against his brogans. First one, then another of the miniature troopers sees the colored children in the churchyard.

"Look at the jigaboos." a voice behind the flags carries easily.

A chorus. "Hey, niggers."

"Hey, darkies."

"Tar babies."

Freckles, with the American flag, leans forward, laughing. His flag tilts and drops off-center. Balancing it with his hands above his head, face lifted prayer like, he straightens the long wooden pole.

Westminster's youth leader locks the church door and comes toward her charges. The good lady teaches and believes that, "One should always turn the other cheek."On this Saturday morning, she has another nostrum, "Children, remember 'Vengeance is mine, saith the Lord.'" She leads the children toward Central Street to find a spot to watch the parade.

Tally, Gayla, Janis, and other neighborhood children are resting under the pear trees in Mom Dutch's yard. Someone says, "I wish the Japanese had won the war."

"Silly. The Japanese would have put us in concentration camps just like they would have done to the white folks."

Someone whispers, "That's okay. Maybe then the whites would see us as Americans, too."

Everyone nods in agreement, except one neighborhood child who is older and smarter. Mom Dutch's pears are sweet.

Carolton's children hear stories that meander, barely touching a point here, coming back there, planting a notion, a caution, or a reminder. They are unaware of a momentum. Seeds fall on the dry ground to await crows or rain. In the dusk Tally, Janis, Gay, and the neighborhood young'uns, listen and soak in half-hidden myths. Gramma Ann can be heard, "Um-huh, yes indeed."

A parade down Central Street is noisy with much laughter and calling out. Gay is riding her pinto, Folly. She is not behind the Scouts, nor with her friends from the cave. She joins the procession behind the white, high school band. It passes the intersection of Central and High where the colored people crowd close to the corner to observe the festivities. No Negroes have been invited to participate, but no one asks Gay to leave; she's Dr. J. C. Hughes' daughter. A few people, who don't know who she is, laugh and point at her as she rides by.

Gay's college boyfriend comes to visit. They will drive back to Pennsylvania for the fall semester. Gayla and George walk through High Street to the Hughes' Buick. Colored Caroltonians nod, smile, and greet the couple. Across the street, in front of the Lyric Colored Theater, a male voice teases, "Hey girl, all right, now. All grown up and got a beau."

A cluster of men in front of the pool hall step aside when the couple reaches them.

Punky, a retarded drifter, yanks off his cap, bows from the waist. Punky wears his thick, kinky hair in tiny plaits cascading in all directions.

George, the new beau, gazes soberly over the top of the car. "When you come home, you walk differently. You walk around as if you own the place."

EPILOGUE

CAROLTON'S COLORED/NEGRO/BLACK/AFRICAN AMERICAN—
AMERICAN—children dreamed of making it and conquering
the world, as children have done since the world began. While
millions came from Europe and Asia to the "new world" and
also left a village, town, or city to which they may or may not
chose to return, many of them know where the village nestles.
We, Americans of African heritage, have no ancestral village,
just our "Caroltons." We are reluctant refugees, not hope-filled
immigrants.

To remain in "Carolton" meant submission. Leaving was
bittersweet success. Summer and Christmas vacations we went
back home, down South to family and friends, driving a new
Cadillac, Thunderbird, Lincoln Continental, and recently, a
Benz or a "Beemer" that trumpeted, "I made it!" Inside each
driver was, always, a knowing that we had not been wanted and
weren't welcomed by *"them."* Beyond family, neighborhood,
and church we were never sure how far the welcome mat
extended. Down home was a split that was bone deep. "Up
North," "out West," "overseas"—anywhere else—pulled, teased
and promised us. We felt seduced into love-hate alienation, ill
at ease growing up poor or "nigger rich."

-END-